Belgravia

The daughter of the 7th Baron Clanmorris, Charlotte
Bingham published her first book, *Coronet Among
the Weeds*, at the age of twenty. She is married to the
actor and playwright Terence Brady, with whom she
has written over a hundred television plays, including
*Upstairs, Downstairs, Take Three Girls, No –
Honestly, Yes – Honestly, Nanny* and *Pig in the
Middle*. She has a son and a daughter.

Charlotte Bingham

Belgravia

published by Pan Books

First published 1983 by Michael Joseph Ltd
This Pavanne edition published 1984 by
Pan Books Ltd,
Cavaye Place, London SW10 9PG
9 8 7 6 5 4 3 2 1
© Charlotte Bingham 1983
ISBN 0 330 28394 4
Phototypeset by Input Typesetting Ltd, London
Printed and bound in Great Britain by
Collins, Glasgow

*This book is a work of fiction and all characters
in it are imaginary and bear no resemblance to any
real person, alive or dead.*

chapter one

It is possible that when Lucius de Bossuet first called on Lady Mary Lawton, he was, as an American, somewhat puzzled to discover that the address to which she had directed him was not one behind which he might reasonably have expected to find living the daughter of an earl. The street where she lived was neither discreetly smart, nor, as it emerged, fashionably shabby. Frankly, it was nondescript, and situated quite well away from the main squares which constituted the stamping grounds of the oftimes idle but still rich remains of English Society. Naturally Lucius was disappointed, for, despite the occasional visit to England in his youth, he was still quite unprepared for the anonymous façade behind which so many of the English Upper Class find it essential to exist.

Of course he had not expected the house to be grand, but he had expected it to be something, and as he stood looking for the bell on a small faded front door guarded by two wilting bay trees he felt the excitement he had experienced when struggling to fit his old gold cuff-links into his brand new Coles' shirt decidedly ebbing away. The door was on the latch but even so he made a polite effort to activate the old brass bell, which he then discovered to be in a permanently pushed-in position and consequently impossible to operate. Since there was no other device by which he could signal his arrival, he pushed the door open and found himself in the gloom of a small hall. Almost immediately he was confronted by a Filipino manservant. This was slightly more reassuring, as was the large oil painting of what he took to be one of Lady Mary's ancestors which hung above the marble table. Lucius announced himself to the servant, and even as he did so wished his mother had chosen a less nineteenth-century-sounding name for him, because suddenly, right here in England, 'Lucius' didn't seem to have quite the right straightforward ring to it.

The Filipino stood aside and indicated a small green spiral staircase which led downstairs to a room where the party was being held. Lucius hesitated. The manservant smiled, which immediately worried Lucius because he remembered from his mother, who once for a short time had employed a Filipino maid, that Filipinos only smiled from embarrassment. The thought of this made Lucius uncomfortable. To announce oneself by name to an Englishman's servant was no doubt far too outspoken in a country where no one appeared to announce themselves to anyone else, or indeed address each other, by any more precise identity than 'Er'. Eventually, since such things were to become the subject of his book, Lucius would delve more deeply into the real reasons for the English Upper Class's extreme reluctance to identify itself; but just at this minute it occurred to him, as he was about to enter a large gathering of people, none of whom knew him, that it was probably unnecessary since they all knew each other anyway.

No one enters a large gathering anonymously with any degree of optimism except a budding author. Even a budding author, as Lucius quickly realised, is soon faced with the uncomfortable choice of either remaining anonymous and thus learning nothing, or revealing himself and becoming involved in an exchange of trivialities. Lucius had no idea what his hostess looked like, so he stood by the large linen-clothed table which was serving as a bar and merely observed the gathering.

His first feeling was one of relief that he had chosen exactly the right clothes. Most of the men there were wearing suits of various shades of grey, or navy with a slight pinstripe running through it, and a shirt such as he had bought himself that morning. The girls, on the other hand, as if by some secret agreement, were almost outrageous in their choice of dress. Their hair was spun into wonderful shapes, coloured by the occasional feather or comb, and their bodies were clothed in costumes which their ancestors would have considered more suitable for flunkeys and page boys – knee breeches, ruffled shirts, lace jabots, satin knickerbockers and little jackets which Lucius thought used to be called 'pelisses' but wasn't altogether sure.

It was obvious that remaining alone so long with his observations had made him conspicuous, because a woman, not as young as most of those assembled, had detached herself from a small group and was making her way towards him. He was quite sure that this must be Lady Mary – and, if her house was slightly disappointing, she most certainly was not. She was tall, slim, and wore a wide pearl choker at her throat, at the centre of which was a large emerald. When she directed her gaze at him, Lucius realised just how felicitously the emerald was positioned, so close to her face: she had quite magnificent green eyes, one of which was oddly speckled like a duck's egg. Her hair was brushed out fashionably from her face, but her clothes, as befitted someone a little older than most of the other girls present, were more formal (although Lucius noted that her shoes were perhaps the choice of a woman who had a more adventurous side to her nature).

She shook his hand in a way which Lucius would very soon come to identify as a mark of breeding – that is she managed to shake it without appearing to touch it at all – while already turning her head to find him a suitably interesting introduction. As he stood beside her, Lucius found himself wishing he had enough social confidence to tell her that he would prefer to talk to her. Instead he waited meekly, much as he used to wait when he was small while his dancing teacher tried to find a partner for him.

A suitable introduction having been found, his hostess gave him a little wave which hinted more of 'au revoir' than 'adieu' and was gone, leaving Lucius bending to catch the name of a slim girl who for a moment appeared to be the replica of the portrait under which she stood.

The painting itself was of a boy in a wide lace collar holding a white dove and staring out with intense solemnity, as if the act of holding a white dove, even for a portrait, was something of an undertaking. The girl who stood under this serious study also sported a wide lace collar and buckled shoes; but her hair was straight, cut square to frame her large eyes and touch the top of her lace blouse, while her expression was in complete contrast to that of the boy in the painting.

Her name was Georgiana. Lucius wished very much that the noise in the room would soften for he found it unbearable not to be able to catch every nuance of the unconsequentialities which she was directing towards him by way of conversation. For instance, straightaway she pronounced American as 'Merican. And her 'th's had more than a hint of 'f's about them, so that she said fink instead of think, and fought instead of thought. Lucius found this amusing and he toyed with the idea of adopting it himself when he returned to America.

Georgiana was one of Lady Mary's cousins. Lucius felt pleased about this. It strengthened his belief that all the members of English Society did know each other and were most probably also related to each other, which would account for a great deal, particularly the softness in the contours of the faces surrounding him. Here there were no rugged frontier chins or too-high cheekbones, and although admittedly some of the noses were large they were large in such a way as to make you feel they had been passed down deliberately and carefully, for future generations to recognise each other more simply. Perhaps even the way Georgiana smiled, or put her index finger to her chin might be traced back as far as a thousand years. And if this were so, and it was highly probable, then perhaps this is what gave her such youthful confidence. As her relatives and friends arrived and departed, Lucius watched her casually introducing them to him with a vague little wave of her hand: although she drawled her speech slightly, the impression she gave was not of someone precociously at ease, but simply of someone who accepted herself for what she was, the way he supposed she was used to accepting everything that surrounded her – the old portraits, the heavy linen tablecloths, and the fine Chippendale chair upon which she leant her knee every now and then.

Lucius noticed that the girls did not kiss each other but rather the space around each other, thus avoiding any embarrassing lipstick marks which would later need to be removed – or perhaps, more to the point, eschewing any real contact. The words 'boring' and 'tiresome' peppered the conversation, while white hands fluttered through graphic descriptions of the skiing or riding accidents which seemed constantly to befall them. And everyone shook his hand the same way Lady Mary had done, barely touching it. Lucius wondered idly whether it was something their nannies had all taught them as a precaution against infection, or was it simply this English restraint again, which forbade excessive physical contact? Whatever the reason, Lucius decided he found it quite charming as an affectation, just as he really rather liked the way nobody opened their mouths very wide when they spoke, expressing even dismay or trepidation through lips which barely moved. It was all intensely interesting and, as he walked home, having taken great care to leave that little bit earlier than might have been expected, Lucius savoured the impression he had of Lady Mary and her girl friends.

The following morning Lucius walked to Pulbrook and Gould and ordered flowers to be delivered to Lady Mary Lawton. He chose an all-white arrangement because he wasn't quite sure he could remember the exact colours of her rooms. Then he walked back down Sloane Street and he had barely returned inside his front door when his telephone rang. He allowed it to ring for a while before answering it. It was Lady Mary. Lucius was surprised, and very grateful to hear from her so soon. He thanked her for the previous evening but of course said nothing about the flowers. She said she hoped it hadn't been too crowded and noisy for him, then asked him round to lunch, putting the receiver down rather abruptly which made Lucius realise that perhaps her other telephone had rung.

Lucius gazed around his apartment in some satisfaction. Receiving a call so quickly from Lady Mary was more than he could have wished, let alone hoped for. He had imagined that, as an American of no great fortune, it would take him some time to find his feet socially, particularly as people might not feel at ease in the company of a person whose professed reason for being there amongst them was that he was about to write a book about them. If Lady Mary was to be believed, the very opposite was true, and apparently they were all even a little intrigued by his stated purpose of observing the London Social Scene with a view to authorship. And perhaps here again the fact that he was an American was a positive advantage, for it was well known that socially speaking the Americans didn't really count, so therefore what an American wrote about them all wouldn't count either. Lucius considered all these considerations, then rose to change out of his sports coat and flannels and into a suit, because he had read somewhere or other that in England only cads lunched in a sports coat.

When he presented himself for the second time in twenty-four hours at Lady Mary's front door, he felt if anything even more excited than he had the previous evening. This time what he took to be a Portuguese maid answered the door, but even so he did not announce himself as he had the previous evening, and neither did the maid indeed expect him to, instead indicating a door to the left of the hall wherein, Lucius supposed, he would find Lady Mary. But he was wrong, for the room was empty, and Lucius was left alone while the maid clattered off noisily down the iron spiral staircase.

The small study in which he found himself was a treasure trove of *objets* both *trouvès* and otherwise. Little tables bore collections of stones and snuff boxes and photographs of friends and relatives in every assortment

10

of frame, some Victorian, some Georgian, some ceramic, and some in silver with complicated arrangements of initial or coronets on them. Over the chimneypiece was a painting of a horse, its eye rolling, held fast at the head by a groom. Somewhere among all the photographs a clock ticked delicately, and outside a taxi passed. Just for a second Lucius imagined it was going to stop outside the front door; but it only paused before driving on and Lucius found to his surprise that he was relieved, and consequently even more excited. A telephone on a small table at the far side of the room rang and was picked up almost immediately by someone in another room, then replaced again shortly afterwards. He opened a book and found himself, somewhat guiltily, reading the inscription, which was 'To Mary' from someone called 'Piers'. There was also a postscript, to the effect that he, Piers, had written in it to stop her giving it to anyone else. Lucius smiled, replaced it and resumed his waiting.

He was almost beginning to lose his state of pleasurable anticipation when the door opened and Lady Mary entered. This time she left her hand slightly longer in his before turning quickly away, a habit which Lucius already thought of as one of her charming little characteristics. Perhaps she had adopted it to hide her eye, that funny speckled eye which once, when she was younger, might have been an embarrassment to her. Whatever the reason, it was most appealing. Because he was thinking of this and of nothing else, he found his mind a blank when she asked him what he would like to drink, and so he asked for a small scotch and Perrier, which was normally something he never drank until evening. She also decided on scotch, which, he noted, she drank somewhat dashingly only with ice. He didn't know quite why but he found the sight of her, sitting there drinking (rather than sipping) her scotch, in her high-necked dress and sleeveless cashmere, extremely sensual. She knew how to put him at his ease and yet remain distant enough to excite his curiosity. She asked him questions and, which was unusual, listened to his replies. She was interested in him

11

but not so interested that it became impossible to be interesting, and she was quite, quite bored when it came to supplying any information about herself. By the time they rose and moved into the dining room, Lucius had fallen madly in love with her.

After lunch they walked round to her mother's house. Lucius could not quite believe his luck. To be entering one of the few remaining houses in Belgravia still with its own private ballroom on only his second day in England was unbelievably thrilling. Even his own mother, who always pretended to be excessively bored by her son's experiences, even Mother would have to be a little intrigued by this. He smiled to himself as he pictured her sitting in the bed with its white cotton sheets, in her cashmere robe, reading the letter he would pen to her in his best Italic handwriting. He thought how cross and jealous she would be. It would be several weeks before he would receive a reply from her, no doubt of that.

Lady Mary's mother the Countess, had been a famous beauty in her time – and not only then, for she was still quite remarkably good looking – and, Lucius noted approvingly, she had a famous beauty's arrogance, and a stylised disinterest. She gave Lucius a tiny touch of her hand and then proceeded to grumble vociferously to her daughter about someone who, it seemed, was any minute about to arrive in order to inspect her ballroom, which, it further transpired, the Countess hired out for dances.

'I just hope she doesn't bring her wretched daughter with her,' the Countess told Lady Mary. 'I have – ' (and here she touched her forehead, just above her right eyebrow) – 'I have such a headache coming on, just here, at the very thought of it.'

Lucius reflected with fascination that the Countess was the first person he had met who could pinpoint an imminent headache quite so precisely.

Almost immediately, the maid showed the already unfortunate woman into the drawing room and Lucius turned his full attention to a scene which for days afterwards, whenever he thought of it – which was often –

gave him the most delicious *frisson*. Everything that happened was so cold, so detached, so English.

The visitor was a Mrs Aidan Parker-Jones. The Countess did not bother to introduce her either to her daughters or to Lucius, but proceeded to interview her much as if she had come in search of a position in the household.

The manner of the interview surprised Mrs Parker-Jones. She had of course envisaged the scene. In fact only the previous morning at breakfast, as she opened the letter from the Countess inviting her to inspect the ball-room, she had at once thought of her own little scenario: namely, how amusing it would be to inspect the Countess's ballroom and find it too small for her purpose.

'A little pokey, alas,' she had heard herself saying, as she watched her husband Aidan's elephantine backview disappearing out of the dining room door. But now, sitting opposite the Countess on the eighteenth-century sofa (a replica of which she had just ordered from Liberty's), she found all such thoughts vanishing from her head; and she found herself thankful, as she saw the Countess run a disapproving eye over her, that she had put on a light silk two-piece, rather than the wool-mix frock and matching coat. The wool-mix frock and matching coat would have been much too warm, the way things were turning out.

It was not as if her introduction to the Countess had not already cost her. She had just paid a quite substantial sum, to an Old Etonian named Andrew Gillott, to be sitting where she sat now. Gillott hired himself out to various people for the sole purpose of effecting introductions to people of social influence and standing. He and the Countess had produced, privately, a little book to help just such ladies as herself to understand what he vulgarly described, with accompanying bronchial laugh, as the 'current market'. The book had arrived on Mrs Parker-Jones' breakfast table some weeks ago and when she first opened it she had to admit that she hadn't experienced such a thrill since Aidan gave her her very first diamond. Here it all was. Everything she needed to know about all the people who didn't need to know her, together with details about their houses, and from where and from what they derived their incomes, not to mention the intimate history of their families, and such relevant and riveting facts as whether or not there were any ancestral weaknesses – although when she looked at the land holdings that were due to accrue to the heir of one prominent Duke she had felt she might be persuaded to overlook the little matter of insanity in that particular family, which her book informed her was the result of a misalliance in the eighteenth century.

Even the names of the families described in the little volume gave her intense pleasure, reminiscent as they were of the great London Squares. Russell, Cavendish, Grosvenor, Portland . . . she repeated most of them out aloud when she was alone in her bedroom, much as a gourmet might privately murmur *filet de boeuf truffé à la mode*, or *les rougets pochés à la nage*. And then she would close the book with a sigh. The sheer richness of the information would overcome her, and she would find herself wishing once again that her daughter Jennifer had inherited her looks and not Aidan's. But then that was how it always seemed to be. Very few beautiful women had beautiful daughters, and Jennifer most certainly had not got the sort of looks which alone would guarantee her immediate entry into the upper echelons. If the name of Parker-Jones was to feature in the future among the pedigrees of these other illustrious families, an enormous effort would be needed: Mrs Parker-Jones knew that she herself was well up to any sacrifice which might be necessary.

Now, as she found herself answering the Countess' questions, her foremost feelings were of bewilderment. Until this afternoon, she had always thought that a person who arrived in a chauffeur-driven Rolls would be treated accordingly; but here was the Countess sitting opposite her, on old furniture which quite obviously had never been re-covered since the day it was made, here she was sitting there making it perfectly plain to one and all, and in particular to Mrs Parker-Jones herself, that she wasn't at all sure if she was even going to show Mrs Parker-Jones the ballroom, let alone rent it to her for her daughter's dance. Mrs Parker-Jones found herself clicking the gold top of her crocodile handbag open and shut as she answered the Countess' endless questions. She had no idea people could talk to one in this way, and she very much wanted to get up and go. But the memory of Aidan saying to her, only that morning, that he was not – as he vulgarly put it – 'made of money', delayed her exit. To hold Jennifer's dance – and, one had to face it, with Aidan holding the purse strings it was never going to be a ball – to hold it anywhere like an hotel was simply out of the question, particularly if the champagne was to be champagne and not, that dread of all social dreads, a sparkling wine with napkins covering the labels.

'I do hope,' said the Countess as she opened the doors of the ballroom, 'that you are not thinking of turning the room into a zoo or anything frightful.'

Lucius noted that Mrs Parker-Jones, whose fingers he thought must be quite numb from all that opening and closing of her handbag, answered 'No' a little too quickly to this question. In fact, Mrs Parker-Jones had been rather taken with the idea of turning the ballroom into something – not a zoo, perhaps, but something with an Oriental theme, with little paper lanterns and bells which tinkled in the draught – but the way the Countess' extraordinarily sculpted nostrils had flared momentarily at the word 'zoo' instantly dispelled such notions.

They all fell silent. The ballroom was indeed beautiful. They stood there in the late afternoon half light as travellers from another planet might stand, trying to understand the place they had come to. It wasn't hard for any of them, surrounded as they were by faded frescoes and palely painted panelling, to imagine they could hear the music playing, and see the couples of yesteryear foxtrotting or quick-stepping their way nimbly across the floor and into the future. Lady Mary wondered how much the course of history, perhaps even of the world, might have been changed here by some wonderfully insignificant event – someone deflected from their destiny by a change of hairstyle, or a corsage saucily placed, or by a sudden decision not to wear the oyster pink but the silver Molyneux. She glanced at her mother. The Countess was standing some way apart from Mrs Parker-Jones, either because she, like Mary, found the smell of Chanel No. 5 a little too sweet for her taste, or perhaps because she alone amongst the four of them not only saw the ghosts but had known them.

They turned to go, the four of them, as if on cue. But before they left the ballroom the Countess made it quite plain to Mrs Parker-Jones that, were she to hire the room, then she had better make up her mind at once and confirm her intention with a cash payment the following day. Mrs Parker-Jones, feeling more flustered than she remembered feeling for years, at once ratified the booking, adding that her chauffeur would bring the money round in the Rolls the following morning. At this, the Countess winced both audibly and visibly, and Mrs Parker-Jones was shown speedily out of the house before she had time even to wonder what it was she had said which had made the Countess look at her so very oddly.

'Send the chauffeur round with the Rolls indeed,' said the Countess, lengthily exhaling cigarette smoke through her nostrils.

She looked at Lucius.

'Of course, you Americans are most fortunate, because you're all common. It's so much easier when everybody's common, because then one doesn't notice people like Mrs Parker-Jones.'

Lady Mary looked at Lucius for the first time full in the face, silently imploring forgiveness for her mother. But there was no need, because Lucius would not have missed a moment of it. And besides, Lady Mary had most unusually beautiful eyes.

The Countess' large antique sapphire-and-diamond ring flashed in the firelight as she chain-lit another cigarette.

It was strange, she observed to no one in particular, how London's Social Life was always being killed off, only to be revived once more the following year. And indeed why not? she continued. What would happen to all those hundreds of small businesses which depended on the Season for their livelihood? The milliners, the dressmakers, the couturiers, the hotels, the restaurants, good heavens, even the chair-hire people – where would they all be without it? She shrugged eloquently and held out her tea cup for her daughter to half fill. No one mentioned, to add to her list of small businesses, the small business of hiring out one's ballroom.

The custom of only half-filling the tea cup was fascinating Lucius. And no less fascinating was the way Lady Mary allowed herself to be dominated by her mother, and how gravely and respectfully she addressed her as 'Mamma'. And how she hardly sat down in her presence but, instinctively occupying the gap left by not having a ladies' maid, hovered around her constantly, one moment putting another log on the fire, the next ringing for someone to collect the tea things. It was quite extraordinary to witness how this tall and potentially self-possessed woman became a gawky, anxious daughter in the presence of her mother. Lucius felt uncomfortable. He wanted to help Lady Mary. Tell her that her funny flecked eye was terribly attractive, that she mustn't keep trying to hide it from people. That she must stand up to her mother, and not allow her to order her about as if she was a servant. And above all, naturally, make her realise that he, Lucius, was exactly what she was looking for, and what she needed more than anything in her life at this moment. As they took their leave of the Countess, he touched Lady Mary lightly on the elbow, guiding her out of the front door. To his intense disappointment, she did not appear to notice.

The Countess watched their departure without enormous interest. Mary had a way of adopting foreign wild flowers, sometimes for weeks, sometimes for months. Sometimes they were painters, sometimes, as in this case, they were writers. Although why an American thought he could write a book on the Season, she couldn't imagine. She lit a small Turkish cigarette, and rang the bell for what she was still pleased to describe as her 'maid', although 'thing' would be more appropriate.

The following morning Mrs Parker-Jones, once more seated at breakfast opposite her husband, was feeling understandably anxious about this business with the Countess and her ballroom. She was feeling so anxious, in fact, that she had not even opened the pile of bread-and-butter letters lying on her side plate. She knew they were bread-and-butter letters because such letters were invariably written with Parker-51 pens on bright blue paper, with the exception of those that came from Lady T, who always appeared to have written hers on her housekeeper's paper, something which Mrs Parker-Jones would have taken as a slight had she not heard Elizabeth Alney complain of the very same thing. She fanned idly through the envelopes, then looked across at Aidan who was noisily consuming his bacon and eggs, something he did when he didn't want to listen to her, which was nearly always. Another thing he did was constantly repeat whatever question she asked him, if the question had anything to do with money. Mrs Parker-Jones sighed inwardly. Among the countless mortifications attendant upon Jennifer's launch into Society, one of the worst was dealing with Aidan and his inability to see the supreme importance of his daughter's debut. Jennifer was his only daughter, and the sheer selfishness of someone like Aidan when it came to his only daughter was barely creditable. Quite frankly, from the first moment Jennifer's dance had been mentioned, her life had been one long struggle to get him to part with a single penny. However she, Clarissa, was made of steel when it came to matters concerning her daughter's future, and nothing Aidan could do would deter her from her purpose.

She watched as he finished his bacon and eggs and embarked on a plate of toast and Oxford marmalade. It was sad to think that the things one admired in someone when young turned out to be the very things you despised once they got older. When she first met Aidan, she had truly loved the way he was such an indoor person, loving to stop off at the slightest excuse for a lunch, tea, dinner or cocktail. Now it was the self-same indoor quality which repelled her so much. She remembered how she had felt it such a great relief not to be engaged to an Englishman who was hell-bent on bringing you down with a sharp rugby tackle or was forever breaking the strings of your tennis racket with his serve; but now, looking at the way Aidan sat at the table, sideways to allow room for his stomach, she thought how much wiser it would have been to have married Freddie, her mother's choice. Funnily enough she had seen Freddie only a couple of days before, sprinting down the Old Brompton Road after a taxi. Nowadays Freddie might not have Aidan's money, but he could still sprint after a taxi.

Aidan, of course, had predictably enough put up objections to sending round the chauffeur with the cash. He said he needed Gurney himself that morning, and when Mrs Parker-Jones had pointed out that he was going to spend all morning in a board meeting so he couldn't possibly need Gurney, Aidan said the real reason was he couldn't trust Gurney with all that money, which also was nonsensical and well he knew it. Then he went banging on about a receipt. He must have a receipt from the Countess, or there would never be any proof that he had indeed paid her.

This made Mrs Parker-Jones even more uneasy. For once she could see her husband's point of view. It was not an enormous sum of money, but it was enough. Nevertheless, after that encounter the previous afternoon, she had the feeling that the Countess most certainly was not the sort of person who would take kindly to being asked for a receipt.

So when Gurney returned later that morning from delivering the cash, and Mrs Parker-Jones opened the envelope he handed to her, she was not surprised to find

19

that it did not contain the receipt requested. Instead it contained a handwritten card from the Countess, scrawled in her overlarge hand. The Countess thanked Mrs Parker-Jones for her 'packet' but regretted it was impossible to send her a receipt. Perhaps Mrs Parker-Jones had not noticed but she was not in fact Harrods, and thus did not issue 'receipts'. She signed herself merely with her initials. Mrs Parker-Jones screwed the card up in something approaching a frenzy of fury. To be snubbed in this manner when she had just been made to pay in cash was agonising. The Countess might not be a department store, as she stated, but she didn't mind receiving money like one, and if she didn't mind receiving money like one and not only money but cash, then she should certainly be prepared to issue a receipt. The whole thing was quite horrendous, and if she had not seen for herself the photograph of the Countess in her court dress on the piano, quite frankly she would have doubted that she was a lady, let alone a Countess. She allowed herself a few moments to fantasise on this theme, then decided reluctantly that she had better straighten out the Countess' card, since Aidan would be sure to want to give it to his accountant, or something equally tedious. And then, as she went upstairs to powder her nose before lunch, she sighed. She had had a very hard life, of that there was no doubt, and if it did not culminate in some sort of social triumph for her daughter then she would pass away a deeply disappointed woman.

The person with whom she was lunching today was Andrew Gillott, the man who had 'introduced' her to the frightful Countess. Fortunately, she found the Old Etonian really quite amusing. He was always teasing her, and once last week he had even pinched her when Aidan wasn't looking, although admittedly it was after four rather large martinis. She liked him because he didn't put on any airs and graces, and he didn't seem to mind answering any of her questions. In fact, and in contrast to Aidan's perpetually voiced opinion, her own was that Andrew was worth every penny of whatever it was Aidan was paying him in his efforts to help improve their daughter's social standing.

Today, for instance, perhaps because of that interesting little book he had sent her, Mrs Parker-Jones asked Andrew why it was that his uncle, the Earl of Streatfield, had his seat in Devon, when since he was the Earl of Streatfield surely he should live in – well – Streatfield?

Andrew Gillott drew hard on his untipped cigarette and brushed some ash off his trousers.

'Not really,' he replied. 'No. Norfolk lives in Sussex, Devonshire lives in Derbyshire, and the previous Duke of St Arrans appeared to live in a paper bag.'

He gave a loud laugh and brushed some more ash off himself.

'Really?' cooed Mrs Parker-Jones. 'How amusing.'

It was perfectly thrilling to hear so many Dukes mentioned in one short sentence.

'Do any of them have gels of Jennifer's age?'

Mrs Parker-Jones had carefully learned to say gels for girls and goff for golf. Andrew wasn't quite sure whether this was altogether a good thing or not. But this was hardly relevant to the real crux of the matter, namely that no one really 'proper' would be the slightest bit interested in meeting her Jennifer.

'No, no,' he replied. 'None of them have girls of Jennifer's age, far as I know.'

'Oh dear,' said Mrs Parker-Jones, and to cover her disappointment carefully put a cigarette into her holder. She smiled at Andrew. He smiled back. Then there was a slight pause in the conversational proceedings, during which Andrew regretted for perhaps the ten thousandth time in his life that his father had left him such a small private income.

After what seemed like an eternity, Mrs Parker-Jones adjusted her skirts for the umpteenth time.

'Jennifer should be here soon,' she said brightly.

Andrew rose and wandered over to her cocktail cabinet in search of another gin. Meeting the beloved only daughter of Mrs Parker-Jones was about as appetising a social treat as a dinner party in Reading. He stared into the cocktail cabinet in an attempt to hide the dread he was feeling, and watched the miniature ballerina pirouette beneath him as he pulled up the shelves in search of the Gordons. If the daughter was as unappealing as the cocktail cabinet he'd be a confirmed alcoholic by the end of the Season and that was for sure.

'Ah. Here she is,' Mrs Parker-Jones announced as the door suddenly opened. 'Here's my daughter, Andrew.'

For a moment, as he was being introduced to her, Andrew thought of handing back the money. Jennifer was really quite, quite frightful. She wasn't very large, but she was very round, and her teeth stuck out when she smiled. She was obviously excruciatingly shy because, as she gripped Andrew's hand moistly, she blushed furiously and turned such a bright red that Andrew felt he could almost warm his hands by her. He could hear the voice of that dreary little doctor he'd been to see in Cadogan Square only last week coming back to him again.

'The body can't pickle for ever, you know, old chap,' the silly bastard had warned him. 'The old body can't pickle forever.'

Well it's going to have to take its chance, Andrew thought, as he steadfastly regarded the crimson Jennifer.

'Jennifer has just finished a flower-arranging course in Sunningdale,' said Mrs Parker-Jones. Then she smiled at her daughter and wondered why pale pink didn't suit her as much as it did other girls. It was extraordinary. She herself had always looked most becoming in pale pink. She sighed to herself and put out her cigarette. It was because of such little things that it was so important to try and launch Jennifer properly, for she certainly wasn't capable of setting sail on her own.

Mrs Parker-Jones looked over at Andrew, who drained his gin in one and followed his hostess through into the dining room.

It was not long after this unimportant social event that another engagement of similar insignificance was held near by, namely a tea-party given by Lady Mary Lawton for her cousin Lady Georgiana. Lucius was present, naturally, in his now acceptable role as author-to-be, and to help hand round very small asparagus sandwiches and little fondants in pleated paper cases.

There can be few, if any, social functions less interesting than a Society tea-party: the most dramatic thing that happened all afternoon was the impaling of a miniature éclair on someone's stiletto. The party was well attended, but not by any of the faces that regularly graced the social pages of *Tatler* or *Harpers*; there were no arms manufacturers with double-barrelled names, or pop singers who had shot to million-dollar fame on the strength of a song with one verse. No one stayed very long, no longer than it took to drink a demitasse and to write down with miniature gold biros in small leather notebooks the address and telephone number of everyone present. Then, amidst a flutter of white hands and mono-syllabic farewells, the guests departed as swiftly as they had arrived.

Mary had told Lucius beforehand that it was very unfortunate but highly necessary for her cousin Georgiana to go through this ritual. For it was by the giving of and the going to teas and luncheons that socially ambitious girls in London still got to know each other, and without those functions they would remain, it would seem, in dry dock. She admitted that it was regrettable that her cousin had to go through this ritual, but as an Upper Class girl with no money, there was nothing else she could do; for with the sole exception of Mary, it seemed that all necessary family connections had long since been severed, and her parents were quite unable to lift a hand to help her. Furthermore, Lucius gathered that Georgiana was not gifted in any way which was discernible to those about her, and that therefore there was no alternative but to find her a rich husband. If nothing else it would be a start, for once she had one rich husband, others, as everyone knew, would be sure to follow.

As he hovered with the fondants, Lucius found himself

wondering which of the girls present was the daughter of Mrs Aidan Parker-Jones. He had not so far come across the luckless Jennifer amongst the teacups, the trays and the flurry of anxious mothers, but he knew he would recognise her as soon as he did, for undoubtedly she would be vulgar and pushy just like her frightful mother.

It turned out, however, that he was wrong, for Jennifer Parker-Jones was neither vulgar nor pushy. Unfortunately perhaps, but without any outward resemblance to the creature who had called on the Countess a few weeks earlier, any more than Lady Georgiana could be said to have any resemblance to her cousin Lady Mary.

Jennifer Parker-Jones was too large to be pretty, but no doubt she would become handsome in time, and far from suffering from too much confidence she appeared to blush at the slightest attention, in direct contrast to Lady Georgiana, whose manner suffered from a great deal of social confidence, and who seemed able to find charm in the dullest remarks, and amusement in nothing at all. Naturally, Georgiana had taken to Jennifer at once. The two girls were so unalike that they were bound to become best friends immediately. And whereas all the other girls, having noted Georgiana's slender good looks and dark shining hair, her slim ankles and her tiny wrists, had put her telephone number in their little leather books with some reluctance, they all eagerly copied out Jennifer's for the very opposite reasons. Plain rich girls in horrid clothes would always be popular among other girls, and Jennifer quite obviously was to be no exception. Georgiana, on the other hand, for all her connections, would have a harder time. In this, as in so many things, life could be really quite fair.

chapter two

Considering her background it would have been surprising for Georgiana not to have been born on her father's large estate in the country. When Lucius first saw her, standing beneath a portrait of some vaguely *arrière* ancestor and tapping him lightly on the arm every now and then to be sure of his complete attention, this was precisely the circumstance he himself would have designed for her. And if he had then asked her about her childhood and she had been prepared to have talked about it, which in itself was doubtful, she would have described her parents, her nanny and her early circumstances in the same lightly fond manner that she might use to describe the death of some old pony, long since destroyed. Naturally Lucius attributed her self-assurance to the fact that she had been brought up in a world of affluence, a world which in spite of all the auguries still survived and enabled children brought up within it to learn the confidence which springs from hundreds of years of privilege.

In reality, however, what people at first took to be confidence in Georgiana was merely a desperate desire to please, which in itself was born out of a willingness to make the best of what had not always been so. For although Georgiana had indeed been born on her father's large estate in the country, the estate was now sadly depleted – not by time, although time had indeed worked against Longborough as much as it had worked for it, but by the continuous mismanagement of generations. Georgiana did not come from a long line of brilliant states-men, but from a family whose constant profligacy had required them regularly to marry heiresses, although by the time Georgiana was held by the vicar over the font in the family chapel, a tiny head lost among the ancient robes, there was very little left for her to inherit beyond a mass of long-standing debts and the blue blood running in her veins.

It was ironic that, in spite of a history of wealthy marriages, her family had apparently for a few hundred years totally eschewed the subject of money. Perhaps, thanks to the endless stream of judicious marriages, it was something they took so much for granted that they found it not only bad form to discuss it but, worse, tedious. And so, even when the storm of taxes and death duties broke over their heads, they continued stoically to ignore the disasters which were upon them and to regard the matter of finance as something which, since they had never discussed it when it was present, they were most certainly not going to discuss when it was absent.

Naturally Georgiana was aware of the lack of affluence in her existence as a child, for it would have been impossible not to be aware of the cold in the rooms, or the way the children on the estate had had more to eat for tea or breakfast than either Nanny or she. She saw their crowded tea tables through the cottage windows each day as she returned from her afternoon walk, knowing that on her own plate, once she climbed the cold linoleum stairs leading to the nursery floor, there would be one paste sandwich and beside it a glass of milk with a thick skin on it in winter, and with large lumps of soured cream in summer. And of course she had known that this was because she was privileged, because she lived in the big house and was not like other children. She knew this because Nanny told her so.

And so she would sit, thoughtfully chewing the stale paste sandwich with its indigestible crust, and wish that she was not privileged, and that she was not 'such a lucky little girl', and dream what it might be like if she was unlucky, for the unlucky children she saw on her walks had mothers and not nannies, and plates crowded with food and tables laid with butter and jam, even though, which she found slightly muddling, their milk and their butter came from the cows her father owned and not theirs. For there never was any butter in her paste sandwich, and the warm smell of home-made bread was something she was privileged to experience only when passing the windows of the less privileged.

Her life in the nursery might have been tolerable had Nanny loved her. But Nanny did not love her, because she was a girl. She did things for her, of course, dutifully; but she was a girl, so Nanny could not love Georgiana, because, as she was forever telling her charge, boys were more affectionate. Georgiana accepted this, just as she accepted the fact that it was privilege which prevented her from having any butter on her sandwiches, or fresh milk in her glass. And so the two of them, Nanny and she, lived together on the nursery floor in a sad and cold imitation of a relationship which Georgiana constantly saw portrayed idyllically in the few books she was allowed to read. Other children seemed to have nice nannies. Christopher Robin had one who took him to Buckingham Palace and allowed him to jump about when his hair was being brushed and even apparently allowed him to keep a beetle in a box.

In her books there were children who had counterpanes upon which they played soldiers, and views from their nursery windows of lamplighters passing by. But she had only a fourposter bed and to see out of her nursery window you had to drag across a very heavy chest and stand on it; and when you did, there was no lamplighter, nor even a lamp, but just trees, and branches growing very close to your windows, forever scratching them on windy nights with long witches' nails.

Sometimes, on her twice daily walks, it seemed to her that everywhere on the estate there were happier people than the people who inhabited her small world. Her world was cold and still, with only the sound of the nursery clock ticking away the hours, because she was not allowed to watch television except on Sundays and, although once an aunt sent her a record of nursery rhymes for Christmas, she had never played it because there was nothing to play records on. She knew this wasn't true of other children, because she could hear their radios and their televisions on her walks, and occasionally, which was blissful, workmen would come up to the nursery floor to do some maintenance and bring their radios with them, which they played very loudly. And sometimes, on Nanny's day off, when Mrs Miles was meant to be in charge but wasn't, she would creep off down to the staff room and stand at the doorway watching their television undetected. Again, here was a world where people seemed to be enjoying themselves. There was nothing silent here, nothing silent and cold in this flickering black-and-white world which kept Mr and Mrs Miles entertained and happy, comfortable in their old chintz-covered chairs.

When she was six, the coldness of it all finally overcame her and she became ill. She crept up into her lonely, dark, terrifying fourposter bed and she started to die, because, although she had never inhabited any place else except this dim and cheerless world, she knew that there was another, and in that knowledge lay a despair as suffocating as the curtains they pulled around her bed when the doctor examined her. Day after day, although the branches scratched at the windows and Nanny mechanically stuck a thermometer in and out of her mouth, she barely moved, as her mind reached out longingly for this other world. She thought about death, and the idea of dying seemed wonderful, a lot less frightening than the bed in which she lay. And as she closed her eyes she imagined the clear blue skies she had only seen in her books, and heard the skylark which she knew sang somewhere far above the frightening trees, and imagined that she had a dog, and that it was running beside her, and that she would never ever have to return again to this cold world of privilege and differences, and that she would have people called Mum and Dad in her life and she would see them every day, and they wouldn't be far below her in rooms which you never entered, or away on a shoot, or abroad, or at the races. They would be with you, and with them you would do things like fly kites and blow out candles on birthday cakes, because if you had a

Mum and a Dad instead of a Mamma and Papa that's what they did.

At first, naturally, she didn't go to school, because girls from her family had never gone to school. She was taught in the school room, by herself. But after she was ill they sent her away because, if she was going to be ill like that again, they thought it would be much better all round if she was ill away from them and with children her own age. Nanny could stay to help with the sewing, and anyway they needed Nanny. But the child must go. And so name-tapes were sent for, which Nanny stitched most carefully onto her school clothes, and new shoes were marked off on lists, and heavy linen sheets and large white towels were carefully placed in an old leather-bound trunk which bore the labels of pre-war ocean liners and exotic-sounding railway trains. And Mr Miles sat on the trunk while Nanny locked it, and then drove her to her new school in a state of great excitement because they all told her she would like school, that school was better for someone like her.

It only dawned on her some weeks after being at her new school that she didn't in fact like it at all. It wasn't because it was worse than life at home, because it wasn't. There still was no television, and no butter in the sandwiches, and girls of her tender age went to bed as early as she did at Longborough; but what made it worse was that there were other children there. On her own, with Nanny in the nursery, the worst she could imagine was that Mamma and Papa would come and visit: for although Nanny didn't like her, and she often heard Mrs Miles remark that she wasn't like a child at all, Georgiana knew her parents liked her even less. She knew this from their expressions of extreme embarrassment whenever they saw her. She knew it because they never kissed her, or spoke directly to her, but always through Nanny or some other intermediary. Then once more they would thankfully withdraw, having indirectly enquired how she was getting on, or if her health was holding up, and Georgiana, with even greater gratitude, would hear their footsteps receding down the linoed corridors again, and the whole horrid business would be over for another few weeks. But school was even worse, because now to add to her list of miseries, there were other little girls who refused to be friends with you, who said you had a silly name, and who were only nice to you when your jam arrived from Harrods, or on your birthday when the cook baked you a small sponge to share with the other girls in your form.

On Georgiana's seventh birthday, the other girls gave her a present. There was nothing from her parents, and although Nanny remembered and sent her some gloves she had made by the afternoon post, on the table there was nothing for her but a large brown-papered box, lovingly inscribed by the head of her form and by all her classmates. Georgiana looked at it and was quite hopelessly excited.

She undid the outside layer of paper, and then the next, and as more and more paper came away in her hands, and as she fumbled with more and more knotted string, she heard the occasional giggle in the now silent dining room, and then, undid more and more paper and more and more string until she came to a tiny box in the middle of the parcel which she opened to now quite unsuppressed giggling and which she found to be empty.

It was from that moment on, although Georgiana was only seven, that she realised quite clearly that it would be the height of foolishness any more to stretch out a hand in the dark and hope to find something there. She later became fascinated by a story of a boy with an icicle in his heart, because she saw in this child a mirror image of herself and her own inability to love anyone she knew. She gave up any hope of finding a hero or a heroine, and adopted a justifiably truculent attitude towards childhood. After all, if she could not die, then she would sit astride this business of being a child and take whatever it cared to throw at her with straight shoulders and a determined eye, in the sure knowledge that one day, in the not too distant future, it would all be over.

She often wondered if other children felt as she did.

Not those whose parents wrote to them twice weekly, and came to visit them every Sunday with sweets and fresh eggs and runny home-made marmalade, because she knew those children couldn't feel as she did. But there were others, others as institutionalised as Georgiana herself, whose parents never wrote or visited, but yet with whom she had no desire to be friends: they were outcasts like her, and like her they wanted acceptance rather than friendship, acceptance into the world of the confident élite. Often Georgiana would smuggle small antique objects which she stole from Longborough back to school in order to try and attract them; because even though she was never successful, she found stealing thrilling, and even though the precious objects were merely taken as their due by the majority of the girls, sometimes for as much as half a day Georgiana would be accepted, like some cur who is allowed a place by the fire before being unceremoniously booted out again into the cold.

As she grew older, however, she saw that in order to survive she would have to forge a new sort of relationship, one based not on small silver animals, snuff boxes and cigarette cases, but on a totally different commodity – herself. As her femininity blossomed, she realised with sublime gratitude that the purgatory of childhood was nearly over. No more would there be rules to be obeyed blindly, life would no longer be regimented by the sound of bells, instead she could go where she pleased and do what she liked. On this sexual playing field which she now saw in front of her, she realised you might sustain an occasional light bruising but, if you were careful and kept yourself just out of reach, she knew there was no reason why she shouldn't score just where and when she wished.

She was pretty. Her looking glass told her that. She wasn't very tall, but she was slender and had beautiful thick shiny hair that she always wore straight which, as Lucius later annotated in one of his notebooks, gave her the air of a mischievous Lord Fauntleroy. When she went to France, to Finishing School, the French would murmur '*très mignonne*' with gratifying frequency. In France she learned to toss her hair a little, and to touch whoever she was talking to lightly on the arm, and to open her eyes very wide when someone was telling her something completely uninteresting.

On her return to England she made a list of things she liked. The list included Modigliani, Egyptian cats, Arab horses, silk underwear, Persian rugs, eighteenth-century silver, arum lilies, Vuitton luggage and vintage champagne. None of these things were to be found at Longborough, not even the silver. In fact on her return she was seized with a certain guilty feeling that her petty thefts had somewhat contributed to the despoilation of the great house, and each dusty space where once stood wine coolers, or candlesticks, or some other noble piece, now stared reproachfully up at her, as if accusing her of complicity.

Nanny was still there, naturally, up the linoed stairs, mistress of a now gratifyingly empty nursery wing. She greeted Georgiana with little enthusiasm, switching on the television news at a tremendous volume as soon as she had enquired politely and without interest about her former charge's stay in France.

Unlike a lot of people whose return to their childhood home is marked by surprise at its smallness, Georgiana's return to Longborough was notable for her surprise at its magnitude. It was simply enormous, especially after her Paris apartment, and in fact, with so many of the great rooms now empty, it even appeared to have grown. Her boots clattered now across bare boards and as she walked through the house, her steps echoing, their sound brought to mind gentlemen callers from years ago who must have come to Longborough in search of an improvement in rank or a plain heiress badly in need of a husband. She opened the lid of the grand piano and played one note, and in the weak sunlight that filtered through the unwashed windows a faint mist arose from the keyboard. She closed the lid and wrote her name in the thick dust, delaying the inevitable moment when in some room or other somewhere she would find the people responsible for her birth.

The brass studs on the baize door leading to the kitchen had grown rusty. Georgiana passed through and remembered how on Nanny's day off she had been allowed to help Miles lay out the knives and forks, and how he would polish the spoons on his apron, breathing on them occasionally beforehand. Those were her favourite days, the days when Nanny was off, when Mrs Miles would give her a little bit of pastry to roll, and she would roll it and re-roll it until it turned pale grey, admirably setting off the raspberry jam which she would carefully place in the middle. It was on these days, days Georgiana thought of as holidays, that she would sometimes overhear Mrs Miles saying that she wasn't like a child at all, but more like a little old lady. And Miles would say mysteriously that he thought it was a shame, and stare at her for a moment with small grey eyes which Georgiana liked to pretend belonged to an elephant when he carried her back upstairs to the nursery and returned her into Nanny's care.

But now Miles was gone, and with him Mrs Miles, retired to their bungalow by the sea. And the floor was no longer polished 'hands and knees' and when you pulled the staff bells in any of the rooms, they would come away in your hands, as if since there now was no one to answer them, there was no point in them functioning. Georgiana walked past the rows of empty jam jars in the larder, and the rusty flour bin which she used to have to put on top of a chair in order to reach the table when rolling her pastry, and which now stood empty except for weevils. On the very top shelf stood a row of Fortnum and Mason Christmas puddings which somehow had escaped boiling and eating, and now sat side by side in rows waiting for the return of the days when at least half a dozen of them would have to be cooked to feed the crowd upstairs.

Back in the kitchen, behind odd doors, mops and dishcloths had petrified into strange distorted shapes, no longer candidates in Mrs Miles' constant quest to find exactly the right polisher; and with Mrs Miles' crusading spirit long gone from the kitchens, vermin could now be heard behind the wainscot. For now there were no cats, and no traps, because Mrs Miles' army of tabbies had retired with her to Wittering, to a well-earned rest, sea air and tinned food. Georgiana sighed. Much as she had hated the traps, and the cats, she hated the mice even more.

Yet still she delayed the moment when she would have to go and greet her parents. Perhaps she dreaded that they too, like the once-proud kitchens, would be covered in dust and droppings, or would be seated in their chairs behind cobwebs, trapped like the flies she had seen in the spiders' webs which now hung everywhere. Finally she braced herself and made her way back upstairs.

She found them in a small room on the far side of the house. Her mother inspected her from a distance, nervous, vague and quite unprepared for her return. She regarded her daughter rather as if she were a hunter being led out from a box for her inspection, and she was a rider caught without her jodphurs. Her father on the other hand, while treating her in much the same way, passing a quick eye over her to see if she'd done a leg or developed any curbs, finding nothing promptly and silently returned to his *Times*.

They still changed for dinner of course, as did Georgiana. She and her mother trailed about the kitchen in their evening clothes as they prepared the food, and then climbed back upstairs to the dining room where her father sat in solitary splendour. After dinner they still retired, leaving him to his port while they drank their coffee in the morning room off the main hall – which was full of eye-stinging smoke because the logs on the fire no longer fitted the grate the way they should – and their desultory conversation was as damp as the smouldering firewood. By the time she went to bed, Georgiana was exhausted, tired out by the lack of conversation. Yet she was unable to sleep, so obsessed was she by the idea of how soon she could return to London. She knew that Longborough presented her with problems she was totally incapable of solving, and her parents were now as unfamiliar to her as most of the people in the photographs in the old copies of *Horse and Hound* which lay beside her bed. Georgiana flicked through a copy with little interest, except to notice how extraordinary it was that, like most of the gentry in the photographs, her parents still managed to look immaculate even though the house was falling down around their ears. It was Nanny, of course, Georgiana remembered. Nanny never would help in the house, but she did do the sewing, and just as the china they used was beautifully riveted, so were her parents beautifully mended, with not a cuff left unturned, nor a starched collar frayed.

The next morning, as Georgiana continued her pilgrimage through the house, she realised it was just as well that Longborough was so large, for she noticed most of the rooms bore traces of having been used some time or other by her parents. They quite obviously occupied each room in turn until the build-up of dust and debris attracted the Tittlemouse family en masse, which forced her parents to set up camp elsewhere in the house, leaving the rooms they had once occupied to the smallest of tenants and only the occasional sign of human occupation, such as a belt left dangling from an old and torn silk-covered hanger in a cupboard, or a china bowl somewhere that still held the remains of the loose face powder which her mother favoured.

Of course her parents never referred to the 'build-up' any more than they had apparently referred to rationing during the war, or to the loss of friends, or to the fact that the roof of the West Wing had fallen in. They accepted the conditions under which they now lived in much the same way as they accepted Georgiana's sudden reappearance, or the vicissitudes of the weather, or a warning from the Trustees – without any outward display of emotion. And Georgiana, as she walked from room to room viewing the decline, found that she too remained outwardly unmoved, until she reached the stables, and then she found it impossible not to feel a quite overwhelming sense of loss, for here were boxed her few happy childhood memories. Here she had enacted her only genuinely sad farewells before departing for boarding school and from here she had led out on sharp winter mornings her one best friend, mane and tail painstakingly plaited, dark coat gleaming. Now only a crooked name plate bearing the name 'Bantry Bay' hung over his box, the tack room door swung on one hinge and the feed buckets lay buckled and upended in a corner. Here too the Tittlemouses ruled and Thomasina and her kin ran around freely and unhindered, rulers of yet another previously unconquerable kingdom.

Georgiana walked back into the autumn sunshine and towards the woods that lay beyond the ha-ha, but even as she walked away from the stables she felt she could still hear the scratching and the pattering of the mice. They seemed to be running in and out of her head, just as they were running in and out of everywhere else. Her mind seemed like a wainscot, and her imagination could no more hold out any solace to her fearful loneliness and desperation than could the floorboards in the great house any longer seemingly hold her weight.

The woods were full of leaves which clung to her boots as she walked. The colours, perhaps tempting to a painter, to her seemed almost garish, so she walked with her head down, breaking twigs and small branches with a sadistic satisfaction. Self-pity was not an emotion she had ever been encouraged to indulge herself in, yet she found at this moment that her over-all feeling was one of precisely that, self-pity. To find yourself at last grown up, to have escaped the horrors of childhood, and then to discover as you look around you that all the secrets the adults appeared to have been hiding from you are only yet another series of disappointments was almost unbearable. But only almost: for later, when Georgiana took a bath prior to leaving Longborough, and stood naked in front of her looking glass, she looked at a future which need not, she thought, be quite as hopeless as it appeared to be that minute.

She went and said goodbye to Nanny, not out of affection but out of a sense of duty. But when for the first time ever Nanny kissed her, Georgiana felt a slight tremor of guilt that she was leaving so soon. Nanny then sniffed and returned to watching her soap opera and turning the collar of the shirt which lay in her lap.

Her parents, when she went to say goodbye, were as silently reproachful as the house itself. They said they quite understood why she had to go back to London, in such a way that Georgiana knew that they wanted her to understand that they didn't. She packed her suitcase and her basket into the back of the village taxi, then gave a little wave of her hand from the back as it drove away. Her parents remained on the steps of the house. As the distance increased between her and them, they looked so perfect standing on the steps of what now appeared to be a perfect house that she wondered for a moment whether she was exaggerating the need for such a sudden departure. Perhaps really they were perfectly all right, and so was Longborough, and the next time she came down, maybe even next weekend, she would find the house as it used to be, with no leaking roof, no broken panes of glass in the Orangery, no lead guttering hanging broken at right angles, no rusty studs on the pass door, and no mice in the now-deserted rooms. She hoped this could be so, as she sat back in the taxi, but she knew it was quite impossible. For only last night as she and her mother were washing up in the kitchen, a small pipe had burst somewhere under the sink, and as the water lay in ever-increasing puddles on the dirty flagstone floor, seeping into the soles of her thin evening shoes, Georgiana knew that she would never again allow life to do this to her. Never again would she let herself be depressed by something not of her own choosing – and as the skirt on her evening dress gathered a black tide mark from the rising water, and as she searched in vain for mops and water-tight buckets, she knew something would have to be done and that she was the only person who could do it. And so, like everyone else who seeks their – or in Georgiana's case – someone else's fortune, she came to London, or at least to the couple of square miles which make up the only piece of that city which matters to those who descend upon it from the country.

For the first few weeks she stayed at home with Mary, because she did not wish to be accused of merely using her cousin, especially because they both knew that that was exactly what she was doing. And so she acted as a young cousin should, answering the telephone, making spinach quiches and above all diplomatically fading upstairs to her room the moment she felt Mary needed some privacy. A young cousin to help around the house was a pleasure; but a social rival, Georgiana sensed, would be extremely irritating.

After Longborough, Mary's house was a source of sensual pleasure to Georgiana, for she appeared to spend more money at the florist than she did even at the hairdresser. Upon every available surface she would place bowls of flowers, or plants with green waxy leaves and white fingershaped flowers with a strange scent and reminiscent of the flowers on Art Nouveau postcards, and whose odd odour would be drowned in the evening by the pungent smell of old roses which Mary, with a fervent, almost religious regularity, would drop from a small Floris bottle onto special little rings which she had placed upon the lamps, so that an overpowering incense would fill the house as dusk fell.

Naturally, since it was in town, the house was done up entirely in country style. There was a presently fashionable form of sisal matting upon the staircases, and festoons in the windows, which to Georgiana, who had only known large heavy curtains which always smelt of dust, were a joy to lower gently in the evening and raise again back into their silken clouds in the morning.

The cat was called Nefertiti, and liked to come and stare at Georgiana, and Georgiana would deliberately encourage her by pretending to ignore her. Sometimes, in those early days, Georgiana and the cat would sit staring out of the window at the street below. The cat would perch precariously upon the window ledge with Georgiana seated less precariously inside the open window, and together they would watch the Rollses, Ferraris and Porsches that nightly passed by, often stopping outside Mary's, sometimes on their way to other nearby houses; and occasionally Nefertiti would nidder and growl as she spied an especially fat London pigeon, and Georgiana would look at her and sympathise.

Eventually it fell to Mary to realise, as Georgiana well knew it would, that her young cousin was an indispensable asset to her household. When her maid was off, or when the extra chairs for a buffet had not arrived, when they ran completely out of Perrier water, or when Mary had no one to pick up her clothes from the cleaners, Georgiana went willingly, and Mary was grateful; and naturally, once Mary felt grateful, it occurred to her that she really should do something in return for Georgiana, poor little Georgiana whose future was so uncertain, and whose parents were so uncaring that they hadn't even been able to organise an inheritance for her.

Mary's house had for Georgiana, coming from her classic country upbringing, a decidedly Bohemian air to it, in spite of its richesse of flowers and silks, and its stippled walls, its tented bathroom and its daily maid. The front door was never shut, music played on every floor (nearly always Mozart), and the visitors who came and went although often aristocratic were not required to be so. If they were amusing they needed only to be rich, or occasionally just talented. Sometimes, rarely, they were all three.

Americans, Australians and South Americans over for the Polo season, all called on Mary as soon as they arrived in London. This new kind of man impressed Georgiana, for with their even teeth, their brown skins, their blue-tinted contact lenses and the small silver or gold spoons so many of them wore on thin chains round their necks, they appeared to be members of a different sex. She could not help noticing how supple and lithe they were, their bodies free from the encumbrance of heavy suiting, in direct contrast to all the men she had been used to meeting, men who to a man were buttoned, waistcoated and cuff-linked into their suits and shirts as firmly as babies into their pram sets.

This other breed of men were all exquisitely mannered and free and easy, and (like so many of the visitors to the house) members of Mary's favourite category, 'the Sometime Famous' – a label which meant that sometime in the future or in the past, these people had been or were going to be famous for something, which qualification was sufficient for them to use Mary's house whenever they wished, either to meet and make friends with more people of their kind, or to do business, or merely to amuse themselves or Mary. Thus Georgiana came to regard Mary's way of life as everything a way of life should be. Mary appeared to have a total disregard for sex but a profound regard for sensuality, which attracted Georgiana enormously, and which Georgiana attributed to Mary's broken marriage to someone she described as Beastly Geoffrey.

Georgiana dwelt on the subject of Mary's ex-husband a great deal. She imagined he must have had some perfectly dreadful peculiarity, or sexual tastes which poor Mary could not share. Or perhaps he had merely been something which Georgiana once heard her mother say of a large labrador who would not stop clinging to the vicar's trousers – a social nuisance – and if that were so, it would account for Mary's *femme seule* existence. Once, when they were dining alone, Georgiana dared ask Mary what she so disliked about her ex-husband.

'His three-buttoned suits in hairy materials,' she replied, looking her straight in the eye. 'Never marry a man's man,' she then continued. 'Anything – a mother's boy, even a wild flower – anything is preferable to a typical English public-school male in a thornproof suit.'

Georgiana remembered this advice, and if anything her admiration for Mary increased. It seemed the height of chic to abandon one's husband not on account of some unspeakable perversion, but for his taste in three-buttoned thornproofs.

From the moment Mary decided to take Georgiana under her wing, she encouraged Georgiana to think of herself as beautiful, not so much because she was but more because Mary could not bear to have anything around her for long which was neither beautiful nor stylish to a large degree. Decorative was one of her favourite words; and here again Georgiana sensed that it was because she did not find them decorative that Mary did not indulge in the current fashion for what was called live-in lovers. She loved the idea of romance but not of sex. She adored people ringing her with small items of scandal but she would have been horrified to be even remotely associated with one. When they were alone in the evenings, which was seldom, she would amuse herself and her young cousin by describing her ideal of the perfect existence, which of course in reality was hers, but which she pretended for the sake of their table game was some other lucky person's, in some other time. It was true that she did long for other eras when she imagined things might have been easier, but Georgiana soon came to realise that Mary was in fact the most thoroughly contented person she knew, in that she led precisely the kind of life she most enjoyed, in exactly the sort of manner she most preferred. If she had any broader vision of a life other than her own, it was as an opera, with arias of such sweet perfection that she would be moved to the most pleasurable of tears, but not to the point that it would spoil her enjoyment, for she would no more have wished to get nearer the emotions which lay at the centre of great opera than she would enjoy being told the details of causes she supported through her charity work. Child cruelty, or starvation in the Third World were things you fought against by serving on committees and by attending endless balls, but your familiarity with them extended no further than the special headings on the paper you used to write to your friends soliciting their support. Of course she knew these things happened, but did not wish to be told about them, any more than she wished to be reminded that drains ran under her house.

'I don't wish to know about that,' she would gently remind anyone who raised a subject which she found unpleasant. And if they were tactless enough still to continue, she would leave either them or the room. It was as if she had taken a vow of silence about reality, and insisted that any who came within her circule must belong to the same Order. In her house only pleasant and amusing subjects were discussed and contemplated. Georgiana, in total sympathy, became a most willing novice.

It was shortly after Georgiana had learned that she had inherited a small trust from a distant but loving godmother that Lucius came into their life – and he was welcomed not only by Mary but by Georgiana herself. Life has a habit of tidying itself into a series of neat coincidences, and the coincidence of Lucius wishing to research his forthcoming book at precisely the same time that Mary decided she must help Georgiana make a rich alliance was gratifying to all concerned. Naturally Lucius had style or Mary would not have taken him up, and since Mary's life was totally devoted to the pursuit of style, it was not long before they both turned their attentions to Georgiana. Lucius knew exactly how Georgiana should look, and so did Mary, and Georgiana, whose upbringing had been so firmly based on doing as she was told, when she was told, submitted quite willingly to whatever they jointly decided and acquiesced to whatever they were jointly agreed upon. She had never been used to much attention as a child, and now it acted upon her like champagne, without, it seemed, the inevitable thirst that follows. She accepted that, in order to have any social success with the kind of men who were rich enough to afford Longborough, she needed to look as if she could afford it too.

As Lucius spent hours deliberating over her hats, and Mary frowned in earnest concentration over the exact placing of a pocket in a tailor-made jacket, Georgiana thought of how when she was a child she had so often dreamed about someone taking her away and changing her, making her into someone who would be quite unrecognisable, the sort of child of which her parents could be proud. Now, as she swung down Beauchamp Place with Mary and Lucius almost daily, or climbed up small dark back stairways into fitting rooms, a sense of mystical exultation ran through her, for this was what she had dreamed life could possibly be – a world of toiles, wool, cashmere, velvet, silk, organdy and taffeta.

One afternoon they took her to fit shoes and match handbags in Bond Street, and having matched and fitted, as many as fifteen boxes were put into the taxi and driven gleefully back to Mary's house. Later, in her room alone, Georgiana took out each pair of shoes and stroked them, before putting them back in their boxes, the way she had with her toys only a few years before. But whereas Squeak, and Gump and their other oddly named friends had stared out at her with black button eyes from their sheets made of paper napkins, now the names of famous shoemakers winked at her in gold from their beds of fine tissue paper. Nanny used to say you could always tell a lady, because she kept her shoes in boxes, her nightdress in a case, and never did up her own suspenders. As Georgiana looked at the contents of her shoe cupboard, and took out her new silk pyjamas from their satin case, she thought with satisfaction of how, for once, Nanny would be pleased with her.

And now, since Mary had given first a tea, then a luncheon, and finally a drinks party for her, Georgiana could not only start to wear the clothes and the shoes which Lucius and Mary had so carefully chosen to offset her slight, slim body, her thick, lustrous hair and her mischievous manner, but she could also meet the objects of all their preparations, the young, rich single men, the older, rich married men, and the middle-aged, rich divorced men. There were very few rich widowers available, thanks to the fact that comfort in the form of the late wife's best friend had become the fashionable mode in mourning.

To be truthful, at first Georgiana did not feel greatly attracted to any one of the men presented to her, but instead she felt attracted to them all, for jointly they represented to her such a significant part of her future that she had great difficulty distinguishing one eligible male from the next, and rather as someone who is ignorant of the finer points of horses but in love with the mere sight of them will at first see only that one is a bay and another a chestnut, Georgiana at first found it difficult not to feel immediately attracted to every person of the opposite sex who spent more than a few moments in her company. This was partly due to her natural optimism, and partly due to the fact that she felt, at first, that anyone who wore a pair of trousers and spoke in a deeper register than herself was by necessity delightful.

In this way she was the complete opposite to Jennifer Parker-Jones, whom Georgiana noticed was completely unable to pretend that she liked someone when she didn't. Jennifer thus succeeded in deterring everyone except her own sex. In this way she was vitally useful to all the other girls and her friendship was much fought over; and if Georgiana's telephone number was sought after by gentlemen of all ages, it was Jennifer's morning mail which became stiffest with invitations from other girls begging her to attend their parties. However, Georgiana knew she had first call on Jennifer's services because Jennifer's dance was to be held in Georgiana's aunt's house just off Belgrave Square.

Such was Jennifer's good nature that she gave no indication she was aware this was the reason for her popularity, or that she was liked for any other reason than for herself. Although she had not been to the same school as Georgiana, she and Georgiana became as close as two girls will whose attractions are at such variance. It was not long after they had exchanged telephone numbers that it occurred to Georgiana that she really should try to help Jennifer improve her looks, in the same way that

Lucius and Mary had helped her improve her own. Jennifer really was too large in every way, and this was something which could quite quickly be rectified simply by eating spinach without the accompanying quiche. And her teeth needed to be straightened. And her choice in clothes improved. Once all this was done Georgiana had no doubt that Jennifer would not be unattractive. Neither would she be too attractive.

The Countess was giving a drinks party, and since she had asked Georgiana to submit a list of 'young' for inclusion, naturally Georgiana included Jennifer Parker-Jones in the list. She also of course included certain other names which would make more sense to her aunt; the sons and daughters of families whose parents the Countess had been used to including on her own lists. This was diplomatic, for since the day the note had arrived with the chauffeur, the slightest mention of Mrs Parker-Jones' name had become the signal for much nostril-flaring on the part of the Countess, although the Parker-Jones 'hop', as the Countess insisted upon calling it, remained a firm fixture in everyone's diaries, just as the rental money for the ballroom remained in the Countess' deposit account at Coutts.

Jennifer pressed her face against the glass of her small gold compact.

'I'm always so afraid my face will go red as soon as I take a sip of my first drink.'

Georgiana didn't answer because she had become quite fascinated by her own image in the looking glass. Surely, she thought, everyone must fall in love with her tonight, for she had never looked better. Earlier, when she had presented herself to Lucius and Mary for the usual inspection, he had expressed unease over her choice of pearls, and Mary over her choice of belt. They had stood looking at her from different angles, Mary squinting slightly with her funny eye turned away from Georgiana, and Lucius holding up one hand, two fingers of which he held against his thumb, a habit of his when he was feeling uncertain.

Georgiana had allowed Mary to retie her belt and then had returned dutifully to her bedroom to change the pearls for a gold necklace in the form of a serpent, a piece which her mother had been given by some admirer a long time ago. As she put on the necklace, Georgiana thought how odd it was that her mother had once had admirers, for to Georgiana she seemed always to have been how she appeared to her now, stooped, grey and embattled, without any discernible charm. This serpent which now lay round Georgiana's throat, winking stone-green emerald eyes at her, could surely only have been given to a girl at least as fascinating as Georgiana herself. Georgiana could not connect such a creature with her mother, the present châtelaine of Longborough.

The Countess, carefully fitting a Sobranie into the top of her cigarette holder, surveyed the necklace around Georgiana's throat and recollected, to her inner satisfaction, exactly when it had been given to her mother, and, more to the point, by whom.

'Of course I had quite forgotten,' she announced loudly, 'that Georgiana's mamma came across with Archie Bryanston.'

'Mamma!' said Mary, sotto, in the vain hope that by dropping her voice she could encourage her mother to do the same. But the Countess, teeth firmly clamped on her cigarette holder and eyes narrowed against her own smoke, continued to stare implacably at Georgiana.

Nowadays, when so many of the Countess' friends' bifocals seemed to be fitted with rose-coloured lenses, Mary would only too often find her mother throwing down some Sunday newspaper which was currently serialising the lifetime reminiscences of one of her old chums, with a cry of: 'He was always a silly bugger.'

Or, as she skim-read the life story of some famous former beauty who was busy publicly proclaiming her total disinterest in sex, she would say to her daughter:

'Poor little thing. And to think that all that time she was in the bedroom she was hating every minute of it.'

Mary found this sort of thing most awkward but Georgiana was not at all put out. In fact she rather liked the Countess: partly because she had been brought up to like and respect her relations, but more because she had style, and nowadays Georgiana only wished to spend her time with people who had style.

Later that night, as Georgiana looked round the party, she thought it was a great pity that Jennifer Parker-Jones had been made to bring her mother, because Mrs Parker-Jones had no style at all. Immediately upon her arrival Mary had placed her with a small collection of bores tucked away by the chimneypiece where she was in no danger of being noticed. Her daughter Jennifer, on the other hand, was introduced into a circle of younger men at whom she was now staring with fiery timidity, her cheeks ablaze.

Georgiana was very happy with the way things were going, surrounded first by Mary's choices, and then gradually by her own. Eventually, however, she realised that there was somebody new in the room, someone in fact who was the only man to whom she wished to talk. Which was why she took great care to move away every time he approached.

The following day, when one dozen red roses wrapped in cellophane arrived at the house, and Mary and Georgiana opened them together, her cousin remarked that Georgiana seemed to have made a conquest. Georgiana diplomatically placed the roses in Mary's study and kept the card, carefully fitting it into the side of her looking glass. She hoped there would be others.

Later, Mary remarked quite casually to Lucius that perhaps Georgiana was really a little young for John Pemberton; she had to be careful, for both their respective ages were far nearer Pemberton's than Georgiana's.

'But of course, he does have money,' Mary added.

Pemberton indeed had money, a lot of money, some of which, unusually for a man of his means, he was quite prepared to spend on Georgiana. He took her to lunch at the Ritz, and bought her a silk scarf in a velvety box from Hermes. He quite surprised her with a teddy bear, dressed in a Victorian costume and small straw hat and holding a basket of flowers, from a shop in Hay Hill.

Georgiana appreciated all this. Just as she appreciated his distinguished good looks, his deep voice and his tall physique. He was doing everything in exactly the right way and, which was even more important, Mary approved of him. Furthermore he did not constantly telephone her, which would have been embarrassing, nor did he try to make love to her until they had achieved a kind of affectionate intimacy. Yet when he leant towards her one evening smelling of the delicate mixture of cigars and expensive aftershave with which she was soon to become all too familiar, she found herself thinking not of love but of Longborough, and of its corridors, its dust, its spiders, its mice, its crumbling roof and rising damp, so desperately in need of Pemberton and his millions. As he put his arms around her, Georgiana thought it was not so much a case of close your eyes and think of England, but close your eyes and think of Longborough.

chapter three

Mrs Parker-Jones sat at her desk. She had just been to the stationers, which was normally not an agreeable experience, particularly since nowadays stationers appeared to delight in stocking absolutely everything except stationery. Today, however, she had willingly shopped at several in her search for some liquid eradicator. This, she discovered, was extremely hard to find on any stationer's shelves at the moment, because apparently those perfectly dreadful teenagers one saw lounging around the place everywhere liked to sniff the wretched stuff, a bewildering piece of information which preoccupied Mrs Parker-Jones as she found herself in one of the local shops waiting while the assistant brought the eradicator out from under lock and key at the back of the premises. However, it had been well worth the effort, thought Mrs Parker-Jones, as she sat carefully erasing all the 'Misses' on her daughter's many invitation cards and changing them equally carefully all to 'Mrs'. Very soon the invitations on the mantelpiece surrounding the reproduction eighteenth-century ormulu repeating clock were all invitations to her and no longer to her daughter. The fact that most of them were in the recent past mattered not one whit to Mrs Parker-Jones, because she knew people paid scant attention to the precise dates on invitations because they were far too busy trying to spot at a few paces whether or not the invitations were engraved.

The only invitation to which she did not have to apply her newly found counterfeiting skills was one Mrs Parker-Jones was particularly proud of, the one from Jennifer's great friend Georgiana, which was personally addressed to Jennifer's mother and which told the world that Georgiana's aunt the Countess had been At Home personally, to her, Mrs Parker-Jones, on the Second of May.

Mrs Parker-Jones liked to remember that cocktail party. She had worn her pink two-piece which had a slight suggestion of sequins over the right bosom, and had found herself placed by the Countess' daughter Lady Mary, who unlike her mother was truly charming, amongst a set of the most interesting people. The fact that one of the group was a woman who really did not seem to know even where she was, and apparently had only recently been discharged from a private nursing home in Roehampton, did nothing to spoil her evening. It had all been intensely interesting, and at the end of it she had been able to return home to dinner and Aidan in much better humour than of late.

Naturally she didn't tell Aidan anything about the party, and her husband, sensing her euphoria, consequently became even more monosyllabic and sarcastic. Mrs Parker-Jones ignored him. She knew he hated to see her happy. In fact lately, she had noticed, he only had to see her happy and he would immediately think of something utterly dreary and dull to tell her. Being with Aidan was about as cheering as switching on the news. She wondered whether he had always been like this and she had simply just not noticed it before, or if he had become like this since she had decided to spread her wings socially.

Sometimes Mrs Parker-Jones found herself wishing she was single, in some way or another. She could not bring herself to specify the exact nature of her bachelorhood, but she felt it would be such fun to be single at a time of life when she was still young enough, and goodness knows quite vigorous enough, really to be able to enjoy herself. As it was at the moment, it was as much as she could do to get Aidan to read a brochure about a cruise let alone offer to take her out to dinner, without her having to suggest it first. Men were so unspontaneous. For Aidan to change his mind once he had made it up in one way was about as complicated a manoeuvre as an articulated juggernaut backing out of a car park. The male sex simply did not have the right metabolism to enjoy themselves in the way a woman would like them to enjoy themselves. Nothing occurred to them on the spur of the moment. They seemed quite unable to make up their minds quickly, even concerning the basic things which they were meant to find so appealing. In fact when she was first married she had quickly realised that, if she wanted to have any fun, the only way was to give her husband a fortnight's notice, followed by a written reminder a couple of days before. It was a wonder their daughter Jennifer had been born at all.

How many nights in vain had she lain in her best silk negligee and Chanel No. 5 waiting for her appeal to come home to Aidan, only to be answered by the heavy breathing which indicated that her husband had already taken his sleeping pills and that they had worked. Eventually, not long after Jennifer was born, she had stopped pretending and had moved into a separate bedroom, which was the date upon which she started to become widely read, a fact which none other than Andrew Gillott had remarked upon only the other day, she was happy to say, just as Mrs Parker-Jones was handing over the little bit extra Andrew said was necessary to ensure Jennifer's success in Society. She didn't actually ask him what the money was to be used for exactly, because if there was one thing that she did know, she did know she could trust Andrew Gillott, completely. He had such taste. He knew how things should be done, and she was quite certain of this, because Andrew knew everyone, and as everyone knew, someone who knew everyone was somebody in whom you could put your trust. And as Andrew Gillott said, doing things properly cost money, often a great deal of money, but in the end it would be worth it all, when Jennifer walked gracefully down the aisle on the arm of one of those men in her little book, preferably one who could be associated immediately with a well-known London Square.

With this comforting thought she had followed Aidan up to bed, or rather to the landing where their separate bedrooms were situated, with a bathroom interconnecting them. She had paused outside his bedroom for a moment, and already she could hear him snoring. It was not a nice noise. When Aidan snored he put his weight behind it. Then she had closed his bedroom door and gone into her own room. Removing her imitation satin nightdress from her camphor chest, she had surveyed her bedroom with pleasure, remarking to herself that it was like one of those gorgeous bedrooms on the old ocean-going liners. Then she had gone into the interconnecting bathroom.

That evening the state of the bathroom was such that quite honestly, if she'd wished to divorce Aidan there and then, she was certain it would be justified on the grounds of cruelty alone. He had left his flannel crooked, toothpaste all over one of the gold-plated dolphin-shaped taps, and worst of all, he had tinkled all over her Peter Jones shag-pile off-white carpet. Mrs Parker-Jones half closed her eyes. It was enough to make you scream. Then she opened her cosmetic drawer and, finding her gingham vanity case, she removed her nail scissors. It was so ghastly, yet so typical that she should have to end such a triumphant evening on her hands and knees in the bathroom, clipping out the stains Aidan had made on her off-white shag-pile with a small pair of nail scissors. She would have liked to have gone and shaken him awake, and told him just what she thought of him, but she knew it was useless once he had taken his pills. So instead she clipped the carpet free of his marks, and tried to put the whole nasty matter out of her mind by concentrating on Jennifer's dance next month, and what she would wear. Pale green, perhaps, with her emerald pendant at her throat. She snipped away efficiently until all the marks had gone, concentrating solely on this thought. Life did not always have to be quite so basic, she thought.

'Where's your diamond bracelet?' Aidan hissed at her the next morning over breakfast.

When discussing anything to do with their valuables, Aidan always dropped his voice, because he did not want anyone to hear that he had a safe sunk into the wall behind the pastel of Jennifer in the sitting room.

'I had to go to the safe this morning,' he whispered, 'to get out some Krugerrands. And your bracelet wasn't there. Only your pearl and diamond pendants, and that repro pearl choker.'

'My diamond bracelet,' Mrs Parker-Jones replied quite evenly and without inflexion, 'is having its clip mended at Harrods.'

She despised him even more than ever at this moment, for as Andrew Gillott had said to her only yesterday, any man so vulgar as to notice which of his wife's jewellery was present and which was not, was not a gentleman.

Mr Parker-Jones, however, was not satisfied.

'Why have you left your diamond bracelet at Harrods when you normally leave it at Garrards?'

There was a small pause, then Mrs Parker-Jones slowly lowered her *Daily Mail*. She looked at Aidan, which was something she did not enjoy doing, not before the first sherry at lunchtime.

'Aidan, dear. It was you, Aidan, who was worried about the clip. If you remember, it was you who advised me to take it to Harrods and have it mended after the Mike Jackson Memorial Dinner Dance at the Dorchester. Don't you remember?'

Mrs Parker-Jones knew her husband would not remember, as indeed her husband knew all too well himself. The night of the Mike Jackson Dinner Dance at the Dorchester he had had two too many dry martinis and from that moment on remembered very little. He thought it might therefore be better to drop the subject completely, before it turned unpleasant. His wife had a superb knack of turning a perfectly innocent conversation on its head and making it into a cross-examination.

'I just hope it'll be mended for Jennifer's dance next month,' he couldn't help adding. 'It is a very fine piece.'

'For all I know it could be ready next week, Aidan dear,' replied Mrs Parker-Jones. 'And if it is, and should the occasion prove right, I shall wear it for the dance. Should it tone in with the eau de nil dress I am wearing.'

Aidan would have liked to have said that diamonds, in the opinion of the person who had paid for them, could surely be said to 'tone in' with everything, but he had the uneasy feeling that such a remark would be dealt with in an extremely summary way by his wife. So he dabbed his serviette, or napkin as Clarissa now insisted on calling them, on his full lips and slowly rose from the table. As he walked across the red patterned carpet towards the door, he paused, slightly breathless, and thought of happier days, days when his daughter was young and used to come and sit on his knee at the end of breakfast and pop little fingers of marmalade-covered toast into his mouth and pretend that he was a lion. But that was a long time ago now, he thought, as he pushed open the door. In those days his wife seemed to have smiled more. Now, although perhaps it was only his imagination, she rarely seemed to smile, or laugh, except when that damned socialite Gillott or whatever his name was that she had in tow came round. Then he could hear her laughing all the time as he sat in his study in the late afternoon doing his bills, a commodity of which there seemed to be an over-abundance at the moment.

'Hello, Daddy,' said a welcome voice from the darkness of the hall.

Jennifer was standing in the shadows quite deliberately as she did not want her father to see she was wearing a new dress.

'I'm just off to an Art Exhibition with Georgiana.'

She slipped on her coat quickly, because that wasn't new. Her father smiled at her.

'Want a lift?' he asked hopefully.

'Not really, Daddy. Thanks all the same,' Jennifer replied. 'In a bit of a hurry. See you at dinner.'

With that she was gone into the street, leaving Aidan to wonder why someone who was in a hurry didn't accept the offer of a lift. Concluding that the Art Gallery was probably only just round the corner, he rang for his chauffeur then, sitting down in the hall, started to read his *Financial Times*. He examined the day's bad news. Sooner or later he was going to have to tell Clarissa that they were going to have to cut back pretty hard on a few of life's essentials, but the way he felt, and the way he knew she felt at this moment, perhaps it had better be later than sooner. He checked his pocket watch against the grandfather clock in the same way his father always had. Every morning before he went out and every evening when he came in his father had checked his half hunter against the grandfather clock, as if the time that it told was superior to the time told by his pocket watch. It was a fine clock. Solid and dependable, unlike the world they lived in today, which seemed, like his wife, to be impatient, dissatisfied and unforgiving. He dwelt on this thought till Gurney brought the Rolls round, and as Gurney drove, and Aidan walked alongside the car, he continued to dwell on this thought, ignoring the life that swam past him. If he had been able to put a word to his feelings, he would have called them melancholy. But as he couldn't, he didn't. Instead he just dwelt on his

54

thoughts, and walked slowly alongside his motor car, umbrella furled, newspaper folded, and bowler hat straight upon his head, the apotheosis of something in the city.

Andrew Gillott contemplated the yellowed tip of his fat index finger and sighed. He was completely and utterly bored. Mind you, it was the most boring time of day, too late for a coffee and too early for a gin and tonic. Not that the time of day usually inhibited Andrew in his drinking habits, for he quite deplored middle class yobbos who were always banging on about not having a drink till the sun had set behind the jolly old yard arm. What was actually inhibiting him at the moment was the fact that he was sitting in a crummy wine bar, and in crummy wine bars – which unfortunately London was now full of – it was quite impossible to get a decent drink. He loathed wine bars, almost as much as he loathed the people who only drank wine. People who only drank wine were either totally uncivilised, or raving queers. You had only to look around this particular crummy little joint to confirm that point of view. The place was stuffed full of common little model girls with stupid crimped hair, and a lot of tight-arsed queers stuffed into cheap silk shirts and designer jeans, whatever-to-God they might be. Collectively they were enough to make a chap vomit, but at least against this loathsome assortment he would surely be able to pick out Nigel Bruce-Smith, the person he was waiting for, because unless everything had gone completely bloody haywire, articled clerks were not allowed to wander round in plastic shoes and overtight jeans as the rest of the world seemed to be.

Nigel Bruce-Smith had been recommended to Andrew as being ideal for his purpose the previous evening over backgammon at the Claremont. Bruce-Smith was impecunious, which was one of the essential qualifications for the job, was purported to be quite good-looking in a dark sort of a way, and a bit of a dancer, another essential qualification. After the last game of backgammon, which

Andrew deliberately allowed himself to lose, Bruce-Smith's godfather described his godson as the sort of chap ladies liked and chaps didn't, which was also what Gillott wanted, but which was neither here nor there at the moment because all that mattered at the moment to Andrew Gillott was the fact that Nigel Bruce-Smith was bloody late.

Gillott checked that the envelope with the necessary in it was still safely in his inside pocket, then lit another cigarette and wondered how much that silly cow Mrs Parker-Jones had been able to fetch on her diamond bracelet. Not a lot, he dared swear, because the diamond market was about as depressed as everything else right at this moment. Still, at least it was an old piece, not like that quite ghastly modern junk most women sported nowadays which looked more like articles designed for unarmed combat than jewellery. He loathed the stuff, and with good reason, for the last time he'd been to bed with a woman, sometime last year, she'd been wearing a large and dangerous-looking ring which one of her four husbands had given her, most likely as a weapon for self-defence rather than as bodily adornment. He had fallen against it in a moment of bridled passion, and it had quite killed whatever ardour he had been able to muster at that moment, which went to confirm his opinion that modern jewellery, together with much that was rotten in the world today, had fallen into the hands of a lot of pouffy designers who were hell-bent on ruining normal indecent relationships between men and women.

Gillott stubbed out his cigarette in a filthy saucer which lay for that purpose on the bar. One of the fat and unpleasant-looking females serving behind the bar, having finished slicing up the cheesecake with an implement which looked as if it had just been used to ladle out dog food, now put on some music he imagined she thought must be the sort of thing the customers would enjoy. Gillott put a hand to his head. If anyone played a noise like that to him at home and asked him to guess what it was he'd have said a prisoners' protest in Sing-Sing. He was just about to leave the place in complete disgust when he saw what had to be Bruce-Smith come in and look around the dark interior of the wine bar. Gillott gave him a small wave of his hand, and hoped that it was indeed his man, and not some pansy disguised as something in the city, because of course, as everyone knew, the buggers were everywhere. Not like the good old days when they stayed strictly incognito, or emigrated to live abroad on Capri.

Once they had made themselves known to each other, Gillott suggested moving to a more decent hostelry, to which, Gillott was relieved, Bruce-Smith quite readily agreed, because, in his own words, he said he was in need of a pint. As they wandered down the King's Road, Gillott was happy to note that Bruce-Smith's shoes were patently down at heel, his tie was stained, and the edge of his shirt collar most distinctly frayed. This was all to Gillott's liking, because it indicated pretty definitely that Bruce-Smith was his man. Chaps like him spent what little money they had on keeping their dinner jackets clean, and the soles of their shiny slip-on buckled evening shoes in good repair. The daytime attire of chaps like this was always a cast-iron indication. They worked at night, therefore they took great care to shine at night, because that was the time they hoped to catch the eye of some unfortunate plain heiress who could, simply by the act of marriage, transform them from being articled clerks or whatever into people with plenty of eminently desirable possessions and thus completely remove the need to work.

Privately, Gillott despised this particular form of impecunious bachelor. If his own fortunes had not fallen so low he would not need to have anything to do with people like Mrs Parker-Jones, but for someone as young as Bruce-Smith to jump straight into the claggy before he'd even made an effort smacked of sheer turpitude. At that age, in Gillott's day, decent but impoverished bachelors went into the Army, ran up a lot of debts, rode point-to-point on other chaps' horses, but most certainly did not boff plain girls for money. They might boff a plain girl by mistake when they got pissed, but not for money. This was one of the many drawbacks of Gillott's present existence, that he had to deal with detestable little people like this, people to whom in the old days he'd never have even lent his copy of *The Life*.

Gillott sat himself down at the bar in the pub they'd found and put the leather-covered elbow of his sports jacket straight into a small pool of brown ale. It didn't matter. At least they were out of that frightful poufs' parlour with its horrid mauve tablecloths and matching carnations. He lit a cigarette.

'Tell you what she's like, old chap,' he said to Bruce-Smith. 'You can't miss.'

'Right,' Bruce-Smith replied, as Gillott shoved a pint across at him.

Gillott sipped his large gin and tonic, and wondered why all the young men nowadays said that: 'Right.' Didn't they realise it made them sound like bloody air hostesses?

'She's fat,' he informed the younger man. 'Fat, got a bit of a squint, her teeth stick out and her legs look as if she's played too much hockey.'

'Right.'

'Mother's a beast of the first water. Sort of woman – well, not even jumped-up. Just trying to leg it up, know what I mean?'

Bruce-Smith nodded. He knew what Gillott meant.

'Sort of silly cow who puts tea cosies on everything. Even on telephones, you know? Thinks that by pushing her daughter around things might open up socially for her, for the daughter. Course it won't, but that's not for the likes of us to tell her.'

The conspirators drank, and Gillott took two tickets from his pocket and gave them to Bruce-Smith. Just the start, he explained to his employee. Mustn't make things too obvious at the off. The plan was for Bruce-Smith to take some other bird to this particular charity bun-fight, and then later on in the evening to come on strong with Miss Parker-Jones who, if past form was anything to go by, would have spent most of the evening up till then in the ladies' powder room. The rest was up to him.

'Right,' said Bruce-Smith, taking the envelope which Gillott now offered him.

During the ensuing silence, Gillott finished his gin and studied the young man. He wondered whether Miss Parker-Jones would allow herself to be led like a lamb not only round the dance floor but actually to the slaughter by this contemptible creature, who now sat quite publicly counting what he rather coyly described as 'his fee' right under Gillott's nose. Or would she not go for broke but content herself with going home early in a taxi? Gillott almost felt a twinge of pity for the silly, plain girl, the victim of her mother, and perhaps about to be the victim of this small-time gigolo in watermarked suede shoes. But then he dismissed any such feelings of pity, for pity had no place in the social calendar and, anyway, what option did he have at the moment? If Miss Parker-Jones went for too long without some form of male attention, her mother would surely start complaining, even asking him for her money back, and God knows most of that was long since gone. He knew. It had happened all too often before. Anyway, the wretched girl might benefit from the experience, from a bit of attention from the opposite sex. The exact form this attention would take was finally entirely up to her, and the fact that Gillott might be indirectly instrumental in her maidenly downfall didn't really disturb him, any more than the idea that the roast beef in his sandwich had once been a blue-eyed cow.

Jennifer Parker-Jones did not like people. She had not been very old when she made this discovery. Even as a child she had never enjoyed meeting people. At her father's house in Surrey, whenever she saw a car approaching up the drive, even if it belonged to someone she knew, she would immediately run away and hide, and watch the new arrivals from the secrecy of the rhododendron bushes. She knew she was required to speak to the visitors, to say hello and, worst of all, look them in the face. She particularly hated doing the latter, because she always noticed everyone not noticing her squint. And not noticing her plain round face, and her round dumpy body. And trying not to look at her mother and wonder how such a pretty woman could possibly have given birth to such a plain, round child. One of her grandfathers took great delight in saying, preferably well within her hearing, that beautiful women always gave birth to plain daughters, and that it was Nature's way of redressing the balance. Unfortunately for Jennifer, the knowledge that she was part of Nature's plan to keep the world from being overrun with great beauties was not a personally comforting thought, and as she grew older she became less and less able to disassociate herself from all that was unappealing. Often she would play a game where she chose some particularly loathsome object and pretended to be it, like a dustbin, or a train seat. After a short but intense period of fantasy she would return to being herself with a slightly lessened sense of revulsion.

At all times she was a prisoner staring out at a world which required that females of her age should have some sort of physical appeal, and she clung to the bars of her body in despair, as she increasingly realised she had not been sent down for a long stretch but sentenced for life. She knew she was popular with other girls only in the same way as a pedestal or a large vase of flowers was in a photographer's studio, as a useful background. Standing beside Jennifer at a drinks or a tea party, no man could fail to notice how pretty the other girls were in contrast to her.

And so, as her mother's mantelpiece became thick with invitations originally addressed to her, summonses from other girls who were eager to have her as background material, it kept occurring to Jennifer that she should run away from home rather than submit to the humiliating experience of her mother pushing her through the Season. But she didn't, because she loved her father, and it would be impossible for Jennifer to hurt his feelings, feelings which her mother had damaged badly enough over the years. She could not add to those wounds knowing full well that in the arid atmosphere of his marriage, she was the only perfume on the breeze.

Lately her father had developed the habit of feigning sleep until he heard his beloved daughter come home, when he would rise and shuffle to her bedroom door, and stand staring in silent love at her. Jennifer would tell him lies about what fun the evening had been, and about all the exciting new people she was meeting, and when they had finished their half-whispered conversation he would turn his bulky frame once more towards his own bedroom, satisfied that his Jennifer was doing all right.

'Kept your end up all right tonight, then?' he would regularly enquire before retiring. 'That's all right then.'

On her own, Jennifer would often bury her head in her hands as if weighed down by the guilt of the lies she supplied him with, but then the truth was something her father both wouldn't and couldn't understand. To him Jennifer was beautiful. She had to be, she looked like him.

Often, when she walked into a room, she would have the terrifying sensation that her hands and feet were suddenly becoming grossly enlarged. She particularly felt this in the company of Georgiana, perhaps because Georgiana was so petite, so *raffinée* as Lucius called it, and moved with such a natural grace, that watching her at parties Jennifer often thought a stranger could be forgiven for thinking that Georgiana was a dancer. Georgiana, she felt sure, could never in her life have experienced the sensation that her hands and feet were suddenly becoming enormous. She could never have had to clasp her hands so tightly in front of her that her nails dug into her palms, to prevent them from becoming even bigger and bigger. And all this before she had even opened her mouth to speak. She would stand there, quite frozen, while people just talked and talked at her, all the time quite incapable of giving them a reply in case when she opened her mouth she should suddenly and unaccountably vomit.

At very large gatherings she would spend the entire

time in the bathroom with her head stuck out of the window, safe from everyone, listening to the traffic below, and blocking out the noise of the party. If the event went on long enough, she would get to know every object in the room as if she was playing Kim's tray – the pictures, the patterns on the walls, the bobbles on the curtains, the colours and names of the various bars of soap. And eventually she would be able to shut her eyes and remember them all on her lonely taxi-ride back to her home, often even down to the name of the manufacturer of the sanitaryware.

Now, tonight, as she waited at home to be picked up by her escort for the evening, Jennifer regarded herself in the reproduction gilt mirror gloomily. Somehow whatever she put on she still managed to look almost common. Not totally common, but almost. She had none of Georgiana's patrician ability to rise above her clothes, so that even something cheap looked expensive and chic. Real pearls on Jennifer looked false, while false pearls on Georgiana looked real. Tonight Jennifer's taffeta dress, which revealed her slightly freckled shoulders, was of undoubted quality. Indeed her mother had carefully taken her to the self-same shop where Georgiana had purchased hers. But of course on Jennifer the same sort of dress made by the same designer looked quite, quite different. Not so much mutton dressed as lamb, Jennifer thought, but more pork dressed as bacon.

She turned away from her mirrored image, because she could no longer contemplate it without getting an attack of what Georgiana referred to as 'cold porridge on your chest'. There was no doubt about it. She was as attractive to herself as she quite obviously was to the opposite sex.

When they arrived at the ball Jennifer realised, from her few weeks of socialising, that she already knew practically everyone in the party by sight, with the exception of someone called Nigel Bruce-Smith, who arrived with a rather giggly model who kept taking out one of her front teeth which made everybody laugh, Nigel Bruce-Smith particularly. Jennifer's escort was in commodities, and couldn't dance any better than she could. Obviously commodities were not doing very well, for he did not hesitate to let Jennifer buy her own bitter lemons, while he himself drank regularly from a silver Georgian hip flask which he kept in an inside pocket of his dinner jacket. Jennifer went, as usual, as often as possible to the powder room, which caused her partner to wonder loudly if she had something wrong with her. He was extremely rude. Most of the people she had met recently were extremely rude. They did not talk to her, they talked at her, or past her, about themselves, which her old headmistress at Grantley Abbey had always said was a sure sign of bad manners. They also talked about money, which again she had understood from the teachings at Grantley Abbey, was bad form of the very worst kind. Her mother talked about herself and about money a great deal, but her mother was common, which Jennifer understood was the reason why she was taking quite so much trouble to ensure that her daughter was not.

'Would you like to dance?' said a voice suddenly from beside her.

Jennifer looked up and saw Nigel Bruce-Smith standing next to her chair. Jennifer's already well-reddened cheeks went an even deeper hue. She could not believe he was addressing her, and so glanced around apprehensively. But there was no one else in the vicinity, just the wall and a large potted plant. She rose to her feet, quickly quelling the sensation that they were rapidly enlarging themselves, and followed him onto the dance floor.

He held her tightly, but expertly. He guided her most skilfully between the other dancing couples, all the time listening with interest to her conversation. By the time the dance number was over, Jennifer's eyes were shining as brightly as the buckles on Nigel's highly polished slip-on evening shoes, and for the first time that evening she found it unnecessary to fetch and pay for her own bitter lemon.

The model girl with whom Nigel had arrived had disappeared, false tooth and all, early, as people so often did at Charity Balls once they knew the result of the tombola. She wondered whether instead of returning to her Nigel too would slip away. This had happened to her on countless occasions. Someone would dance with her once, and then on the pretext of fetching drinks would disappear into the party in search of prettier girls upon which to prey. Jennifer found herself praying. Praying for Nigel to come back. Just for once not to be abandoned. Panic rose up almost uncontrollably inside her. Of course, were she Georgiana she would just laugh, go to the bar and fetch her own drink. Georgiana never seemed to notice or even care about such things. Georgiana appeared to assume that if a man had not the intelligence to notice her appeal, then as far as Georgiana was concerned, he was a person of no substance and certainly of no taste.

A hand placed a bitter lemon in front of her. Nigel's hand. Jennifer looked gratefully up at him. He was really quite handsome in a dark sort of way, and he had a way of appearing to listen to you intently, even when you weren't saying anything. He told her in a minute they would dance again, and Jennifer found this difficult to believe. But he was smiling quite genuinely and Jennifer found herself smiling quite genuinely back. For the first time in she didn't know how long, Jennifer felt another emotion inside her besides despondency, and if she had not been so utterly fascinated by Nigel she would have known it at that moment to be happiness.

Later, after she had paid off the taxi she had shared home with him, and after he had left her at her door and walked off back home to Pimlico, Jennifer knew she couldn't possibly sleep and so she walked slowly up and down Sloane Street. She felt desperately excited. But although she knew she was unsophisticated compared to Georgiana, she was not so unsophisticated as to confide to Nigel that he was the first member of the opposite sex with whom she had found herself alone. She knew that would have been a great mistake, she said to herself, as she walked slowly up and down, up and down, in search of some sort of inner calm. But inner peace was not to be forthcoming, for at that moment her life was in a turmoil. She had been brought home by a dark-haired man called Nigel, and he had promised to telephone her tomorrow. Her father would never believe it.

Aidan heard Jennifer come in, and rose and shuffled to his bedroom door. Jennifer came up the stairs and smiled at him. He looked back at her in silent adoration. She was worth everything. The endless bills, the worry, the constant nagging of his wife, Jennifer was worth every damned penny. She kissed him goodnight and he watched her go into her bedroom. And then he went back to his bed, at precisely the same time as Nigel jumped happily into bed with his false-toothed model girl beside him. Nigel laughed again as Bella again removed her tooth and stuck her little pink tongue at him through the gap, and the dawn light faintly illuminated her hastily-discarded clothes, his frayed blue shirt and the shabby room where they both lay. As the sound of the first bus rumbled up to them from the street far below, so the sound of their love-making filtered through the thin walls to the land-lady, who banged angrily on the wall with a shoe.

chapter four

The Countess put on her spectacles and checked her guest list for luncheon, just a little anxiously, because nowadays she did have a little trouble in remembering whom she had invited, and even though Mary would be there, she might not always be to hand. There would be herself and Mary of course, and Mary's popinjay Lucius, still rumoured to be researching for a book on the English Social Scene which he was subsequently to return to America to write. Naturally she didn't believe a word of it. She had known far too many people who had crashed around English Society under the pretext either of writing a book or painting (as her husband Freddie always used to say, either 'your whores or your horses'). But there it was. Even since Mary had turned Beastly Geoffrey out – and the fact that Geoffrey was beastly was one thing upon which they never had any trouble in agreeing – ever since she had turned him out Mary had spent her time in the company of popinjays. At least this Lucius was American, which was an enormous improvement on those dreadful Australians.

Next on the guest list she had written Dick and Jane. She had no difficulty remembering who they were. They were very old friends of hers who in the past had been thought rather jumped up, but who now weren't, for the simple reason that they both had outlived all the people who had originally thought them to be jumped up, and now there was no one left to ostracise them. So that was all right, she thought. She had used to find them both infernally dull, but now she was always rather glad to see them, and even the business of them being boring she found quite soothing, for it was a constant at a time in her life when very little else was. Then there were the Weavers. The Countess sniffed. Colonel and Mrs Weaver were the village stalwarts, and Mrs Weaver did not approve of the Countess, except when she wanted a donation for the Pony Club, or to borrow her garden for the annual Fete. The Colonel, however, *c'etait autre chose*.

Mrs Weaver always looked right through the Countess, just as if each time she saw her she was conjuring up the Countess' lurid past. But the Countess didn't mind, because she disliked Mrs Weaver as intensely as Mrs Weaver disliked her. The Colonel however, although inclined to be endlessly boring on the subject of his ancestors (totally ignoring the rule that the only ancestors worth talking about must be either funny, or rude, or preferably both) was a pink-cheeked flirt, whose favourite social occupation was squeezing knees – usually the wrong ones – under the table when given the chance. This often had the most amusing results, such as the time he had squeezed his wife's knee when taking it to be the

Countess', and Mrs Weaver had remained icily aware of the error for the rest of the luncheon. The Countess decided to put Mrs Weaver between her next two guests, two happily married wild flowers called Fulton and Elliott, who had been together now for years. She thought what fun it would be to place one on either side of the wretched woman if only because Mrs Weaver loathed queers almost as much as she loathed the Countess. She could just see Fulton listening to her, pursing his lips in mock approval as she voiced her latest second-hand *Daily Telegraph* opinions, while Elliott would stare at her intently in between frowning slightly at the tops of his fingers, a little habit he had because he was mad on fingers, especially his own.

Having completed the checking of the guest list, the Countess walked across the hall, with its rush woven matting, its oak armoury chest, its portrait of Freddie's mother by Sargent, and entered the dining room. How glad she was that she had allowed Mary to redecorate the dining room last year, for it looked so pretty, all laid and ready for her luncheon party. The room was now yellow, and with its long eighteenth-century windows and direct southern aspect seemed to fill the eye with sunshine, even on the greyest of days.

She checked the table, particularly that the flowers in its centre were of the right height, because Dorothy from the village who always did the flowers for her at the weekend, also did the Church flowers and sometimes forgot that a dining table was not a high altar. She then made sure that each chair had been placed at the right distance from the table, and next went to the side and lifted the lids which covered the hors d'oeuvre. She liked to match the food to the flowers and the linen as often as possible. At any rate she liked to play about with making everything tone in with everything else. It was a little trick she was quite sure very few people noticed, but which she greatly enjoyed. In the old days of course, a visiting chef would have done the food for her, but nowadays she had to make do with Dorothy's sister who was rather inclined to think of a crown of lamb as the height of culinary achievement.

Once she had done the *placement*, there was nothing left to do but ring for Teresa who was to place the tulip-shaped champagne glasses upon the side so that the Countess herself could prepare the brandy, sugar and bitters in the bottom of each glass. For she was not such a fool that she did not know just how important it was to give people champagne on Sunday mornings, more especially when their hostess was an old lady. People did not lunch with the old unless they were rich, famous or served champagne. Besides, champagne cocktails were indisputably the best way of opening up a social event, however intimate.

Freddie had taught her how to mix them. He loved to drink champagne. On the subject of champagne he would wax, for Freddie, quite eloquent.

'Champagne's not a drink,' he always used to say. 'Champagne's a remedy. But you must be careful when you drink it. You must only drink it mid-morning, before lunch, in the middle of the afternoon, before dinner, during dinner, after dinner with the dessert, upon the arrival of a friend, upon the announcement of good news, on the birth of a baby – or at any other time.'

It was Freddie's set piece. Mercifully, he did not have many, unlike her first husband, poor Perry. Even now she had only to see him in an old sepia photograph mounted on his polo pony for a yawn to start. No one who had not been married to Perry could ever really have known ennui. He had only to walk into someone's box, even a horse's, for it to empty within seconds. You could be quite certain that as Perry's wife, if he accompanied you to Ascot, or Goodwood, or anywhere in the world, you had not the least chance of fainting in the subsequent crush.

Poor Perry. He had had a nice, open face which reflected his eagerness to be liked to such an extent that nobody did. What a good thing he had died young, for it gave everyone the chance to respect his memory without having to be bored by his presence.

After a respectable period of widowhood, which she had spent improving her mind in Florence and Venice, the Countess had taken some lovers. This was perfectly proper once a woman had been widowed, whatever the Mrs Weavers of this world might think. Her first was a passionate Italian, except that it turned out he wasn't in the least. The only real physical activity he indulged in was combing his hair. He combed his hair a great deal and had a habit of resting his long Florentine fingers upon his lips (somewhat à la Elliott), in order to draw attention to the fact that he had a manicure every day. Elliott and Fulton would have approved of him quite dreadfully, but the Countess had never come to terms with him. Although it had to be admitted that when caught between his hair-dressing and his manicure appointments his fractured English could be quite amusing.

Certainly he amused many of the people who were staying on the Lido. In between their bouts of frantic swimming they would sit and listen to Sergio's happy gossip. Frantic swimming had been all the rage among the English that year on the Lido, on account of the fact that the early rejuvenating treatments required it. The 'Swiss Treatment', as it was vaguely denominated, which made it sound as if it was all just a question of plenty of exercise and fresh mountain air, in fact involved rather more real medical practices, such as injections of a hideous nature that were designed to undo the damage of years and turn the recipients back instantly into youthful and vigorous satyrs. The side effect of the treatment was that everyone had to keep frightfully active in order to avoid decay setting in, at least that was the *on dit*. Hence the shoals of old ladies and gentlemen who could be seen splashing past each other at every moment of the day; hence the frantic swimming.

It had been an amusing sight, watching people who hitherto had only thought of water as being something kept in bottles marked Malvern by their bedsides, swimming frantically about in it like some of Neptune's own.

But not amusing enough, and so it was not too long before the Countess decided that now she was in mauve mourning, she could leave her old, half-restored palazzo and return quite correctly to England, where she would set about the serious business of finding herself a new husband, someone who would amuse her not only in the drawing room, but also in the bedroom. She had not been at all squeamish about such matters, as many of her friends so often were, pretending that it was all a beastly bore and that marriage was only intended for producing heirs. This to the Countess was sheer nonsense, for everyone knew a man was an animal, and if you found it difficult to become an animal with him then you would never make a brilliant match. And having failed once, she was quite determined not to fail again.

And thus she found Freddie, who loved sex only second to hunting. He used to say he didn't mind how he spent his days as long as he was mounted. And he saw to it that he always was, one way or the other. He had never bored of her, which was probably why she had never bored of him. It helped of course that he was both rich and an Earl, being slightly better born than even she. And he had everything she had ever wanted, and was sensible enough to realise it from the moment she met him. She was quite happy to forgive the fact he had never read a book, and would gaily introduce his two topics of conversation as 'horses and horses'. Nowadays of course she rarely talked about Freddie, for she had noted that to be a slightly ageing habit and, more importantly, she still missed him. She missed hearing his laugh. She missed the trail of mud up the stairs which he left behind him when he couldn't find the boot jack. She missed him backing his car into the moat when he got drunk, and then delightedly taking photographs of it the next morning, before summoning the tractor up to pull it back out. She missed his endless tales of days out in the field, and missed his genuine laugh. The laugh that belongs to a real man, not the giggles she would be hearing over luncheon. But then old women must be grateful for laughter, of whatever kind.

Elliott and Fulton arrived first, driving a very dull motor car. She gave Elliott the first bottle of champagne to open because it seemed to her he might put those long fingers to some sort of use. He broke a fingernail opening it, and made a dreadful fuss about it by pretending not to make a fuss about it, which is always a sure-fire way of getting yourself noticed. Teresa had to be summoned, plus Elastoplast and antiseptic ointment, and Fulton practically had to kiss the poor finger better before they could all relax and enjoy their cocktails.

Things brightened up after that little *crise*. Elliott and Fulton became quite jolly, walking slim-hipped round her drawing room, noticing what was new and giving each other little secret looks.

The Countess knew what each of the looks meant. She could also interpret their cryptic little remarks. For instance, 'most *recherché*' from Fulton about the flowers meant that he didn't like them. She and he could never see eye to eye about colours. She loved colour to be daring, and his choices to her were merely pallid. Fulton was currently considering an all-white drawing room, which really was frightfully old hat, and the Countess was obviously going to have to be the one to tell him, one way or the other.

'The trouble with all-white drawing rooms,' she said, 'is that they make people look grey, their teeth yellow and their hair dyed.'

She saw Fulton's bottom, tucked neatly into hand-woven Italian trousers, contract tightly. But Elliott took the point seriously, as he was meant to do.

'Before the war,' the Countess continued, 'we all had white drawing rooms, until we discovered they were quite hopeless unless you were sure all your guests had bathed from head to toe before entering the room. We had one in Chelsea, and one could never relax, not even for a minute, simply because one always knew that someone would have just stepped in a puddle, or sat on a dusty cab seat. It really was quite impossible.'

Fulton pursed his lips and looked at her without a word for a full minute. She could see him trying to work out whether she was stopping him having a more elegant drawing room than hers, or speaking – which was the truth – as a friend. Colonel and Mrs Weaver arrived as he was trying to make up his mind, and just as the Countess had started to wonder why it was that Fulton, like so many wild flowers of his age, had started to look exactly like his mother at the same age. Perhaps it was something to do with glands, she thought, or because he was the wife in the marriage, and twenty or thirty years in an apron, doing all the shopping and the housework (Elliott never helped with any chores because of his hands), must take their toll just as they do on any woman. Of course he did not always look like his dear mamma, who had been a great friend of the Countess'. Sometimes when he was in a bad mood he looked just like his aunt Enid, who had not been a friend of anyone's.

There was a slight lull while the Weavers were introduced, Mrs Weaver having strode in very much ahead of the Colonel as if she wanted to tell everyone something she did not want him to hear. But sadly this was not to be the case, as Elliott discovered when she sat down next to him on the sofa and drank her first glass of champagne far too quickly. This annoyed the Countess because it was vintage, and should be sipped, not gulped. And Mrs Weaver jiggled her foot about in that dreadful way some people have, which annoyed Elliott. So all was set fair for everyone to be irritated by her, which pleased Fulton. Because after all it was *de rigeur* for every party, and certainly every house party, to include at least one highly irritating person among the number against whom everyone else could unite. Which in turn meant that all the rest of the guests could, in contrast, find each other far more interesting than they actually were. The Countess was also well aware of the value of such a guest on the list. When she was young this type of person used to be known as a Robinson, after a perfectly dreadful little man, naturally called Robinson, who got hold of the idea that he was being asked everywhere because he was amusing, when in fact the very opposite was the case. Perhaps from now on Mrs Weaver would take her place alongside Mr Robinson in Social History, and guests who were asked specifically to supply the right ingredient of ennui would be known as Weavers.

Mary's popinjay was the next to arrive, wearing what the Countess considered to be quite extraordinary trousers. They were far too tight at one point, and far too loose at another, which meant that he had to keep standing with his legs pushed slightly forward as if posing in a shop window. It made him look a little silly.

Naturally Lucius knew Elliott, and greeted him as 'El-y-ot'. They had, it seemed, only just seen each other that same morning at High Mass in the Oratory. It really was extraordinary how many popinjays were left-footers. High Mass at the Oratory nowadays must be more like the Finoccio market on Capri, nothing but violets and pansies waving their heads in the breeze to the sound of the consecration bell. It was such a frightful thought that the Countess rang her own bell, and they all went through to luncheon.

The Countess always tried to orchestrate the conversation at her table. Anyone telling stories was not to be encouraged, nor was – which was even worse – the telling of jokes. In fact, if ever anyone even started telling one she always made it a practice to drop her fork and pretend not to be able to find it. And if that didn't always work, she had, on occasions, even taken refuge behind a mild attack of palpitations. No one had ever dared finish a joke in front of her after an attack of her palpitations. It had never ever been attempted.

It was just as Teresa was serving the *tonne e fagioli* that the Countess became aware that Mary was in love with Lucius. This did not surprise her. Mary nearly always fell in love with her popinjays, at least for a short while. It

73

was a very safe form of romance, and she never usually had any fears for her daughter on this account. Mary in love never got further than a little light hand-holding in the theatre, an exchange of small, hand-bound and privately printed books of poetry bought second hand, and a great deal of Mozart on the gramophone, although listening to Lucius' elegant New England tones it occurred to her that for once it could well be Schubert. Even so, there was something about this one, this particular popinjay, which worried the Countess, and it wasn't just his rather silly trousers. Perhaps it was because this one was intelligent, which popinjays usually weren't, and because he was pretending not to be as clever as he was, while the others had all struggled with the opposite problem? Whatever it was, there was something in his presence that made the Countess fear for her daughter.

Mrs Weaver took so long over her fagioli, practically picking up each bean one by one with her fork, that the Countess signalled quite openly for Teresa not to wait for her but to start clearing away.

'If we all wait for Mrs Weaver,' she said mock-jokingly, 'we shall all be here until Christmas.'

'Tonne e fagioli is probably just a little real for her,' Elliott whispered to Mary.

Mary smiled. Lucius was talking, and she wasn't really listening to Elliott, so she smiled. Elliott thought that Mary's one odd eye looked even odder when she smiled. She reminded him of a cat he had had when he was a small boy. Strange how little boys all like cats, he reflected. This cat had been called Tomato, and Elliott had loved it quite frantically. His step-father had had Tomato destroyed when he was away at boarding school. Elliott still carried a photograph of the cat in his wallet. It was his Achilles heel. Once, when Fulton had found out about one of Elliott's indiscretions, he had torn Tomato's picture into tiny pieces. It was by far the worst thing Fulton had ever done, and nothing had ever been quite the same since. Even though they still lived together, and even though Fulton as a penitence had immediately had another copy of the photograph made and put especially and expensively into a new Asprey's wallet as a please-forgive-me present. Nothing could fully erase the memory of a torn Tomato, an eye here, a bit of tail there, and as Elliott had run around the room sobbing his heart out while he picked up every single piece of the photograph, he was all at once six years old again, running round his nursery in a paroxysm of grief. And for Fulton, just as for his step-father, there had been no final forgiveness.

There was a lull in the conversation while baby lamb, cooked in garlic and herbs and served with a pretty side salad, was produced.

'I gather you are writing a book, Mr de Bossuet,' someone asked Lucius.

'Not exactly a book, no,' replied Lucius, with a slight frown. 'Perhaps more of a novel.'

'What fun,' said Fulton, picking up his knife and fork even though only half the table had been served, because Fulton knew his manners, and the best manners were no manners, and one could hardly get any more chic than that.

'I should love to write a novel,' he added.

'You will, Oscar,' said Elliott. 'You will.'

'I think I'd quite like to write a novel,' agreed Mary, 'but I should never know quite where to begin.'

'You begin at the beginning,' replied Lucius, 'and you go right on to the end, when you stop.'

Everyone smiled.

'I suppose it's all right to write novels nowadays, is it?' enquired Colonel Weaver of no one in particular. 'In my day we weren't allowed to, but I suppose like most things it's all right nowadays.'

'No, it most certainly is not "all right",' said the Countess. 'Writing professionally is no way for proper persons to conduct themselves. It is no more a way of going on, in my opinion, than writing one's diary and then publishing it for money.'

Mary paid no attention to this remark. To run to Lucius' defence would be quite the wrong move at this precise moment, particularly since Mary realised this was precisely what her mother wished her to to.

'No more virtue in it than publishing one's diary,' said the Countess again.

Elliott looked at Lucius and admired his fingers. They were long and white, just like Elliott's. He might be an American, but he certainly wasn't in the habit of doing the chores, not with hands like that.

'I should have thought,' Elliott said to Lucius, 'that writing a novel could be great fun. To be able to pour out all one's feelings onto the page, and to unleash all one's emotions in such a way that afterwards one would achieve a magnificent calm. I can think of nothing more satisfying.'

Lucius sipped his wine and gave a small smile.

'Writing a novel,' he replied, and for a second all stopped eating their fennel salad so that they might hear what he had to say on the subject, 'writing a novel is comparable only to being lowered down a well in a bucket every morning, and being left there, uncertain as to whether or not towards evening anyone will come along and haul you back up.'

Everyone was silent. With the exception of the Weavers, who never read anything except train time-tables, they had all thought that writing a novel sounded rather nice, like playing the piano, or painting in water-colours. Being lowered in a bucket didn't sound much fun. In fact it sounded most extraordinary. They consoled themselves that Lucius probably only felt like that because he was an American, and everyone knew Americans had not been at anything very long, not even writing novels.

The Countess worried silently in case the popinjay wrote those frightful books where people were always making love to each other on the floor.

'I can't understand modern novels,' she then said out loud. 'They've replaced class with sex, and it's so much less amusing, don't you think?'

Lucius laughed, which was encouragement enough.

'Before the war,' the Countess continued, 'everyone

was miserable because there was too much class. And now everyone is miserable for the opposite reason. Which is only to be expected since no one knows where they stand any more. No wonder the poor creatures keep swallowing National Health tranquillisers all day long. I know I most certainly should if I didn't know who I was.'

'I'm sorry,' said Lucius, 'but I'm not quite sure I understand what you're saying.'

'I am merely saying,' replied the Countess, 'that there is a lot to be said for knowing one's place.'

And she smiled graciously at everyone.

After lunch they walked around the grounds. Lucius had learnt to say 'parterre' and he said it a little too often perhaps, he thought afterwards. Elliott quite hated hostas and dared to say so once, which even Fulton had to admire.

'Mamma is quite outrageous,' Mary said to Lucius as they walked a little ahead of the other guests. She said it with a certain justifiable pride, and then she looked back at her mother, who was bending over a plant in one of the borders demanding that Mrs Weaver should tell her what it was called. Mrs Weaver was bound to be the only person who would know what species it was because she was the only person who had donned galoshes for the walk.

'Do you know about valerian smelling of cats?' Fulton asked.

'You're showing off again,' Elliott replied, quoting automatically.

'So what is it then, if it's not what I said it was?' the Countess asked Mrs Weaver, as if she had asked her to lunch solely so as she could identify the mystery plant.

'Stipangigantea,' essayed Mrs Weaver, a little nervously. 'Yes, I'm sure it's Stipangigantea.'

'But just a moment ago you were equally sure that it wasn't,' said the Countess. 'Come along; I thought this was your subject.'

Mary leant against one of the trees on the lawn.

'This is one of the oldest cedars in England,' she said to Lucius.

She put her arms round its trunk, and Lucius did the same, and still their fingers could not touch. It was surprising how young Mary looked, more especially since the light in the country was clearer than it was in town, and it was now mid-afternoon. But it seemed to Lucius that she had shed years now that she was away from her two outside lines, her household intercom, her large engagement diary, her list of weekly recipes and her singular preoccupation with the social success of Georgiana. Suddenly, here against the background of Clayton Manor, with its old stone walls, its deep flowered borders, and its wealth of fine paintings, she had not unnaturally become quite irresistible to him.

She drove him back to town in her maroon Porsche, using the straight-armed driving position which with her slim bare legs made her look immensely attractive. Lucius was well aware of course that the very act of a man being driven by a woman was in itself highly sexual, but what he was not aware of was whether or not she shared this particular awareness. He had no idea of her sexuality because she was so impossibly English, and he had not dared to try and breach her defences lest he should lose his one really valuable contact in England, an event which would have terrible repercussions on his book, naturally. He had absolutely no idea how she felt or thought, even though he had known her for a great many weeks now. They had dined together, sometimes daily, they had shared the same experiences, they had exchanged small gifts, and they had even now and then discreetly held hands. He knew she liked the poems of Robert Frost, the operas of Mozart, and Chopin as played by Rubinstein. But he did not know at all whether she would be thrilled or appalled if he tried to make love to her.

Afterwards, of course, he wondered why it had taken him so long to recognise the signs. But up until the moment she turned from the door and looked straight at him, standing in her dark hall as uncertainly as he had stood when he first arrived earlier that year, he was in total ignorance as to how she felt for him sexually, if indeed she felt for him at all.

He started simply by undoing the top button of her linen dress, and her response was a gasp of total pleasure. He was quite unprepared for such a reaction, and for a moment almost mistook it for a gasp of outrage. But it wasn't. He knew this, because for the first time ever she was looking at him full in the face, not bothering to try and hide her funny speckled eye, and he was suddenly aware that she desired him as strongly as he desired her. It was as if, after many weeks of trying to find a key which would open a secret door, that door had suddenly sprung open at the lightest touch, and had sprung open almost by mistake. He slowly undid each of her buttons and her dress slid with what appeared to be a glad sigh to the floor.

It was like a fantasy, Lucius thought, as he made love to her under the portraits of her ancestors. He looked up at some of the former châtelaines of Clayton Manor as they stared back haughtily at the two of them from their heavy gilt frames. Why had he waited for so long before making love to her? And yet if he had not waited for so long, could it possibly have been this exciting? Would he have had such an instant and breathtaking success? As he took her upstairs to the bedroom he thought not, but that was all academic now. What was infinitely more exciting was the discovery that she would now do whatever he wished her to do and whenever he wished it. He knew it from the way she looked at him the moment he started to make love to her, and it made the time they both took to climb the stairs to the bedroom almost unbearable.

Later Mary awoke in the half-light that surrounds all moments worth remembering – blue-pink dawns creeping back through the estate gates with shoes in hand, cold dew upon the feet, dogs warm in their beds smelling of biscuits, and dog blankets; silver-grey evenings along the shore by their beach house, making little boats out of match-sticks, placing Viking figures in them, and then setting them alight and floating them on the sea; shade under trees, girls with innocent arms round each other, poetry upon their laps – all these half-lights crowded in behind her eyes in the few seconds it took her to open them and see Lucius beside her, asleep on the pillow.

He was very handsome. Dark, curly-haired, smooth-skinned and, as she had discovered an hour or so earlier, of a quite astonishing virility. She couldn't believe she had mistaken him for what her mother called a 'popinjay'. Was it because Beastly Geoffrey making love to her had been so appalling that she had not really considered being made love to since? Or was it because she had simply just not met anybody who attracted her before? Why was she now lying in her large, ornate bed which was rumoured once to have belonged to a Borghese, with one arm crushed beneath Lucius' body, the other lying abandoned across his back? She could not answer, and in truth she realised she did not want to answer. For once in her life she knew she had to abandon thinking, as where she now lay and with whom had nothing at all to do with the orderly process of thought.

Lucius opened his eyes and looked at her. He was thirsty and wanted a cold drink. She gently removed her arm from under him and slipped on her crushed velvet robe, then went downstairs to fetch him an iced Perrier water with a slice of lemon in it. Lucius smiled to himself and closed his eyes. Soon he would send her out for some food and she would serve it in the bedroom on a basket tray. Finally, it had all really been very simple.

chapter five

Georgiana, on those unfortunate weekends when she was not asked away by other, more fortunate people, usually had to return home to Longborough. She realised that she was fortunate in that she did at least, unlike some girls she knew, have somewhere to go. Those who were forced to stay in London at weekends crouched in their Pimlico flats, living off Marmite sandwiches and ginger biscuits until Monday morning, when they were at last able to show their faces again around Peter Jones without a feeling of social disgrace. Not to be asked away for the weekend was bad enough, but to be forced to stay in London because your parents didn't even have a crumbling country house was quite inconceivable.

There were no such unpleasant experiences for Georgiana, however, and even her enforced weekends at Longborough were few and far between, for although she might have a shortage of what was necessary to restore her family home to its former beauty, she did have an abundance of the other commodity which is quite indispensable if one is to maintain any sort of position in Society – cousins. Some of these, unhappily, were even poorer than Georgiana herself, which made weekend visits to them rather indistinguishable from weekend visits to her own home, living as they did off even worse forms of dog food than her parents, while others, though rich, were just boring, which often made Georgiana long for a more amusing time with rather worse food. But happily she had one or two sets of quite exceptional cousins, who did not serve dog food or hold dull conversations, and the best of these were the Sydmouths.

Even as a child when Georgiana went to stay with the Sydmouths she would pray that she would fall sick and be obliged to stay with them for another deliriously happy few days. In any other family, perhaps, being such a much poorer relation might have proved embarrassing, but at Sydmouth Castle wealth was so much in evidence that even the richest of visitors was cut down to size. When Georgiana thought of what it was to be a Sydmouth, she automatically thought it meant you took a bath in a bathroom with paintings on the walls which other people had to go to large museums to see. And although money alone might purchase such paintings, only time could give them that indefinable air which Sydmouth did, of having hung for so long that no one could remember when they hadn't been there. As they were a Saxon family, time was another of the Sydmouths' quite astonishing riches, a constant in the family's history, like the red hair, the sly green eyes and the white skin that had characterised its members for the past eleven hundred years.

The Sydmouths were famous in English history for their cruelty as well as for their political tenacity, and that too was thrilling. To be closely related to a family who had absolutely no compunction about killing, and who were not kept awake at nights by guilty thoughts of the blood they had shed, was a stabilising thought to Georgiana when she was a child, and Nanny Sydmouth often would brush her hair in the evenings while telling young Georgiana stories of the frightful deeds that had been done in order to secure the fortunes of the family within whose house she was presently staying.

Her cousin Poppy was the main reason why Georgiana went quite so often to stay at Sydmouth. Georgiana was said by Nanny Sydmouth to have a stabilising effect on Poppy, with the consequence that Georgiana was frequently called to come and stay at the Castle. What Nanny Sydmouth said went, for Lord Sydmouth had left Poppy's upbringing entirely in her hands, there being no real alternative since Poppy's mother had run off with some black crooner shortly after Poppy was born – a moment in Poppy's family history which Georgiana had always greatly envied, since Georgiana could never imagine her own mother running off with a jobbing gardener, let alone a black crooner. Sadly Poppy had never been allowed to meet her mother, but she knew all about her from Nanny, who in turn knew all about her from the staff, whose information was unimpeachable since they made it their business to hold readings of Lord Sydmouth's private diaries whenever he was away somewhere.

One of the most intriguing facts to come to light from the reading of the diaries was that Lord Sydmouth had tried to have the black crooner murdered by a well-known firm of assassins who had been warmly recommended to him for this purpose. It appeared that for a really rather reasonable sum of money – considering the risk involved – it was possible to eliminate one's wife's lover in such a way as to arouse no suspicion, so naturally Lord Sydmouth had given the murderers the green light – naturally since his Lordship felt particularly badly about the chap, whom he had hired to perform the cabaret, not run off with his wife.

However, fortune conspired against the murderous firm when it came to the crunch, for Lady Sydmouth's dark lover had elected to take his new paramour to Harlem, where white assassins were about as easy to spot as black crooners were difficult, with the end result that Lady Sydmouth was able to settle down quite happily with her lover and produce six children, before her lover in turn ran off with his manager to California, leaving Poppy's mother with a large set of bills to pay, including one for rhinestone evening jackets.

Of course the first thing Lady Sydmouth did was to turn back to her husband and his family for help, who duly and without rancour paid off her bills, including the one for the rhinestone evening jackets, in the hope of encouraging Lady Sydmouth to do the decent thing and return the family jewellery, which was quite beyond price and had been in the family since the beginning of the eighteenth century, when the Sydmouths had stolen it from a friend's house in lieu of a questionable gambling debt. However, although she was a fool, Poppy's mother was certainly not an idiot, and so she allowed the family to settle her debts, but kept the jewellery. And then, to add insult quite purposefully to injury, as soon as the children of her liaison with the black crooner had grown up enough to earn their own livings, she placed them all as maids and butlers in the Bahamian holiday houses of all the Sydmouths' friends, thereby making it if not impossible, highly uncomfortable for a Sydmouth to visit anyone in that part of the world.

Georgiana, who delighted in this story, was of course told it by Poppy, who had learnt it from Nanny Sydmouth, who was now waiting to greet Georgiana in the Great Hall. As Georgiana kissed her, she thought of how much she had preferred Poppy's nanny to her own, and how guilty she had always felt in loving Nanny Sydmouth more, far more than she had ever loved her own mother replacement. She was then shown to her room, which of course was the room in the castle to which she was always shown, Regency yellow, Chinese Chippendale, and with her favourite portrait of the Hon. Miss Sydmouth staring down at her from the wall above her bed. Nanny bustled off to run her a bath, and Georgiana wandered over to the biscuit box on the table and took, from force of habit, a tiny vanilla-tasting heart, remembering how as a child she had been so unused to the trappings of great wealth that her first night at Sydmouth she had sat up eating all the fruit and biscuits left by her bedside, unable to get over their very presence in her room.

Shortly after Georgiana had changed into her silk dressing gown, Poppy came into her room, smiling slyly. She sat down on Georgiana's bed and lit a cigarette, carefully blowing the smoke near Georgiana. Georgiana, who hated the smell of cigarettes, said nothing, knowing that Poppy knew she hated it, which made it *de rigeur* that Poppy should therefore smoke all over her and her bedroom.

Poppy started to talk to Georgiana, and Georgiana listened. Her cousin had a way of talking that made the most ordinary information sound intriguing and the most extraordinary news banal. She could tell you someone had just cold-bloodedly murdered their gamekeeper, and you accepted the news without emotion, and then in the next breath she could tell you exactly where to get your underwear and precisely what to pay for it in such an intense way that, if you didn't know her better, you would rush off the following day and buy up the shop. Which would be exactly what Poppy would want you to do since naturally she herself would be clothed in a completely different brand of underwear. She also had a habit of looking away when she was listening intently, and staring at you very hard when she wasn't. She looked at Georgiana intently when questioning her cousin about her relationship with John Pemberton, and turned away when informing her Pemberton was a fellow house guest that weekend. And then she rose quite abruptly and left the room, leaving behind the acrid smell of stale cigarettes which even the pot-pourri scented air freshener could not altogether drown.

After a while, Georgiana went and had her bath, first pouring in some Floris bath oil before climbing into the large white tub. She liked large old white baths with worn patches by the plug, large claw feet, and old gnarled brass taps, which was just as well since there were about a dozen back at Longborough. She lay in the oiled water and thought about the conversation with her cousin. Poppy obviously had been anxious to tell her that Pemberton was a guest, because she knew that Georgiana might not be so anxious to see him. Or that she might be too anxious to see him, which Poppy wouldn't like either. As it happened, Georgiana had been careful not to show either pleasure or displeasure at the news concerning her fellow house guest, not because she enjoyed evading Poppy's curiosity, which she did, but because she actually did not know herself how she felt. Over the past few weeks, Pemberton had become rather a permanent fixture in her life, and Georgiana realised she was in a way beginning to take him for granted. But now that Poppy had asked him for the weekend with her, it suddenly seemed that she might be forced to think of him as a more permanent fixture than he actually was, and not just as a temporary bridge, which she deeply suspected was what she actually wanted.

She had lain in her bath now so long that her fingers were turning to parchment in the water, but still she turned on the hot tap yet again. She knew she should have got out ages ago, but she forced herself to stay in the water until she had overcome her sense of indecision about Pemberton. She could not possibly go down to the library for drinks wearing the scent he had given her, and the silk shirt he had so recently admired, until she knew exactly how she felt, not only about him, but about her life. And she could not think about her life without including him, because he was her first lover, and not only had he opened a brand new chapter, he had also closed another.

She stared up at the high ceiling. She knew she had hurt his feelings. Even though she was considerably younger than he was, she knew at once from the expression on his face. Of course they had both drunk a considerable amount of champagne, and her tactlessness could well have been caused by that, but she had not meant to hurt him, and hurt him she had. Why had she laughed? She had seen men naked before, so why had Pemberton naked induced in her such a strong desire to laugh? Perhaps it was because Pemberton's clothes were so much part of him; once out of them he was not so much naked as denuded. And then when he started to make love to her, he seemed to lose the very qualities which Georgiana had so admired in him. She realised it was very difficult for a man, even a gentleman as sophisticated as John Pemberton, to remain cool, witty, and aloof when he was making love, but somehow Pemberton had not retained even a trace of his finer qualities. And although Georgiana realised that love-making naturally demands a certain loss of cool, and the temporary abandonment of a sense of humour, she really rather regretted quite how totally Pemberton had lost his hitherto beautifully preserved composure. And so if the First Duke of Wellington had reminded Harriet Wilson of a rat catcher, so it was that the Seventh Marquis of Pemberton had reminded Georgiana of a picture she had once seen of George IV, large and white, but unhappily, as she now realised, she had discovered this fact just a bit too late.

Afterwards, when he had tried to get her to stay the whole night with him, Georgiana had not been able to conceal her emotions from him, much to his hurt astonishment. So she ran from his house in Belgrave Square back to Mary's; with the knowledge that it was at such times, when life was at its most real, that she most disliked it. She felt ashamed now, as she lay there in her slowly chilling bath, regretting that she had left him so abruptly, and that she had so openly shown him her dismay. But most of all she regretted the fact that she had perhaps been using him, and that life was not quite as simple as she would like it to be. She thought of how he would probably be downstairs in the library already, waiting for her, and she tried to put out of her mind the image of him lying against the pillows of his bed, naked, watching her dressing, his face still dazed from the shock of what she had just confessed to him. But then she realised that downstairs, in the library, he would be dressed again. He would once more be part of his clothes, and thus surely he would have recovered the witty, aloof and charming manner she had originally so admired, and even once or twice been quite thrilled by. Pemberton would be himself again, and this would make everything much, much simpler, because Pemberton was very rich, and Longborough was very decrepit, and the unhappiness of that one night was all her own doing and none of his – and so at last she was able to get out of the bath.

Later, as she went down the stairs, Georgiana looked carefully at all the portraits of hers and Poppy's ancestors. She knew it was her duty to suppress her feelings, as it had probably been their duty to suppress theirs. Who knew what sacrifices they had all made for their family's fortunes, for the houses they had to live in, and for the children they were forced to bear? As she opened the library door, Georgiana lifted her small rounded chin, and faced the assembled company with a renewed sense of determination. Perhaps if she had been a little older, she would have realised that life has a way of springing surprises at the least expected moments, and conversely of not springing any when most expected, concealing them instead from the person or persons concerned. Rather as the actor or singer who wishes to surprise her audience does so by choosing to lead them vocally in one direction, only to astonish everybody by changing her tone or pitch at the least expected moment, or as the magician who causes the audience to look in one direction as he effects his concealment in another, so was that weekend at Sydmouth.

Georgiana felt immense relief at seeing Pemberton back in his clothes. They were very well-cut clothes, but not ostentatiously so. They were an English gentleman's clothes and, within them, Pemberton was himself once more – cool, charmingly aloof and even occasionally witty, so that very soon Georgiana and he were able to resume their former easy relationship. Georgiana felt quite securely that their association might now continue without any reference to her erstwhile tactlessness, which judging by his silence on the matter she presumed he had completely forgiven.

There were other guests of course. One or two of them spoke very loudly which made Georgiana wonder why it was that people did, and one or two of them spoke very much out of the sides of their mouths, which made Pemberton wonder out loud to Georgiana on two occasions where such people got their accents. The two of them felt united in their bewilderment, because of course Pemberton was referring to 'County', and they both shared a mutual Upper Class loathing for County.

'What exactly are the County, do you think?' Georgiana asked him.

'People,' replied Pemberton, 'who in the last century made money in coal, in the previous century made their money from wool, and in the one previous to that made money from ships.'

'And who nowadays?'

'People who nowadays,' he continued, 'just make money. A person's place in the County is nowadays judged purely on the level of his income, that's all. With the right income, he can rise to being Lord of the Manor, and in the space of a generation he will not only have found himself some ancestors to go with his acres, bought at auction at Sotheby's on a rainy day, but sometimes even acquired some manners too, although the latter are considerably more difficult to come by. And so within a very short space of time his children will become the cream of the County, riding to hounds, and despising their neighbours in such a way that they will be able to go to bed every night safe in the knowledge that they are so hated by everyone that they must by now be Upper Class. That's the County nowadays.'

Georgiana looked at Pemberton with quite passionate fondness. They each knew without speaking not just what they liked, but what they could never understand. Furthermore, she felt that such a passionate fondness must in turn mean something, and such a sense of mutuality must once more lead to love.

'Have you noticed,' said Pemberton, with his easy laugh, 'how many of the silly asses think that if they say "orf" it means they're not?'

Georgiana was separated from Pemberton during dinner, and sat next to a gentleman who was so anxious to prove that he was more than he actually was that he refused to say anything at all, having perhaps come to the conclusion that by behaving in such a way a person most definitely could not be found out. Georgiana tried in vain to make conversation on every subject upon which she was certain she was totally ignorant, in line with a theory of hers that people who will not talk easily can be lured into conversation by the profession of utter ignorance, insomuch that if you maintain long enough and loudly enough that the world is flat, or that horses with three legs run faster, they will eventually be forced to correct you. Unfortunately this was not true tonight of the person on her right, who remained completely silent throughout the whole first course until the butler, perhaps sensing her desperation, came to her rescue while removing her unfinished hors d'oeuvre.

'Try goff,' he whispered knowingly, which Georgiana did with quite alarming success.

The gentleman on her left was of a totally different

calibre. He was slightly titled and immensely rude, whether because he felt slighted by the littleness of his title in such august company, or because he was just by nature rude did not bother Georgiana. What irked was that he was rude. He made a great point of discussing anything he had to say with the lady on his right, and then at the very last moment, just before the ladies rose to leave, turned to Georgiana.

'I'm so sorry,' he said finally to her. 'I don't believe I've really had a chance to talk to you.'

'Haven't you?' said Georgiana sweetly. 'I'm afraid I didn't really notice.'

She wished she was older, and didn't blush quite so fiercely with the effort of being rude.

'Who is he and why was he so horrid?' she asked Poppy as she followed her up the stairs to comb her hair while the gentlemen passed the port.

'Oh, he's nobody,' Poppy replied vaguely. 'He's just stupid and a bit jumped up.'

'Well he was frightfully rude,' said Georgiana. 'Nearly as rude as that dreadful Lord Brough of Brightlingsea I had to sit next to last week at the Kavanaghs.'

Poppy looked away, because she was listening.

'I've never actually met an "of" that I've liked,' she said. 'Well, maybe one, but not many.'

'What's an "of", Poppy·' asked one of the other ladies, rather loudly.

'Oh – you know –' said Poppy, grinning slyly, 'those frightfully silly titles Socialists take because they want to get into the House of Lords and draw their pin money. Papa calls them the Gannex brigade.'

She said it with a malicious grin because both she and Georgiana knew that the husband of one of the ladies present was about to accept a life peerage, after a political career devoted to a campaign for the lowering of the Upper Classes.

'Everybody has been "jumped up", as you call it, sometime or other,' said the lady in question, in an attempt to squash their snobbery.

90

'Absolutely,' agreed Poppy. 'Georgiana's jumped up because her family's only Norman.'

'That's quite true,' Georgiana admitted with a straight face. 'Poppy's Saxon, you see. So she's not at all jumped up.'

For a moment they were back as children, playing blood-curdling games of Saxons and Normans, and Poppy was being allowed to win as usual.

After that there was little more to be said on the subject of ancestors, so the ladies, freshly powdered, coiffured and scented, once more descended to the saloon where they sat for what seemed like an age waiting for the reappearance of the gentlemen and some mixed conversation. To while away the time, Poppy, who by now was in a thoroughly mischievous mood, told a story she knew would not make all the ladies present laugh, and would certainly shock at least one. Georgiana knew the story of course, but she enjoyed it again, if only for the way Poppy told it; and besides, there never was any point stopping Poppy once she had decided there was someone present who was visibly vulnerable to shock.

'I had a great-aunt once,' she announced, 'who was always consumed with curiosity as to what the gentlemen actually did when the ladies retired, and one day she was bribed by one of her six elder sisters to find out. In fear and trepidation she crossed the hall, opened the dining room door and peered into the room where the gentlemen had been incarcerated for the previous two hours. Having seen what she'd been sent to see, she then fled back to this room, to her sisters who were waiting in a state of hysterical suspense.

Poppy paused and surveyed her captive audience. Georgiana admired her technique more than ever.

' "Well?" said the sisters. "So what were they all doing?"

' "Doing?" replied Great-Aunt Clara. "Doing? Why they was pissing in the wine coolers!" '

Georgiana led the laughter, which was voluble from the County and predictably muted from the rest of the ladies.

Poppy was delighted, because the jagged edges of her nature required her to shock people, but only in such a way that she could not be criticised for being anything more than a little daring.

'I wonder what the gentlemen talk about now?' one of the County ladies asked brightly. 'Shall we dare ask them?'

'No,' said Poppy. 'Not unless we all want to die from boredom. And I'm far too young for that.'

Georgiana watched each of the other ladies watching Poppy, and thinking that not only was she, regrettably, far too young to die of boredom, she was also far too precocious for her age. The habit that her father had fallen into of using her as hostess for his parties was not something of which they could approve, particularly since she made no attempt to conceal her contempt for their age and situations. Perhaps even more discourteously, she never hid from them the fact that she knew they disliked her, and yet still they accepted her invitations to dine. Evenings at Sydmouth might not be their favourite evenings, but not to be invited would be an even worse fate, so they went, and Poppy's knowledge of the reason why they went made her more intimidating than the most formidable Dowager.

The gentlemen finally joined them, and Georgiana regretted that Pemberton was not able to sit near her, because she missed his easy conversation, and instead had to submit to the attentions of the gentleman who had been sitting on her right, whom she had opened up so successfully on the subject of 'goff', and who was now apparently determined to stay by her side until the end of time, taking her around the old course at St Andrews for the fifth time and driving Georgiana to such a state of frantic boredom that she found herself hoping he would suddenly be struck dumb as he stood on the eighteenth tee needing only a five for his best score ever, and thus put everyone listening out of their immediate misery.

And so the evening ended for Georgiana in a state of abject boredom, and without her having exchanged with Pemberton anything more profound than the expression of their mutual dislike of the County. Naturally she felt cheated. It might even have been preferable, she thought on her way upstairs, to have initially received a more distant reception from Pemberton, because that at least would have given some edge to the evening. Instead he had shown her nothing but courtesy and charm, and this she had to admit to herself she found a little bewildering. As she lay in bed listening to the owls hooting in the castle grounds, and the silent patter of feet in the corridor as the guests tiptoed backwards and forwards to each other's bedrooms, Georgiana realised that she still had a lot to learn, and she also recognised that a lot of her confusion lay in the fact that she did not know what it was she had to learn. If she had known the word 'pragmatic', she might well have used it to describe herself and her attitude to life. But since she did not know the word she fell asleep, and it never occurred to her to wonder whose feet were pattering up and down the corridor and whose doors were being opened.

Next morning, Nanny Sydmouth brought Georgiana breakfast on a wicker tray, and sat on her bed talking while she ate her hot buttered toast. It was too early in the day to concentrate on conversation, so Georgiana let her thoughts drift as she stared at the portrait of the Hon. Miss Sydmouth in her chip-straw hat which was reflected in her dressing table mirror. What had her life been like, she wondered? Was it a succession of masked balls and discreet liaisons, and had she had a little black sambo for a page? Had she married someone she didn't love and given her life in childbirth, or had she had a tragic succession of still-born babies? Had she always favoured such cheeky little hats, and did absolutely everyone fall in love with that enigmatic smile? And why had Nanny suddenly stopped talking? She looked at the old nursery maid now silently reflected in the glass.

'Sorry, Nanny. What did you say?'

'I said anyway, that's what I'm hoping,' Nanny replied, folding her red hands in her lap. 'That's what I'm hoping, Lady Georgie. For my Poppy.'

Georgiana picked up her hairbrush from the table by her bed and started to brush her hair very slowly. She had actually heard what Nanny had just said, but she wanted to make absolutely sure.

'What is it that you're hoping, Nanny?'

Nanny sighed with the slight irritation of someone being forced to repeat themselves.

'That it will not be too long before they announce their engagement.'

Georgiana continued to brush out her hair.

'They?'

'My Poppy and Lord Pemberton.'

Georgiana turned and carefully replaced the hairbrush on the bedside table.

'Do they know each other very well then, Nanny?' she asked.

'Well no, darling. Not very well. But they're madly in love. I know that because my little darling told me so herself only this morning.'

Her little darling's cousin stared for a moment at Nanny. Nanny's wording 'madly in love' could only mean one thing, and Georgiana knew it. She also knew that the opening and closing of doors and the tip-tap-tip of bare feet in the corridor last night could only underwrite that knowledge. Poppy had invited Pemberton to stay not for Georgiana but for herself. That was why he had been so affable and charming to her, and that was why Georgiana had gone to bed the previous night with that slight sense of unease as if she had suddenly lost her grasp on a situation she had previously had well under control. As she stared at Nanny, who was now beaming fondly at her, Georgiana suddenly wanted to scream. She wanted to throw the beastly little Beatrix Potter teapot on her tray to the floor, throw the covers off her bed and run around her room screaming very loudly. Which of course she didn't because it would be quite unforgivable, though not quite so unforgivable as the deed just perpetrated by her cousin. However, it was not altogether surprising, because when they were small Poppy had always wanted Georgiana's toys even though Georgiana's toys were never as nice as her own. And now Poppy, who was the heiress to one of the largest and most valuable estates left in England and didn't need Pemberton the way Georgiana needed Pemberton, had to take him off her cousin simply because her cousin had him.

'Is something the matter, pet?' asked Nanny.

Georgiana assured Nanny that there was not, but she had to push her clenched fist very hard against her chin in an effort not to break into angry sobs. Why should Poppy have what she wanted when Poppy didn't even need it? Life was so unfair. She knew Nanny was busy whitewashing the whole situation, because Poppy had sent her to do so. Poppy had always used Nanny as her messenger, and to clear up everything she left in her spoilt wake, and now she was just using her to tell Georgiana indirectly that she must give way to her. Poppy was no more in love with Pemberton than Georgiana was, but what was worse was she didn't need him. She was rich and would never be poor, while Georgiana was poor and would quite probably never be rich, because quite probably she would never attract someone of Pemberton's vast wealth again. And as for Nanny talking about love – love just never came into it with someone like Poppy, because she had never known it, except from Nanny, which didn't count because as everyone knew Nannies loved one because that's what they were paid to do.

Nanny finally left her, her mission accomplished. Georgiana could imagine Poppy questioning her on her return and Nanny giving all the reassuring replies Poppy wanted to hear.

'Lady Georgie is delighted, pet,' Nanny would tell her. 'She thinks Lord Pemberton's a most suitable choice. She told me so herself.'

And then she would fuss round her charge, pouring her out her fresh orange and laying out a set of clean underwear. And Poppy would just lie there in bed, watching Nanny with those bright green eyes, happy in the knowledge that Georgiana now knew that what had almost been hers was now Poppy's, and that she could do nothing at all about it, because to admit she cared for Pemberton would be quite ludicrous after the way she had behaved towards him. And even if Pemberton had only fallen into Poppy's bed on the rebound, or from hurt pride, or whatever, it didn't matter. What mattered was that Poppy had stolen one of Georgiana's toys while Georgiana was still not quite sure that she had finished playing with it, and that Georgiana's pride had been hurt, and Poppy knew that Georgiana's pride was something she cared about even more than her life.

Later that morning all three of them went for a ride, which in the circumstances was quite fortunate for Georgiana, since it gave her a chance to observe Pemberton on a horse. Georgiana was fascinated. Pemberton was not a subtle rider. He might not have shown any embarrassment when he met her in the stable yard, and he might have had the delicacy to treat her just a little more distantly than he had the night before, but his seat and his hands showed no delicacy whatsoever. Her father would have described him as a huntsman, and so, she thought gleefully, would she. By the time they returned to the stables and dismounted, Georgiana realised that Pemberton as a rider was exactly the same as Pemberton as a lover, and she was no more able to admire his technique on a horse than she was his technique in bed.

After that, it became a matter of some urgency for Georgiana to leave early, and alone. However, she was coerced into having lunch with Poppy and her now ex-lover before she left, over which she watched Poppy carefully not watching Pemberton and Pemberton pretending very unsuccessfully to be interested in everything Georgiana said, which anyway was little. It was not much fun, and had she not seen Pemberton riding she realised she might have had some sense of regret. As it was she had none, so she wished Poppy well, playing the fox to her huntsman. Later, on the train back to London, Georgiana felt relieved – mostly because now that she had shown that she no longer cared for Pemberton, Poppy could no longer hurt her, and thus she had removed herself from her cousin's grasp. But the euphoria was shortlived, as the images of the weekend were all too soon replaced in her mind by images of Longborough, with its gardens and stables overgrown with weeds and moss, and the house's crumbling and peeling façade. She could see her mother bent over the smouldering fire throwing on yet another green and damp log, while her father, wrapped in a moth-eaten old cashmere rug, sat by under damp-stained ceilings watching without hope. And once again despair rose within her, because she knew she had been robbed; and Poppy, who had everything, it was Poppy who had robbed her.

She arrived back at Mary's house in what Lucius now described as 'downtown Belgravia' with a sense of great relief. As she stood in the hall she could hear nothing but the sounds of the birds outside, and the fountain in the courtyard splashing as it played. She stood there quite happily for a while, drinking in the peace of the house. Then she heard a tread on the stairs leading up from the kitchen below, and turning saw Mary in her crushed velvet robe coming towards her, carrying a laden wicker tray similar to the one off which Georgiana had breakfasted earlier that day. She looked beautiful as she sometimes could when caught unawares, in that crushed velvet robe which Georgiana secretly coveted, and with her long hair hanging down in loose curly clusters. Georgiana just had time to notice how smooth and clear her skin was before she disappeared with a small smile back upstairs to her room.

It was not unusual for Mary to entertain a friend in the privacy of her room, just as it was not unusual for her to take trays of food and drink up there at odd hours. People from all over the world called to see Mary, and she would often treat them to what she called a little *fête champêtre* in her room. But there was something different happening up there this evening, and Georgiana sensed it straight away. It wasn't so much the unfamiliar composer now being favoured on the gramophone playing behind the stippled door, but more the different smell upon the lamps. It was no longer the usual stephanotis, nor musk roses, but a denser, mustier scent, reminiscent of dead flowers.

chapter six

It was now early June, a hot day when all over town morning-dressed gentlemen were hurling their toppers onto the back shelves of their limousines and motor cars, many of them meanwhile wondering if full morning dress on such a day, even for the Derby, was not really a fearful price to pay for the *style anglaise*. However, for those who had suffered the privations of a privileged upbringing, discomfort would always be equated with pleasure, and consequently the idea of sitting at home and watching the race on television in comfort and shirt-sleeved order was quite out of the question. So they were all making their chauffeured way out towards the Downs, their ladies plumed and preening beside them, as unable to break with the tradition and pattern of their forefathers as migrating birds.

Andrew Gillott was no exception to this rule, and the thought of not putting on his tail coat and not hurling his topper onto the back shelf of his hired limousine simply never occurred to him as he struggled for some time to fit into his morning dress, which was still far too tight for him, even though John Bell and Croydon had fitted him up with a corset the previous season. This season however, he now found to his consternation that even the corset was too tight. Consequently he was now concerned lest once he had made the ascent to his private box without undue incident, his stays would burst should he find himself in the unlikely situation of cheering home some long-priced nag upon which he'd had a substantial wager. As he finished dressing, he found himself looking forward to the end of the day, when he could return home, remove the beastly thing and have a damned good scratch.

His stays, however, were not the only blot on that morning's otherwise clear horizon. His guests were the other. He knew nobody that he knew would want to speak to Mrs Parker-Jones and her daughter Jennifer, and to think that the dreadful woman would not be prominent in his box would be to underestimate her sadly. He knew full well that she would make a point of hanging out of the box waving to everyone she both knew and didn't know, and if any chum was foolhardy enough to venture into the box to see Andrew, there she'd be, at the ready, waiting to bore the knickers off one and all like there was no tomorrow, which quite frankly at this particular moment in time Andrew personally wished there were.

Another person in the party whom Andrew was not looking forward greatly to seeing was the frightful accountant he had hired to escort Jennifer, because only the night before the greedy little sod had rung Andrew and informed him of his fee for Derby week. It had been just as well for Andrew that he had not been wearing his corset when he received the call for had he been he was in little doubt he would have had a massive coronary on the spot and died subsequently from constriction. In all his years in Society he had never heard of hired escorts charging for the Derby. It was quite incredible how things had gone to the wall nowadays.

Andrew directed his driver to the Parker-Jones' Knightsbridge flat where mother and daughter were waiting for him to pick them up. Mrs Parker-Jones emerged from the building wearing the first of her new Season's outfits, a startler in purple and green with matching accessories. Andrew gave as elaborate a shudder as his stays permitted. He had an almost Italianate loathing of purple, considering it a colour only worn by the most lurid of women. He quickly put on his

99

dark glasses, but not before observing that Jennifer, in direct contrast to her mother, was dressed from head to toe in bright tangerine. Andrew thought for a moment he was going to throw up. He got out to greet them, and Nigel beat him back into the car and the favoured seat up in front by the chauffeur. Andrew clambered gracelessly into the back and had to seat himself between the two violently colour-clashing women. At that moment he deeply cursed whichever fool it was who had first invented the Season.

Mrs Parker-Jones herself had been more than a little pleased with her choice of outfit for the day, until Aidan had informed her that she reminded him of an air hostess. She closed her eyes at the memory. After all this time and trouble, there she was, expensively turned out, doing for once the right thing at the right time and he had to go and tell her she looked like someone who distributed plastic trays and sick bags. It really was the end. Had she been Jennifer's age she wold have burst into tears. But age had taught her some self-control, and anyway she knew Aidan was only saying horrid things because he was mean and resented what he was being forced to spend on his daughter's social life. Clarissa had from the start been determined not to listen to his moans, and now she even felt a thrill at the idea that the stupid man didn't know she had pawned her bracelet. It meant he couldn't control every aspect of her life, and although she said nothing to his face, she knew she had some power still to hurt him. Aidan was fat and silly. He was also a social handicap, with his habit of saying serviette, and pronouncing Ascot, As*cot*, and clematis clem*atis*. Not like dear Andrew Gillott, who was always so correct, and so amusing. She and he had had a wonderful time planning poor Jennifer's dance. She had of course left everything to Andrew, because his taste was quite impeccable in everything. He knew exactly who to go to for flowers, and the catering, and the band. The dance, she knew, would be a tremendous boost to her social life, let alone to poor Jennifer's. Of that there was absolutely no doubt. And after it, even

100

the wretched Elizabeth Alney would have to show her some respect.

Mrs Parker-Jones smiled at Andrew. Every sacrifice she was making for poor Jennifer was worthwhile. For not only was she being asked everywhere by everyone nowadays, but she even had a regular escort in the quite charming Nigel Bruce-Smith, who was too good to be even half true, taking her everywhere, hanging on her every word, and refusing to take no for an answer. It was wonderful to see. And Jennifer was blossoming with his attentions, even beginning to look quite pretty. Well no, perhaps not pretty so much as *jolie laide*, but even so, that for Jennifer was something.

Of course Andrew teased her quite dreadfully about Nigel, suggesting that in reality it was the mother not the daughter he was visiting when he called at the flat. But that was just silly. Because he always brought her flowers and obviously far preferred talking to her rather than Jennifer didn't mean a thing. After all, most young men preferred to talk to older women, because for a start they had much more conversation, and knew much better what young men were about. It was only natural.

And so they arrived at Epsom racecourse on its most colourful day of the year, and proceeded to the private box, Andrew walking some way ahead of the two ladies lest his chums should imagine that they were with him. He could well imagine how they would josh him that evening at the Claremont should he be spotted as their escort.

'Run out of Iranians and Ayrabs, eh Gillott?' they would cry. 'Who were you with at Epsom? The *Daily Mirror* Punters' Club?'

The thought of their possible jibes made Gillott put even more distance between him and the rest of his party.

Happily, by an immense stroke of good fortune, he managed to cram the two women and the beastly little accountant into a lift where there was no room for his ample frame. He waved at them briefly as the doors closed and they disappeared from view, and then took off his top hat and wiped the sweat from his brow in relief. It wasn't a moment too soon because he had already spotted the familiar and elegant figure of the Countess heading his way.

She had also already seen him.

'Still got that frightful woman in tow, Andrew?' she enquired, never being one to dissemble.

' 'Fraid so,' sighed Andrew. ' 'Fraid so.'

'Ghastly creature. Going to be a quite terrible season for you then.'

'What season isn't nowadays?'

'Quite right too,' agreed the Countess. 'More dreadful every year. Don't know where they're gettin' the people.'

They both glanced up at the indicator above the lift doors in the ensuing silence.

'Hear Georgiana's got Pemberton,' said the Countess, deciding on a change of subject. 'This true?'

'No idea,' said Andrew. 'Sorry.'

'Bit old for her, isn't he? Wouldn't you say?'

'I know. But then who isn't who's in dibs?'

The Countess nodded.

'True. True. Anyone her own age won't be interested. Not once they've seen Longborough.'

She laughed shortly, and Andrew Gillott did too.

'Now then,' she said, putting a bony hand on his arm, 'what about a tip for the first race?'

Andrew took out his race card and happily went through the runners, back on his favourite ground. Horses might be unpredictable, but they were a great deal more interesting and gave one a lot more sport than women. A lot of them were much better-looking, too. By the time the lift re-descended, Andrew had fully marked the Countess' card and only hoped he didn't bump into her after the last when she would demand to know why they'd all gone down. At the moment, examining his selection, he was well in favour.

By the time Andrew arrived at his box, the carousel was in full swing. Jennifer, because she was looking even more unbecoming than ever, was already being whirled in and out of all her girl friends' private boxes to act as flattering background, and where her daughter was asked, Mrs Parker-Jones followed without compunction, making new enemies at each and every introduction. By the middle of the afternoon people, in their desperation to avoid her, crowded into whichever private box she wasn't disgracing, having discovered early on Mrs Parker-Jones' happy knack of killing conversation and fun with one fell blow.

Jennifer was quite well aware of this as her mother trailed behind her like a cloud of purple and poisonous gas, clearing whole boxes and sometimes even the corridor outside them as soon as she opened her mouth. She was quite well aware of the mockery her mother aroused with her constant references to 'the Rolls', and all her other toe-curling social solecisms. She had been well aware of her mother's embarrassment factor ever since she had been sent to her public school, which had been specifically designed to breed a new generation of ladies out of girls who weren't. Unlike her mother, Jennifer knew that ladies did not refer to their motor cars, nor to their 'bags', that ladies prompted other people to talk, that they did not steamroll other people's conversation, did not drain their champagne as if it was lemonade, and did not laugh in that horribly sudden and very loud way. She regretted knowing all these graces, and had always known her education to have been a great mistake, since otherwise she would never have known that her mother was quite so common, which she would have preferred. But thanks to Grantley Abbey she had been made aware of such social distinctions, and ever since then she had suffered because of her knowledge. But today, Derby Day, was the worst of them all, and as she watched her mother steamrolling her way through the cream of Society, Jennifer turned bright pink beneath her tangerine. If it had not been for Nigel, dear Nigel, she would never have got through it. He was, happily it seemed, quite oblivious to the mockeries of others, and the sillier her mother became, the less he seemed aware of it, only pausing to fuss over her even more, or fetch her yet another glass of champagne. And when thankfully it was time at last to leave the racecourse (her mother in a most unseemly state, with her lipstick all smeared and her hat more than a little crooked), Jennifer resolved that whatever happened she would make absolutely sure her mother did not go to Ascot.

Georgiana on the other hand had a very good Derby. She could see so many rich men from her box that she felt like someone who has just come off a diet and is confronted by the food counters at Fortnum and Mason: they all looked so delicious that she did not know where to begin, or at which counter to start. Somewhere, she thought dreamily after her third or fourth glass of champagne, somewhere down there was a man whose bank balance was so vast that not even the roof at Longborough would present any problems to him, or make an even slightly noticeable hole in his current account. Certainly not as big a hole as there currently was in the Orangery roof. The main problem was to find one who was not of the Moslem faith, and who was used to racing horses rather than camels.

She was, she felt, once more her old self, for although her self-confidence had indeed taken a tiny knock since Poppy had stolen Pemberton from right under her nose, she had quickly recovered and once more found her spirits soaring at the sight of the English in their racing best. It occurred to her, as she surveyed the scene below, that this was probably the greatest concentration of style in the smallest space that anyone was ever likely to see.

The people in her party, since it was Mary's box, were all a little older than she was, but Georgiana preferred this since they were far less likely to throw bread rolls onto the people in the boxes below, and of course did not drink their champagne as Jennifer's mother had, as if it was either their very first glass, or their last before the bar closed forever. Georgiana felt sorry for Jennifer, particularly when she saw her with her frightful mother in tow, and she realised that Jennifer's predicament was if anything slightly worse than her own. She felt it might even be easier to land one of those rich gentlemen below her on the lawns than it would be to shake off a mother such as poor Jennifer sported.

And as for being pushed around town by Andrew Gillott, it was difficult to imagine anything worse. Everyone knew Gillott was in such dire financial straits nowadays that he had to take on either parties of foreigners, or lame ducks such as Jennifer. Georgiana had done her best to help Jennifer, but she knew that even Jennifer realised there was a limit to what one could do for someone when that person had a mother such as Mrs Parker-Jones. There was only one other girl who had a mother as frightful as Jennifer's, but since the girl in question happened to be rather pretty, she never got asked anywhere at all, which only further went to prove that however badly off one considered oneself to be, there was always someone somewhere even worse off than you.

Lucius, of course, was having a ball. Not only was he mining rich material for his book the whole afternoon, he was wearing morning dress for the very first time in his life; and although Mary had hinted that he was better off carrying his top hat rather than wearing it (which he suspected was because in it he looked a little American), he thought he looked rather handsome in it. He certainly felt handsome, and occasionally when no one was looking, he would glance at his reflection in other people's sun glasses and carefully adjust his tie to an even more perfect position.

As for the day itself, nothing could have prepared him better for his first view of an English Derby than starting an affair with Mary. It was superb. To be able to look at her in her elegant silk dress and her little veiled hat, and know what she was capable of doing made him very excited, in exactly the right way. And every now and then he thought of new things that he would make her do, and that was wonderfully unbearable. He loved to watch her cool English manner, knowing how much it was capable of being reversed. And as for the feeling that he could, whenever he wished, order her ladyship to bring him what he wanted when he wanted, like a maid, it was really quite intoxicating.

Naturally she had told him that she had mistaken him for a homosexual, and they had laughed about it and then decided to continue the deception; for they both knew that it would enable Mary to continue her affair with him without the Countess being able to interfere. In fact Lucius liked to encourage this idea of himself, and not just in front of the Countess. He encouraged others to share this misjudgment of character because he relished privacy when it came to sex, and the fact that Mary shared this secret with him meant that they were like naughty children, and like naughty children they could exchange secret looks and experience private frissons.

Fulton and Elliott visited their box after the second race and Lucius flirted mildly with them, knowing that Mary would enjoy it. It was really dreadfully funny, and all the more so because Mary took such care to take it so seriously. The only unfortunate thing about this particular enterprise was that he could not write and tell Mother about it. Instead he would simply write and tell her that Derby Day dawned clear, bright and hot, and stayed that way all day, and that he had had a bet on the Irish-trained favourite and that it had won. That the women looked very pretty, although perhaps not as chic as New York women, but nonetheless pretty, soft and very appealing. That soft apple green (or should he call it soft green apple?) and pale primrose were the most popular colours this year, and that the younger women looked really so charming in their neat straw boaters. That he had met Mr Penny, the famous milliner, and had complimented him on so many charming examples of his craft. That the film director Charles Kaminski was in the next door box, and that he and Lady Mary, as he always referred to her in his letters to mother, had been invited in and introduced.

Charles Kaminski was such a famous film director that even the English had heard of him, Lucius noted approvingly. He was tall, so therefore quite able to compete in physical stature with the rest of his party, and indeed quite unconsciously dominated them, not only by dint of his reputation. He wore his clothes, rather than vice versa, which combined with his height and natural authority to make him a most unusual example of someone in the film business. Lucius recognised that Kaminski was a man of such authority that he had absolutely no need to demonstrate it. He made Lucius feel quite small, and so when he returned to Mary's box it was with a feeling of considerable relief. He liked famous people but he was not sure he liked them to be quite as famous as Kaminski, who seemed to dwarf everyone else around him.

Georgiana, on the other hand, had barely even heard of him. Not only was she a little young to remember his early films, she was not even the kind of girl who would have enjoyed them. They were not intellectual, but they were on such themes as the obscenity of war, or the predicament of man in the age of space exploration, or just the predicament of man, and Georgiana was far too interested in her own predicament, and in man the male, to have had even a passing interest in the grand themes which preoccupied a mind such as Kaminski's.

Lucius told her all about him, leaning over the front of the box while talking in a low tone.

'He is so successful he is classic. And yet he is still famous in spite of being classic.'

This was all a little bewildering to Georgiana who thought of classic as being a book bound in leather with very thin pages and small print, and famous as being something you had to become if you weren't Upper Class.

'How do you know if you're famous, Lucius?' she asked.

There was a pause while Lucius, who himself still longed to be famous considered what his reply should be. It really was the moment to frame an epithet, but on the whole epithets were to be avoided because they always sounded like misquotes from Oscar Wilde, even when they were your own.

'If you're really famous,' he eventually replied, 'no one

need ever mention your first name, nor your achievements.'

Georgiana nodded even though she had not the faintest idea what Lucius could possibly mean. She hoped if she kept silent Lucius would elaborate, which most obligingly he did.

'For instance, people quite unselfconsciously refer to Chaplin, or Picasso, or Shaw, while other people who purport to be famous need to be identified by their first name, and often by their track record.'

Georgiana nodded again, even though she was no longer interested.

'There is your measure of Kaminski's fame,' Lucius concluded. 'You never need to mention his first name.'

Georgiana put her race card up to her face and peered over the top of it to stare at Kaminski, who was now leaning over the front of his box. She saw that he had a beard, which she never liked on men, mostly because it made them look foreign, and Georgiana never really liked looking at anything foreign when she was in England. She went back to studying the horses, which was far more interesting than studying a film director, even if he was so famous that no one had to remember his first name.

chapter seven

During the days which elapsed between the Epsom Derby and the start of Royal Ascot, Jennifer Parker-Jones went to three dances, and at each dance became more and more hopelessly infatuated with Nigel Bruce-Smith. This was hardly surprising since she had never danced with anyone else, nor been escorted by the same escort to more than one social occasion. She was so grateful to Nigel she began quite seriously to consider making some sort of physical commitment to him, and she tried to tell him this on their taxi rides home together, when he would so sweetly allow her to drop him off at his Pimlico flat before she returned to Knightsbridge. But as frequently as they rode in taxis together, so did Nigel assert that he respected her far too much to allow her to give herself to him. Naturally this made Jennifer love him even more ardently, even though sometimes late at night alone in her bed she often wished he wasn't quite so honourable.

It became impossible for Jennifer to pass Harrods without her going in to buy Nigel some little present, because someone as wonderful as Nigel deserved everything she could afford to buy him, and besides, she had never before had someone for whom she could buy presents. She bought him gold cuff links. She bought him Designer ties. She bought him cigarettes and she bought him wine. But when she told Andrew Gillott the depths of her growing love for Nigel, he informed her rather unexpectedly that it was enough to make a chap puke.

And then he walked out of the room, leaving Jennifer to wonder who or what was enough to make him puke. Was it her devotion to Nigel? Or Nigel's devotion to her? It really was rather difficult to know.

That, however, was the least of her problems, her greatest being how to prevent a recurrence at Royal Ascot of her mother's dreadful behaviour at Epsom. She could see no way around it, for her mother had chosen to go to the meeting on all four days, and had bought four different outfits, and four of Mr Penny's hats to go with them, not to mention the shoes and the new handbags she was busy 'wearing in' between three and four o'clock each afternoon when there was nothing else to do. At first she contemplated setting fire to her mother's wardrobe, but the realisation that such a fire would not restrict itself just to her mother's clothes prevented her in the nick of time. Then she thought that she would cause her mother to have an accident. So she tied a piece of twine across her mother's bedroom door in the hope she would fall and break a leg, but instead her mother merely broke the twine and laddered a new pair of stockings, which was not the desired result.

Once or twice she pretended she had not seen her mother on the dark stairs that led to the flat, and she ran down them very fast hoping to knock her down. But each time her mother heard her and stepped aside. At her last attempt her mother stepped aside so quickly that Jennifer crash-landed on the hall floor with a noise which Andrew Gillott later described over backgammon at the Claremont as only comparable to a juggernaut hitting a brick wall. Not unsurprisingly, as a result, Jennifer bruised herself badly and broke a bone in her own foot. Happily, this unintended accident did at least solve the problem, for her mother went to Ascot while Jennifer, on doctor's orders, stayed at home in bed, hearing her mother return each evening much the worse for wear, escorted not only by Andrew but by dear Nigel too. She also learnt a fact of life of which she had hitherto been ignorant, namely that when someone is in bed there is never anything but laughter in the other rooms.

There were, however, compensations. She could lie in bed watching Ascot on television, and glory in the fact that she was not there with her toes curled in embarrassment within her new shoes, and her head lowered beneath her hat in the hopes of avoiding anyone she knew. She did not have to tolerate the sound of people laughing quite openly behind her mother's back, and she wouldn't have to stay in the cloakroom doing and redoing her hair until her head ached with the brushing. Instead she could just lie in her bed listening for Nigel's voice in the hall, and wait for his knock on her door. Each day, after the races, he brought her back a bunch of flowers which he cleverly chose to match the ones she saw on television in the Royal Enclosure. And then he would sit and tell her all about the events of the day.

She was still quite hopelessly in love with him. Just a glimpse of his dark shiny head round the corner of the door made her feel quite faint. She had always hoped that one day she would feel like this about somebody besides her dog, but she never in her wildest dreams thought she would actually feel more than she felt for her dog, and that her feelings might be reciprocated, because she was becoming increasingly sure that Nigel's feelings for her were the same as her feelings for him, and that she was one of the few girls whose Season really would end in marriage. She kept a number of bridal magazines in a locked suitcase under her bed, and when the flat was empty she would take them out and dream of herself and Nigel walking down the aisle together, her ankle mended and Nigel in his morning dress. The only bit of the dream she did not enjoy was when she turned round to hand her bouquet to a bridesmaid and saw her mother. Then she would stop dreaming and return to considering how she could possibly break her mother's ankle and not her own before her wedding day.

Naturally Nigel was coming to her dance, and the dinner beforehand. Jennifer's foot should be better by then, and even if it wasn't, her long Belinda Bellville ballgown would cover it, and she would be able to dance very slowly with Nigel, which was something to which she was looking forward enormously.

She wished her father liked Nigel more, but unfortunately he did not like him at all, associating him for some reason with Andrew Gillott, whom he liked even less, because he took her mother's attention away from him, or so he said. Lately Jennifer had overheard her parents quarrelling a great deal about money, and Jennifer considered this stupid for they all knew they had a great deal of money, and it seemed ridiculous to quarrel about something of which there was plenty. This, it appeared, was another reason why her father so disliked Andrew and Nigel, accusing them of encouraging her mother to 'wanton extravagance'. In this matter, Jennifer was completely on her mother's side; she thought that her father was being both mean and silly, and considered the way he went on about being bled dry by the 'bloodsuckers of Society' most unpalatable, particularly since they all knew who the bloodsuckers were meant to be.

Her mother bore all this with great fortitude and Jennifer was forced to admire her for this. She explained to Jennifer that when a person came from the sort of background her father came from they always thought everyone was after their money, which was of course quite ridiculous. It was just as if there weren't lots of other people in the world who had money.

But the quarrelling continued right up to the morning of Jennifer's dance, and in fact that particular day, which should have been so wonderful and to which Jennifer was looking forward quite inordinately, was in danger of being ruined by her father's persistent beastliness.

It started at breakfast time when Jennifer heard him asking her mother where her diamond bracelet was?

Then she heard her mother leaving the dining room with the announcement that she did not wish to remain there and have another filthy quarrel. Normally her father would not bother to get up and follow her, but this morning for some reason he did, following her round and round the flat, while repeatedly demanding of her the whereabouts of the diamond bracelet. Finally she heard her mother lock her bedroom door against him, and then she heard her father breathing heavily while he banged on his wife's door, and her mother shouting that if he did not stop she would call the police. It was very frightening, because her father was really very big.

Jennifer sat in her room listening to all this with a fast-beating heart. She somehow felt it was all her fault, for being the age she was, and for needing a social life. And when she heard her father roaring that her mother had gone mad and that if she didn't find the diamond bracelet by the time he got home it would be him who would be calling the police, it seemed to Jennifer that the best thing to do would be to run away with Nigel, if he would come with her. It was too horrible for words.

Her father departed for his office soon after this incident, and so she was able to creep out of her bedroom and knock on her mother's door.

She went in in answer to her mother's summons and

saw her sitting at her dressing table, with a tissue held to her nose. She had never as far as she knew felt sorry for her mother before, but seeing her now with her make-up all smudged and her nose all red, she did. She sent Jennifer into the drawing room for the whisky, and then informed her that she had to do something for her. She told her she had to take all the jewellery she had lent her for her dance that night and sell it and bring her back the money at once or they would all be ruined.

Jennifer stared at her mother. It wasn't just the smudged make-up that was unusual. It was the fact that her mother must have done something wrong that astounded her.

'What do you need the money for?' she found herself asking.

'Because I do,' her mother replied abruptly.

'But why?' Jennifer persisted.

'For the diamond bracelet of course, you silly girl!' said her mother, blowing her nose largely on a tissue.

So her father was right, Jennifer thought. Her mother had done something foolish, and now they were all facing ruin because of her action.

'Where do I take the jewellery?' she asked, having decided it was best to do and die and not to reason why under the present circumstances.

Her mother scribbled down the name of a jeweller's in Kensington.

'Say it's your jewellery, Jennifer. Say that you want to sell it, and then come straight back here with the money.'

Her mother handed her the piece of paper bearing the address.

'He'll only give you a third of the value,' she continued. 'They only ever give you a third of the value when you have to sell. Go on – off you go. And hurry! We must have the diamond bracelet back by the time your father gets home or he'll call the police.'

'And accuse you of stealing?' said Jennifer. 'Of course he wouldn't!'

'You don't know your father.'

'But he gave it to you. He gave you the jewellery.'

Jennifer had never felt so confused in her life. And all on the day of her dance, too. Her mother looked up at her and gave what was obviously meant to be a laugh but which sounded much more like a sob.

'You don't know your father,' she repeated. 'Everything, every item of jewellery. It all belongs to him. He bought it all as a hedge against inflation.'

Jennifer saw her father in a new light.

'Now then,' concluded her mother, 'I need a hammer.'

Jennifer, in a sort of daze, followed her mother into the kitchen where she fetched a hammer from a drawer, then into the sitting room and watched in stupified silence while her mother quite deliberately smashed the glass front of a small antique item.

'If anyone asks you where it's gone,' she said to her daughter, 'it is being repaned.'

'What are you going to do with it?' Jennifer asked her.

'Sell it, of course,' replied her mother. 'Together with the money you get for the jewellery I should have enough to get the bracelet back by lunchtime.'

Since they were by now well pressed for time, they left the flat with their respective valuables and waited impatiently for two separate taxis. Jennifer took this chance to ask her mother why the bracelet had to be pawned in the first place.

'Why do you think?' her mother replied quite shortly. 'Andrew needed some more money.'

'But what for?' asked Jennifer, now completely bewildered.

'Why do you think, Jennifer?' said her mother. 'For all sorts of things. You can't have an omelette without breaking a few eggs, you know.'

In the taxi on her way to the jeweller's, Jennifer puzzled over her mother's crypticism. She was perfectly aware that omelettes were the end result of broken eggs, but there was enough of her father's blood in her veins to make her wonder why Andrew needed more money from her mother when she knew he had already been quite handsomely paid by her father right at the beginning of the Season. She knew this for a fact, because her father had grumbled about it quite persistently and out loud to the point that both the women wanted to scream at him to stop. But now, faced with the uncomfortable truth that she was going to have to sell the jewellery to help her mother out of a tight spot, Jennifer realised uncomfortably that her father could be right, and that her mother quite possibly was a rather silly woman who was in the clutches of two people who were perhaps not quite so nice as one other person wished and hoped them to be. This dawning realisation was quite appalling and made Jennifer suddenly wish she was a little girl again, standing on a chair trying to catch sight of her new bonnet in the hall mirror.

The jeweller gave her the exact amount of money that her mother had said he would, and did it in such a way that when he wrote down her name, she had the distinct feeling that it was a name he had written down before, and not so very long ago. Thus she realised with an agonising certainty that her mother must have been calling here to sell jewellery on various other occasions. When she finally escaped from the shop, she stood for a moment just clutching her handbag, which was full of more money than it had ever held before, and thought that she would try not to think about anything at all until after her dance was over, because already the day was in very grave danger of being quite spoilt.

As soon as she got back inside the flat, her mother snatched the money away from her and rushed out to get another taxi, leaving Jennifer instructions to sweep up the broken glass from the drawing room carpet. She was brushing the very last pieces up from the shag pile when her father returned home early from the office.

She tried to make conversation with him, but failed. He merely grunted, and glanced every now and then at the door, and then back at the reproduction ormulu repeating clock on the drawing room mantelpiece.

'She'd better get back with that bracelet,' he kept saying. 'She'd better get back with that bracelet.'

Jennifer sat in silence and tried to ignore a cold fact which was now staring her in the face, namely that the day was slipping away from her. She had just started to pray for her mother's safe return with the bracelet when she heard the front door of the flat open. Her father's expression did not change, as if he no longer cared whether she returned or not. After a moment her mother came in, with a carefully rehearsed and dignified entrance. She stood looking at her husband as he stood looking back at her, then she hurled the diamond bracelet across the room, hitting him full in the face.

'Satisfied?' she demanded.

Her father said nothing, but just stood there. Jennifer was astonished. She had never thought people who were married did things like that to each other, but then she had spent a great deal of time at boarding school.

Her mother turned to go, but before she did, she looked back at her father.

'Just one thing, Aidan,' she said. 'Don't expect me to wear the bloody thing tonight.'

Jennifer thought she was dreaming, for this was incredible. Her mother had sworn. Her mother, Mrs Parker-Jones, a woman who hitherto had been known only for the politeness of her language, who never read a newspaper in bed, or referred to going to the ladies, or powdered her nose without first putting on a mackintosh cape, or took a bath without wearing a Victorian lace bath cap, or put lump sugar in her tea without using tongs, or ate cake without a cake fork, or put lipstick on in public, or took any other action without first considering what was the polite thing to do, had sworn publicly, in front of her daughter and at her husband, and not only that, had thrown a diamond bracelet at him. The whole thing just had to be a frightful dream.

Particularly now that her father had turned such a funny colour. Jennifer stared at him. It wasn't just where the bracelet had hit him, he was turning puce all over his

116

face. Then quite suddenly he staggered, and clutching his collar crashed face down on the shag pile, hitting his head on the imitation Collector's Club fender as he fell.

The noise brought Mrs Parker-Jones back into the room. She stood for a moment and stared at her prostrate husband with a certain amount of satisfaction. Then she went over to Jennifer who was now kneeling beside him.

Jennifer looked up at her mother.

'You've killed him,' she said.

Mrs Parker-Jones stared back at her daughter, and she knew she was right. She didn't have to do all the things Jennifer was now doing, like feeling Aidan's pulse, or loosening his shirt collar. She knew Aidan was dead.

It was typical of him. To die on the very afternoon of the dance. She despised him for it, and could well have kicked his ankle, had not Jennifer been kneeling in front of it. Why, oh why had she been allowed to get this far, have done all this organisation, made all these sacrifices, just for Aidan to go and get a heart attack, or whatever it was that had killed him, right on the day of her greatest social triumph? Of course he had always been a killjoy, he had always been a spoilsport, so in a way this was just typical of him. He had never been a person to think what fun something would be to do, only to think of how much it would cost. He had had the habit, ever since she first met him, of saying whenever she opened a present, be it a bottle of perfume, or a new dress, or whatever, that he hoped she would make it last. It was always the same, whatever the present, and whenever she got it. He hoped she'd make it last. Well, she could quite honestly say that she had, whether it was her crêpe-de-chine pre-war underwear, or her silk stockings during the war, or her bottles of Chanel No. 5 after the war, she had made them all last in the sure and certain knowledge that if she did not there would be no more forthcoming from Aidan. And now there he was, lying on the shag pile like a beached whale with Jennifer sobbing over him, still determined to spoil her fun. She had made it last all right, but he hadn't made himself last.

She was quite sure he had done it on purpose. He had died just like that to spite her, to stop her going to Jennifer's dance, to stop Jennifer going to Jennifer's dance, to stop Andrew going to Jennifer's dance, and to stop Nigel from going. She knew with absolute certainty now that Aidan had done it on purpose.

Clarissa did not ring the doctor straight away. Instead she rang Andrew Gillott and asked him to come round at once, without saying why he was to do so. Andrew, who dearly would have liked to have told her to go to the devil, didn't and couldn't, because the night before Mrs Parker-Jones had loaned him five hundred pounds to pay off a little bad luck he had encountered at the backgammon table. After that she rang the doctor who was of course out. Doctors always seemed to be out, even when they were private, which Mrs Parker-Jones considered cheek because surely the whole point of them being private is that they should be there when one wanted them. She left a message with a central answering service in charge of a girl who sounded as if she didn't feel like taking messages for subscribers just because she was paid to do so, and then finally turned to Jennifer and told her to go up to her room and lie down.

'We must cancel the dance,' Andrew Gillott said as soon as he saw Mr Parker-Jones lying dead on the carpet.

Mrs Parker-Jones looked at Andrew with some distaste. He had just said exactly what she did not wish to hear. It was simply too terrible even to contemplate. If she was to cancel the dance now, she dreaded to think what would happen to her social life. It would be nipped in the bud just as it was about to produce its rarest bloom, a private dance held for the daughter of Mrs Aidan Parker-Jones. It had even appeared in Forthcoming Events.

Andrew, however, felt a sense of enormous relief looking at the shag-pile carpet upon which lay the remains of the very lately deceased Aidan Parker-Jones. He considered it really most sporting of him to choose to depart this life just at the very moment when Andrew was about to have to face the most dreaded of all the Season's

118

events, the Parker-Jones hop. As a matter of fact, now he came to think of it, the poor old chap wasn't that bad. He had never done anybody any harm, not that he knew of anyway. He'd been a bit of a bore, true enough, but then who wouldn't be, married to the dreadful Clarissa? Andrew looked down at the prone figure, and realised that the poor old chap had been a gentleman as Andrew knew he himself could never be. He had neither a lender nor a borrower been. He might not have been over-generous, but Andrew betted he always took his staff out to Christmas lunch, and gave them a yearly bonus when things were good. He'd been one of the old breed of city men, the kind who knew that the best sort of business was built on an honourable reputation, proper distribution of assets, and regularity of habits. He would have prided himself on the fidelity of his secretary, and the fact that he had fought in the war voluntarily, and he would have returned home every evening with the dim hope that his wife might be nice to him and tell him he was dining in for once. He wouldn't have thought himself better than his neighbour, and he wouldn't have thought himself worse. He would have remembered his father with affectionate respect, and would have polished his shoes every morning as his mother had taught him from an early age. He would not have wanted to improve his social standing, but he would have been happy to improve his bank balance. And if he never crossed a road to help another chap in trouble, at least he made sure he kept out of trouble himself so that no one had to cross the road on his account. All in all, he was the embodiment of that familiar expression, 'not a bad sort of chap'.

'Yes,' agreed Mrs Parker-Jones reluctantly. 'Yes, I suppose we must cancel the dance.'

And then she looked down at her dead husband and said nothing.

She knew while she said nothing, there was still a chance. Andrew most certainly would not volunteer to deal with the cancellation, so as long as she kept her mouth tightly shut there was still a chance. She sat down on the sofa and reached inside her handbag for a handkerchief. It really was high time she did some crying.

'Want a scotch?' asked Andrew.

Gillott had been brought up to believe that at times like this, scotch whisky was the great panacea.

'I'd prefer a gin,' Mrs Parker-Jones replied.

'Have a scotch,' Andrew persisted, while pouring himself a very large one. 'Gin's dreadful stuff for ladies. Brings on crying jags, and gives 'em fat arms.'

He poured another large scotch and handing it to her, sat down beside her on the sofa. Clarissa, who secretly was thrilled that Andrew should care whether or not she had fat arms, accepted it, pretending to drink it reluctantly as if she wasn't quite sure of its effect. And then she turned to Andrew and enquired how she was going to be able to cancel three hundred people at such short notice.

'Could put a message out on the wireless, I suppose,' said Andrew after a long silence.

Mrs Parker-Jones sighed happily to herself, for she knew such a proposition to be an idle one.

'I have to be quite honest with you, Andrew,' she said, placing a hand carefully on Andrew's arm. 'I'm not quite sure we're doing the right thing.'

'What do you mean, old girl?' Andrew enquired, more than a little puzzled. 'Can't hold the dance now, you know.'

'I'm really not at all sure, Andrew,' Mrs Parker-Jones continued. 'You see, I'm not altogether sure it's what Aidan would have wanted.'

'Oh, I think he would, old girl,' Andrew replied rather too quickly.

'No, I know he wouldn't, Andrew,' Clarissa persisted. It was after all, her ace in the hole. 'You see, it was Aidan's last wish that he should escort me into the ballroom wearing that diamond bracelet he gave me. He was just saying that when his heart attack arrived.'

She turned and smiled what she hoped was bravely at Andrew, while he wondered whether 'arrived' was quite the right word to describe the onset of a heart attack. It made it sound as if heart attacks were rather like hired cars, or trains coming into Paddington. He looked down at the inert Mr Parker-Jones. He was actually clutching the diamond bracelet that Andrew had made Clarissa pawn a couple of months ago. Andrew felt a sharp pang of guilt. The poor chap had died holding something for which he had probably slaved half his life in order to afford for his wife.

'Is that really what he was saying?' Andrew asked.

Mrs Parker-Jones sniffed tragically in reply and looked down at her handkerchief.

'How extraordinary,' said Andrew. 'I didn't think he was the social type. Always gave me the impression that he'd rather I was out of the way.'

'No, no, no,' said Mrs Parker-Jones. 'He was just very shy.'

'Even so, even so,' said Andrew, pondering, 'we can't really give the dance without him. I mean without him being – with him not being here.'

'He would have wanted it, Andrew,' said Mrs Parker-Jones in a firm voice. 'I know he would.'

'But, dammit, you're a widow,' Andrew said.

'I know,' replied Mrs Parker-Jones.

'Widows don't go to dances,' said Andrew.

It was Andrew's turn to play a trump now, because even though, as he knew, an awful lot had changed concerning the way people carried on nowadays, he was absolutely certain that widows did not go to dances on the day their husbands kicked the bucket.

There was a brief lull while Mrs Parker-Jones thought out her next ploy, and while Andrew drained his second whisky.

'But if Aidan had died tonight instead of this afternoon, Andrew,' Mrs Parker-Jones reasoned, 'we would have been at the dance and would have been none the wiser till we got home. Just because he dies now, don't you see it means poor Jennifer won't have the one thing which she's been looking forward to more than anything? And which her poor father wanted her to have more than anything?'

'Thought you said he was going to escort you to the dance, old girl?' Andrew asked suspiciously.

'Yes, yes he was,' Mrs Parker-Jones replied somewhat hesitantly. 'But then he was going to come home.'

Andrew looked at her for once with a little sympathy. Obviously the stupid woman was suffering from shock, which was why she wasn't making any sense.

'Listen, old girl,' he said as kindly as he could, 'you can't have a dance when someone's just shuffled off.'

Mrs Parker-Jones conceded defeat, and stared into her drink. She knew Andrew was right. He was always right about things like this, so of course she would abide by what he said. She admired him more than ever now, for the sacrifice he himself was making, because of course the dance meant a lot to him as well. After all, had he not been instrumental in organising the whole thing? She sighed and drank the rest of her whisky rather too quickly for such a recently-widowed woman.

Andrew, the victory his, went to the telephone and rang for an ambulance. Then he rang the Countess, since it was her ballroom they had hired, and listened to her trying to keep the relief out of her voice.

'How ghastly, Andrew,' she said, meaning quite the opposite. 'What a pity.'

It wasn't that the Countess didn't feel a little sorry for poor old Nosey-Parker or whatever it was he was called. It was just such a relief not to have all those people in her ballroom. She also realised that it was far too late for the florists to take all the flowers back, and that they would look quite splendid arranged all round her house.

'I will ring all the dinner-party hostesses, Andrew,' she graciously volunteered, 'and they can continue with their dinner parties if they wish, and perhaps everyone can arrange to go on somewhere later if they so please. After all, it's the least I can do.'

The Countess knew that a great many people would in fact be greatly relieved at the cancellation. After all, the

Parker-Jones hop would be the third dance held in her ballroom that season, and one had to be realistic. There were just so many times people could stand seeing the trompe l'oeil, even if it was a Rex Whistler.

'Tell Mrs Parker-Jones I will send the drink back, and I will cancel the band,' she added. 'Tell her she can leave it all to me, and please send her my condolences.'

The Countess rang off, and started to hum to herself, a little snatch of 'Parisian Pierrot'. She was giving a drinks party in two days time she suddenly remembered, so the flowers would come in most useful.

Andrew Gillott looked at Mrs Parker-Jones and patted her hand.

'Everything's being taken care of, old thing,' he said. 'So there's no need to worry. Andrew's taken care of everything for you.'

Mrs Parker-Jones was now weeping quite genuinely, and Andrew was quite surprised by the apparent depth of her feelings. But Mrs Parker-Jones was not in fact weeping for her recently-deceased husband, but rather for her new pink evening gown which she would no longer be able to wear that night. Then she realised there would be other nights she could wear it, and her tears dried up. After all, mourning was not a long time nowadays, unless you were a member of the Royal family. She looked at Andrew, sitting beside her, holding her hand, and attempted to smile what she hoped would look like a brave smile.

'You're so kind, Andrew dear,' she said. 'I'm so sorry about all this.'

She gestured in a hopeless way towards her dead husband who lay sprawled before them, as if he was something somebody had dropped or spilt on the carpet.

'Don't worry, old girl,' said Andrew, getting up and helping himself to another large scotch. 'The ambulance will be here in a moment.'

Later, after the remains of Aidan had been somewhat indiscreetly removed, and after the formalities had been completed, and after Andrew had wobbled somewhat uncertainly off in the direction of the Claremont, Clarissa Parker-Jones, as she prepared herself for bed, remembered something that was really rather nice. Andrew Gillott was a Baron's son. He was an Honourable, and if she was right, he came somewhere like seventy-fifth or sixth in the order of precedence in England and Wales. Lying in her carefully turned-down bed, she opened her bedside copy of Debrett to make absolutely sure. Yes, there he was, seventy-fifth in order of precedence in England and Wales, after:

'The Duke of Edinburgh, The Heir Apparent, The Sovereign's Younger Sons, The Sovereign's Grandsons, The Sovereign's Nephews, The Archbishop of Canterbury, The Lord High Chancellor, The Archbishop of York, The Prime Minister, The Lord High Treasurer (when existing), The Lord President of The Council, The Speaker of the House of Commons, The Lord Privy Seal, Ambassadors and High Commissioners, The Lord Great Chamberlain, The Lord High Constable, The Earl Marshall, The Lord Steward of the Household, The Lord Chamberlain of the Household, The Master of the Horse, The Dukes of England, The Dukes of the United Kingdom and Ireland since the Union, The Eldest Sons of Dukes of the Blood Royal, The Marquesses of England, The Marquesses of Scotland, The Marquesses of Great Britain, The Marquesses of Ireland, The Marquesses of the United Kingdom and Ireland since the Union, The Eldest Sons of Dukes, The Earls of England, The Earls of Scotland, The Earls of Great Britain, The Earls of Ireland, The Earls of the United Kingdom and Ireland since the Union, The Younger Sons of Dukes of the Blood Royal, Marquesses' Eldest Sons, Dukes' Younger Sons, Viscounts of England, Viscounts of Scotland, Viscounts of Great Britain, Viscounts of Ireland, Viscounts of the United Kingdom and Ireland since the Union, Earls' Eldest Sons, Marquesses' Younger Sons, The Bishop of London, The Bishop of Durham, The Bishop of Winchester, Other English Diocesan Bishops according to seniority of Consecration, Secretaries of State (if of Baronial rank), Barons of England, Lords of Parliament (Scotland), Barons of Great Britain, Barons of Ireland, Barons of the United Kingdom and Ireland since the Union including Life Barons and Lords of Appeal in Ordinary, Lords Commissioners of the Great Seal (when existing), Treasurer of The Household, Comptroller of the Household, Vice Chamberlain of the Household, Secretaries of State under Baronial rank, Viscounts' Eldest Sons, Earls' Younger Sons, Barons' Eldest Sons, Knights of The Garter, Privy Counsellors, Chancellor of the Exchequer, Chancellor of the Duchy of Lancaster, Lord Chief Justice of England, Master of The Rolls, President of the Family Division, Lord Justices of Appeal (according to the seniority of appointment), Judges of the High Court of Justice (according to seniority of appointment), Viscounts' Younger Sons ' – and then, at last – 'Barons' Younger Sons'.

Clarissa put the book back on her bedside table with some satisfaction. Dear Andrew – the younger son of a Baron. Her dance might have had to have been cancelled, but there was a very good chance that her life might have just begun.

chapter eight

Over the last few years it had been Kaminski's habit to rise early and be at breakfast by a quarter past seven. He remembered his father telling him once that as a man grew older so he rose earlier and earlier, until at last there was really no reason to go to bed at all, because that was Nature's way of adjusting the clock until the clock needed no more adjusting. That had been his father's idea of a humorous statement.

Karminski breakfasted in a silk dressing gown worn over his shirt and trousers, and with the shirt and trousers he wore handmade Lobb shoes, and plain coloured silk socks of which he had dozens of pairs, for he bought always six pairs in Jermyn Street whenever he came to London.

His clothes bore witness to his cosmopolitan life, for his trousers were Italian, his underwear American, and his silk dressing gown French, from Paris. Like most men of White Russian ancestry he divided his love of cities between Paris and London, but he always felt most at home in London. It was less self-conscious than Paris, and although the food was not as good, the theatre was better.

However, that had not been the reason he had chosen to come to London at this particular moment in his life. Normally at this time of year he would be in Sardinia, normally but not always, for here again he was aware that places such as Sardinia were losing their appeal for him, almost daily. He had come to England because he was starting work on a new film, and the film he was about to work on he had decided to set in England. It was a remake of an early Michel Bolst film, about a man obsessed with a young girl, who in turn is obsessed by the idea that she would like to die at the ultimate moment of love, a moment for which she searches continually, and which she realises the man she loves, the only man she has loved, cannot supply. In his original, Bolst had set the story in a castle built by the mad King Ludwig of Bavaria, but Kaminiski, anxious to update the story and give it a different allegorical feel, decided to change the setting to England in her post-Imperial phase, which he thought would provide the perfect setting. The writer he was working with, E. F. Tyrell, thought so too, but then E. F. was always anxious to work away from home because he had a wife who bored him to tears.

E. F. was a typical script writer, instantly recognisable to anyone in the industry, Kaminiski thought as he watched him alight late as always from his taxi at twenty past ten. He dressed as if he was successful, he talked as if he was successful, and he knew he was a flop. All script writers finally were flops in their own eyes, because what they actually wrote they never saw on the screen as they

126

had written it, and finally they were less important to the film industry than the caterers. However, Kaminski liked to work with E. F. because even though he was talkative and his habits drove Kaminski mad, he was a physical presence in the room, and Kaminski needed that. E. F. in his turn liked to work for Kaminski because at least Kaminski's films got made, and this was always popular with script writers since they did not get paid what they called 'real money' till the first day of shooting. E. F. had a number of excellent credits, but then so had fifty other script writers. Where E. F. finally scored over the other forty-nine writers was that he was good at chess, which was a major obsession with them both.

When they worked together, they would start the morning with coffee which Kaminski would have served in a pot which kept it warm all morning. Kaminski always poured the coffee out himself because he hated anyone else doing it, and the coffee had to be Blue Mountain medium ground from Harrods. He drank his black, and E. F. took his with a great deal of cream and five teaspoons of sugar, which fascinated the fastidious Kaminski. Then, while they drank their coffee – Kaminski slowly, carefully and silently, and E. F. naturally the complete opposite – E. F. would tell him of his experiences of the night before, whom he'd laid, how much he'd lost or won at poker, and which of the well-known London hostesses had venereal disease.

Kaminski was fascinated by these conversations although he never showed it. Sensuality was an important part of his life, and as someone who was currently a bachelor, having had the sense to divorce his wife at an early age and not make the mistake of remarrying, he was not disinterested in amorous exploits, and what was really amazing about E. F. was that he bore out the dictum that when it came to sex, if you didn't mind the quality you could get it in bulk. E. F. was certainly not choosy, with the consequence that he could be flattered into doing it with almost anybody.

Kaminski knew that the recital of the previous night's

activities was an essential part of E. F. winding himself up to work, but sometimes, as indeed he did this morning, Kaminski found it tedious. Being a writer himself he appreciated routine, but sometimes he just could not take E. F.'s routines – for routines, as they both knew it, they most surely were. They were not fantasies, because last year E. F. had evidently managed to get the clap while they were in Rome; but in a way they might as well have been fantasies, because E. F. needed to relate them, or else they did not exist.

The most fascinating part of E. F.'s love life was the fact that he had no difficulty whatsoever in obtaining women. If Kaminski were casting E. F. in a picture, he would be looking for a fat actor, with a protruding belly, receding hair and an underslung jaw, which is hardly a recipe for male beauty. Yet E. F. had no trouble when it came to pulling the opposite sex. Other problems he had, but never that one. Kaminski had often puzzled over this phenomenon. When they were in France, he attributed E. F.'s powers of attraction to the fact that he was American, when they were in Italy to the fact that he was successful, but here in London he admitted defeat, because in London American script writers did not necessarily go down big. Yet here he was, here was E. F. having yet again what he described as a 'helluva good time' with whomever he wished, and not even having to pay for it. He wasn't handsome, he wasn't – outside the film industry – famous. So what gave him this appeal? Finally Kaminski found the answer: E. F. liked women.

In fact he positively adored them. A woman only had to come into his line of sight and E. F. would be putting her into close-up, examining her good points and discovering her bad ones. Frequently, particularly if she had too many, he would dismiss the good points and admire only the bad, and this flattering tactic would have them eating out of his hand in a few minutes. He could instantly spot bad hips, thick ankles or small busts, and having once spotted them he would spend the major part of the evening adoring and praising that particular part of the girl's anatomy.

Kaminski poured his coffee and looked at E. F. as he settled himself in for the morning session. He thought if E. F. had not been a writer he would have been a salesman, and the tales he would tell in the bars every evening would be little different to the tales he told Kaminski in the mornings. In a way he was a travelling salesman, with words instead of goods in his briefcase, ringing bells on doors that belonged not to housewives but to producers. He had once or twice drawn this parallel to the attention of E. F., who in secret had already thought it out for himself, for E. F. was well used to the sensation of doors being slammed on his foot. Which was why he had put his writing to another use. For if his perfectly polished phrases, neatly executed lines and lyrical passages were trodden regularly to death by the bloated bastards he had to work for, he could at least charm another audience with them, he could make someone love him and he did, which made him feel wanted, made him feel happy, neither of which he felt when he awoke every day and faced his work. E. F. reminded Kaminski of a small advertisement he had once seen in a newspaper, extolling the virtues of a pocket size loud-hailer, with the legend: 'Make them listen. Croon anywhere'. If another verb was substituted for the verb 'to croon', that would happily sum up E. F.'s sexual philosophy.

And so once more the two men faced each other over the coffee table, as they had for years faced each other over coffee tables all round the world. Several of the pictures upon which they had colloborated had been highly successful, yet neither of them had any feelings of real affection for the other at all. Perhaps because they were so used to pinning characters up on the wall and dissecting them, or stripping people's motivations so bare that they no longer saw the human dilemma as anything other than a means to an end – that of making motion pictures – perhaps because of this they looked upon each other as they looked upon any of their fictional creations, with academic interest but no real involvement. E. F. liked this in Kaminski and Kaminski liked this in E. F. They had a highly satisfactory *modus operandi*, and because they cared little for each other they could fraternise quite happily without the danger of emotional commitment.

'I found a house which could be sensational,' said E. F., starting the ball rolling.

He threw some photographs down on to the coffee table.

'It's not so much Gothic, it's Visi-Gothic, it's so Gothic.'

Kaminski picked the pictures up and leafed through them. E. F. was right about it being Gothic. It was so Gothic it was a pastiche. There was so much ornamentation it looked as if all it needed was a couple of guys with a smoke machine, the sound of dripping water and Vincent Price to come out of the front door. It was exactly the sort of house he didn't want, and E. F. knew it, and he knew that E. F. knew it, and E. F. knew that he knew he knew it, because this was E. F.'s way of finding out exactly what Kaminski did in fact want.

'Don't you want to know who the house belongs to, Kaminski?' E. F. enquired.

'No,' replied Kaminski. 'Because the house is terrible.'

E. F. picked up a photograph of the Gothic monstrosity and tapped it against his hand.

'It belongs to this fantastic broad I laid last week.'

'You surprise me,' said Kaminski, totally unsurprised.

'You'll never guess what her bag was,' E. F. began.

'The house is useless,' Kaminski interrupted him.

'Okay,' muttered E. F., 'so the house is usless. How the hell am I meant to know what you want till you tell me what you want?'

'I want an old house,' Kaminski informed him. 'One of great grandeur. With simple elevations. I want a house which from the moment we first see it we will realise was built at the height of British Power and Influence. Palladian possibly. Eighteenth-century certainly.'

'Is that right?' E. F. said without real interest, heaping five more spoons of sugar into his new cup of coffee.

'There is someone calling here later this morning with some stills of possible locations.'

E. F. nodded. He liked going on recces, because going to look at locations got him out of Kaminski's apartment, beautiful though it undoubtedly was, and Kaminski's apartment, wherever it was, New York, Paris, Rome or London, Kaminski's apartment meant work. It meant more grinding out of words, more searching for ideas, more self prostitution. E. F. had long ago given up the idea that he would ever be anything but a literary whore, a purveyor not of clap, but of clap-trap. Still, if he was a whore, Kaminski was no better than an artistic pimp, because he lived immorally off the earnings of others. Kaminski was no one without the actors, E. F. told himself nightly, no one without the cameraman, the editor – well, perhaps not the editor because Kaminski did all his own editing – but certainly the designer, and *certainly* the writer! Kaminski depended for his art upon these people, so how could the man possibly be a genius? How could he be the singular visionary all the cinema magazines described him to be? Here was no Chopin of the cinema, here was no Picasso. Here was not even an interpretive soloist. Here simply was a director, and who were directors? Directors were people who invented themselves, they were their own greatest creations, in some cases the *only* creation they had ever made. Yet for Chrissake everyone salaamed before them, as they moved from one international apartment to another in their silk dressing gowns and handmade shoes. One day – the famous one day – one day he'd tell Kaminski this. But not today. Today he would have to sit yet again and listen to his asshole ideas, because Gloria, his bitch of a wife, wanted him to earn enough money for her to move from Connecticut back into Manhattan and lunch at Le Cirque every day. And that meant money, and money meant another day. Another day he really would tell Kaminski. But not today.

'Right,' said Kaminski. 'So we begin. Again.'

And he put his hands into their customary work position, with the tips of his long fingers just touching the end of his nose. It made him look as if he was praying, but it didn't impress E. F. Before he'd even started to work with Kaminski E. F. had seen dozens of pictures of Kaminski in this famous pose. To admirers everywhere it was the portrait of a genius. To E. F., a study of a despot.

'We'll begin,' Kaminski announced, 'by talking about men and women.'

This was Kaminski's way. Whatever the subject, they would talk. Kaminski would talk, and E. F. would listen, then E. F. would talk and Kaminski wouldn't listen. Then E. F. would suggest the rough outline of a scene, which Kaminski would reject, then later, usually about mid-afternoon, Kaminski would suggest the self-same scene and order E. F. to go away and first-draft it. Then E. F. would return having done so and they would talk some more, and the process would be repeated, identically, until finally they had a whole script up in first draft. It was a great way of working, but only if you were Kaminski.

'Young girls or virgins?' E. F. enquired.

'What?'

'Are we talking young girls or are we talking virgins?'

'Young girls,' Kaminski replied somewhat impatiently. 'This girl is no virgin. She's a decadent, and she's looking to "die" at the height of lovemaking.'

E. F. resharpened the end of an already sharp pencil and thought to himself life had been a lot easier all round before women discovered the need for sexual satisfaction. Ever since Gloria had read about such things in her women's magazines she thought the earth should move every time he made love to her. It was garbage, dangerous garbage. Women should concentrate on pleasing men, and then they'd please themselves all right.

'This is not "Lolita", E. F.,' continued Kaminski. 'This is two people with opposing obsessions.'

'Yeah,' said E. F. 'Just like me and this dame last night. She wanted me to make love to her in a drawer. I told her I was quite happy with a bed.'

E. F. paused as he suddenly remembered a girl he'd known once who'd had an obsession with being tickled. Most chicks you fore-, or five-, or maybe even six-played them into making love, but this one you just tickled. She was great. He would have told Kaminski about her, had not the genius just resumed his praying position.

'How much of the English aristocracy have you met, E. F.?'

Kaminski looked at him over his united hands.

'The aristocracy, Kaminski? None. They don't invite writers, because I hear none of them can read.'

'I think this girl should be a British aristocrat.'

'It's very fashionable at the moment,' E. F. conceded.

'She should be aristocratic and decadent. She should have been brought up to have everything, and she should have everything. And so suicide, of the most élite kind of course, suicide is her only escape from a life which anyway is no more than a living death.'

E. F. sighed to himself. Last week it had been a German girl, very Metternich, and very blonde, next week no doubt she'd be a hairy Spanish au pair, and Christ knows what the week after.

'Why do you want to know if I knew the aristocracy, Kaminski?'

Kaminski didn't answer. In some ways he knew he shouldn't be working on this film, as he suspected that his only reason for doing it was because he needed to work. And he needed to work because he was bored, bored because he had reached certain goals, and achieved certain achievements, and now he was searching, like the characters in the film they were creating, he was searching for something to happen to him which hadn't already happened. He had made things happen so often – he had fame, success and money. So now all he could do was to look for something he didn't even know he needed; to look for some experience he didn't even know he hadn't had. He wasn't searching for the secret of life, he was simply looking to find out whether there was any secret at all.

He went out to the bathroom to wash his hands. E. F. knew this was the signal for Kaminski to pick up a pencil and take up a fresh sheet of heavy cream paper. And this meant E. F. would have to pick up a pencil and paper too, and concentrate on the subject in hand, until that much anticipated moment later, much later, when Kaminski would put down his pencil and paper and offer E. F. a much needed dry martini.

But this morning, before they had time to start the work proper, the front doorbell rang, and moments later Kaminski's maid appeared.

'There is someone in the hall,' she announced in broken but not completely fractured English.

'What sort of person, Juanita?' Kaminski enquired.

'A girl,' she replied.

'My very favourite sort of person,' said E. F.

'Show her in then please, Juanita,' ordered Kaminski.

The maid went out and Kaminski looked at E. F.

'Maybe you've been followed, E. F. Who exactly were you with last night?'

'No girl, Kaminski, and that's for certain,' E. F. replied. 'Unless your Juanita's short-sighted.'

Juanita returned with the visitor, who was indeed a girl, a girl carrying a large brown envelope, exactly the same as E. F. used to send off his scripts in.

'Good morning,' she said. 'Mr Kaminski?'

Kaminski remain seated. The visitor smiled. E. F. stood up, because he always stood up for women, although it was admittedly not the position he most enjoyed taking with them. He stood up for them not out of respect, but because he saw each and every one as a potentially new and quite wonderful experience. And because E. F. had stood up, Kaminski also now rose.

'Yes, I am Kaminski,' he said.

'I'm Georgiana Longborough,' said the visitor. 'Lady Mary Lawton? Does that ring a bell? She sent me.'

'I had dinner with Lady Mary Lawton last night,' said Kaminski.

'Yes,' said Georgiana. 'And she promised you some photographs of houses which might be suitable?'

Georgiana gave Kaminski the envelope. She had spent considerable time trying to decide whether to put the photograph of Longborough at the top of Mary's pile of pictures, or at the bottom. The rest of the houses in the collection were those which Mary had had a hand in decorating, or redecorating, or just rearranging at which she was quite expert, and so naturally Longborough was not among them, because it was falling into the ha-ha. But Georgiana had no intention of letting such an opportunity slip without including a picture of Longborough. The question that had obsessed her on her taxi ride to Kaminski's was whether the house would get a better chance seen first or last, and last had won. Luckily Mary had put the photographs in an unsealed envelope, otherwise she would have had to stop and buy another, which would have delayed her. But anyway, there it was now, on the bottom of the pile which Kaminski now had in his hand, and for one awful moment Georgiana thought she might have chosen wrongly because Kaminski had stopped to examine the first one.

'It's beautiful,' he said, passing the photograph to E. F. 'You're very clever.'

'It's not me,' said Georgiana. 'It's my cousin.'

E. F. looked at the house in the photograph. It was beautiful. Perfect. Exactly the sort of place they were looking for. He smiled at the girl.

'My cousin does interior decoration. Mostly for friends. Privately. You know.'

E. F. was pretty used to the English accent, but there was something so cut-glass about this girl's manner that he broke up inside. He looked at Kaminski who was studying the rest of the photographs. He didn't appear to have even noticed the girl, but was going through the pictures slowly and thoughtfully, until he came to the last which he passed over quickly. E. F. wanted him to notice the girl, but Kaminski was too busy noticing houses.

'It's beautiful weather, isn't it?' E. F. asked her, just so he could go on hearing her talk.

'Yes,' she replied. 'Very. Not at all English.'

Kaminski looked up at her.

'Could your cousin find out more about this house for us?' he asked Georgiana, indicating the house at the top of the pile.

'Yes,' said Georgiana smiling. 'I'm sure she could.'

Kaminski now stared at her. He had never had much time for the Mona Lisa, although he acknowledged that the painting was a great work of art. But that smile no man could live with, it made him feel she was holding something back, that she had a secret which, he was quite sure, should she ever choose to tell you, would turn out to be something quite banal. But *this* girl's smile, this girl standing now in front of him, her smile was the smile of Cleopatra to Caesar. It was a smile which both put you in your place, and encouraged at one and the same time. It was a mixture of such mischief and superiority Kaminski wished he could freeze-frame it.

E. F. looked at Kaminski. Brilliant, he thought. He's noticed the girl at last! What was more he was staring at her, and his hand had gone to his beard, which only really happened when he was on the set and watching a scene which he knew was working.

'So,' said Georgiana.

At that, E. F. found himself catching his breath. He tried to imagine how he could describe the sound that her 'so' had made. It was treble C-sharp on a Steinway Grand, it was cut glass breaking, it was diamonds against a mirror. It hovered above Kaminski's head, while she stood looking at him questioningly. It held in the air over where he stood on his Oriental rug, a brightly coloured hummingbird. Then it dived away and was gone, leaving the listener to wonder whether he had really heard it in the first place.

'I'm sorry,' Kaminski said. 'I don't think I caught your name?'

'Georgiana Longborough,' said Georgiana.

'Would you care for a drink, Miss Longborough?'

Georgiana hesitated. Being called 'Miss' always gave her a tiny thrill, as if she was suddenly in disguise, and being with Americans always fascinated her, because they were more than foreign, they were almost dangerously so. She wanted to stay, because she felt it naughty to stay, but she didn't drink and she was quite sure neither Mr Kaminski nor his friend would have any bitter lemon.

'Is something the matter, Miss Longborough?' Kaminski asked her.

'No,' she replied. 'That is, yes.'

She smiled again, and Kaminski found himself staring at her with even greater intensity. There it was again, that smile, that mischief, that condescension.

'What exactly's the matter?'

'I'm sorry.'

'What exactly are you sorry for?'

'I'd love to stay for a drink, but you see, I don't drink.'

'Then have a soft drink. We have soft drinks, don't we, E. F.?'

'Of course we have soft drinks, Kaminski.'

'Goodness. Have you really? That would be wonderful.'

E. F. went to the drinks trolley, trying to keep his face straight. He failed quite utterly to see what was so wonderful about a soft drink, but he hastened to fetch the girl one because he could not bear that she should go. She was something else. She was Mickey Mouse. She was cellophane. He hurried back to her with her lemonade just to hear her say 'thank you'.

Georgiana thanked E. F. and smiled at him. While she did, E. F. imagined he could feel Kaminski's eyes boring into his back, as if he had stepped in front of his camera and ruined a great take. He turned round, almost expecting Kaminski to shout at him to get out of the way because he was in shot, and bossed his eyes at him. He'd got news for the great director. He'd spoil that shot any day just to get Miss Longborough to smile at him again.

Georgiana looked at them both.

'So,' she said once more.

She'd done it again. E. F. looked at Kaminski for a reaction, but Kaminski was just sitting beside the girl on the sofa, his hands beneath his nose in the praying position, as if about to compose a new sequence.

Georgiana looked from one man to the other. She had no idea why they were both staring at her in that way. Just for a second she thought she shouldn't have stayed, particularly since she had promised Mary she would help her prepare lunch for Lucius' publisher. She really should be back in Lyall Street cutting radishes into flower shapes for the salad and chopping the melon into bite-sized pieces. But to be honest, she knew that one of the reasons she had chosen to stay for a bitter lemon was she was getting a little fed up with Lucius lately, because he was becoming rather bossy. She didn't mind him ordering her about, but she objected to the way he ordered Mary about, and found it peculiar that Mary did exactly what he told her to do and when he told her to do it. She found it odd because Mary wasn't like that, and what was even more peculiar was that everyone knew Lucius was a queer, so she just could not understand why Mary should allow a queer to boss her around like that, although of course Lucius was ultimately bound to be dominating, because he was not tall, as Mr Kaminski was tall. Actually, now she was a little nearer Mr Kaminski than she had been at the Derby, she saw that he didn't look quite as foreign as his beard had made him look that day. From a distance he had an almost Armenian look, but close to he had pale eyes, not brown, and his hair was dark, not black, and although he did not look Anglo-Saxon, neither did he look Eastern. But nevertheless he was rather frightening, because he seemed to be staring right through her, and she had the feeling he might even be able to tell what she was thinking, which she sincerely hoped he couldn't.

He had on very nice shoes. He got good marks for those. She always liked those sort of successful slip-ons with little bits on the front. And his socks were a nice silky grey, and although he wasn't thin, he wasn't fat like his writer. She just wished he didn't look quite so serious and frightening; although she seemed to be talking a lot, and his writer-person seemed to be laughing a lot, Kaminski was still staring at her as he had been doing now for fully ten minutes, with his hands positioned below his nose like the Angel Gabriel in a school play.

'So,' she said in an ensuing silence.

E. F. couldn't take it any more. He looked at Kaminski and thought it was incredible. Sometimes art mirrored life in such a way that if you put it in a motion picture people just wouldn't believe it. To be sitting discussing a young English aristocrat with Kaminski that morning and then for this creature to stroll in, it was incredible. He knew Kaminski was thinking the same as him because he hadn't taken his eyes off her since he'd sat down. He imagined Kaminski would now be on to lighting her – from source, of course. Lighting from source was one of Kaminski's trademarks. The next thing he'd do would probably be to shout 'Action!', and she would start her dialogue, and Kaminski, who never looked through the camera, would watch the scene, his right hand placed on his beard, his left arm motionless by his side.

She was very graceful, this girl, graceful and yet at the same time a little unsure. She would make a small gesture with her hand while describing something, then she would turn to look at Kaminski with uncertainty, as if she was hoping he wouldn't suddenly tell her off. Then she started to tease him. E. F. watched fascinated. No one, but no one teased Kaminski. But this girl did, and the effect was mesmeric. Kaminski brought his camera in even closer. He softened the lighting and printed every take. He couldn't get enough.

And then she went.

Kaminski got up first this time, no longer resentful of the interruption to his work. E. F. stood up, and the girl stood by the door and thanked them for her bitter lemon as though she had been given champagne. E. F. thought to listen to her you'd think she'd never been given a lemonade before. It wasn't just charming, it was flabbergasting, simply because quite obviously she wasn't doing it in order to charm them. Anyone could see she was doing it because at that very moment she quite literally felt there had never been quite such kind people as himself and Kaminski, and that the lemonade was positively the most refreshing drink she had ever been given on a hot day. Now that was charm.

After she had gone, Kaminski went slowly over to the drinks trolley and made them both another martini. E. F. followed him over and they both stood silently as Kaminski mixed the drink, E. F. appreciated the fact that Kaminski always poured him exactly the same size martini as he poured for himself. In that respect at least Kaminski was a gentleman. He might be a cold bastard, but he never poured the writer's drink short, which was more than E. F. could say for all the other sods he'd worked for, and for whom, no doubt, he would be working again.

Kaminski went to the window and watched Georgiana walking away from the apartment. She kept glancing behind her to see if she could find a taxi, and then, perhaps because Kaminski was praying for her to do so, she stopped at the kerb and waited so that he was able to see her face, her long hair and her slender body. After a moment a taxi drew up beside her, and she was masked from him. Kaminski wished that he was the taxi driver. He imagined her looking at him from where she stood on the kerb, and thought she would probably have that look of mischievous delight on her face that he had stopped at all, and he would take her back to wherever it was she was going, and wish at the end that the journey had been longer.

He couldn't remember anything she had said to him while she had been there sitting next to him, only that she seemed to be eluding him all the time that she spoke, that she had treated him as if he were a large and fierce dog of whom she was determined not to be afraid, and that she had crept so near to his whiskers that he felt she had been just about to reach out a hand to pull them when she had had to get up and go.

'That was just too much,' E. F. said, gesturing to the now-empty sofa. 'I mean we talk about it, and then in it walks. It's just too much altogether.'

Kaminski walked slowly back from the window.

'Lunch,' he announced, and then threw his glass into the fireplace where it shattered.

E. F. knew the routine. He too threw his glass into the fireplace, once he had drained every last drop from it, and then looked to Kaminski, and couldn't believe it. For the second time that morning the bastard seemed to be smiling.

chapter nine

The Countess put down her *Daily Telegraph*, carefully placing it on the lace cloth which shielded the paper from the cream lace sheets. She supposed she would have to go to the beastly Parker-Jones funeral, although she hardly knew the man, and on what looked as if it was going to be such a hot day as well. The idea of going to a funeral on a hot day was quite intolerable. Somehow funerals on cold days seemed far more in keeping, though she didn't quite know why. She realised she was getting off quite lightly however, because poor Andrew Gillott was actually having to cope with the wretched widow and her fearfully plain daughter. But even so, such obligations in such hot weather were both dreadfully dreary and boring, and doing dreadfully dreary and boring things was dreadfully dreary and boring when one was old, because it was dreadfully dreary and boring enough being old, without having to do dreadfully dreary and boring things that didn't hold any appeal.

She thought she might perhaps have one of her little fainting fits. Not the serious kind that make people rush you into King Edward VII's Hospital for Officers, but the kind which made it quite impossible to attend a funeral on a hot day. After all, there was very little point in being old if one couldn't have a fainting fit and miss some boring funeral. She picked up her telephone and rang her daughter. She would have a fainting fit and Mary, who after all had at least known Mrs Parker-Jones, could represent the family at the funeral. Thus the Countess could stay in bed till just before lunchtime when she would suddenly feel better and be able after all to go and have lunch as planned with Lavinia Fellowes in her new hat.

'Mary,' she said to her daughter when she answered the telephone. 'I have just had another of my little attacks. Nothing to worry about, but I think you had better go to this beastly funeral instead of me.'

'I can't go I'm afraid, Mamma,' Mary replied. 'I have to go to the country.'

'The country? But it's only Tuesday!' the Countess retorted.

'I know it's only Tuesday, Mamma,' said Mary. 'But I have to show someone some houses. A film director.'

'Whatever for?'

'Because I promised.'

'Well you can't. Tell him you have a funeral.'

'I'm afraid that's quite impossible, Mamma. Besides, I didn't even know Mr Parker-Jones.'

This was too much for the Countess, who put the telephone down quite angrily without even saying *au revoir*. Mary seemed to be growing into a completely different type of person ever since that wretched little American had crept into her life. If it wasn't his publisher Mary was busy entertaining, it was his wretched queer friends. And if it wasn't some wretched queer or other, now it was some film director. It really was too much. If Mary hadn't already been left some money by her father, she would

142

have made a move that morning to cut her daughter out of her will, so angry was the Countess feeling. Unfortunately her husband had had the lack of foresight to leave Mary quite a tidy little sum, so that whatever her poor old mamma did it made little difference at all. The Countess felt quite put out. In fact she felt put out enough to feel she really might have a fainting fit after all, as soon as she'd had another cup of coffee.

But the coffee was so good, she forgot about fainting and instead rang Andrew Gillott to tell him she would not be going to the funeral because Mary was being quite beastly, and Mary being beastly always made her feel quite ill, and so that was that. Andrew understood. Andrew had to understand. The Countess was far too useful to him for him not to do so. Then after she had rung him, the Countess rang Fulton and Elliott. Elliott sounded as if he was holding the telephone at least three feet away from his mouth as usual, for it was a habit he had adopted since becoming terrified of germs. Fulton was out shopping, of course, so she told Elliott how beastly Mary has been to her and asked herself round to tea. In return she had to listen to Elliott telling her all about how Fulton was going ahead and redoing the drawing room white, in direct contradiction to everyone's advice, and that already everyone's teeth looked fearfully yellow against the walls because the paint was so white.

'We all look like clowns, dear,' said Elliott from a distance.

'Like what?' demanded the Countess.

'Clowns.'

'Very appropriate, too,' the Countess replied.

'Now then,' said Elliott. 'Naughty. You mustn't be a naughty old tabby. Countess.'

Naturally she had to be told more about the drawing room, because it was going to be such a disaster. The floor was going to be black and white squares, which was quite fatal because they would have to be scrubbed at least twice a week. The walls were bright white, and the windows were to have white curtains.

'Can you imagine?' said Elliott. 'In London?'

The Countess couldn't.

Furthermore, all the furniture was to be white, and Fulton had even ordered a white suit for their first all-white cocktail party, and was presently working on an all-white cocktail. The Countess put the telephone down and practically jumped out of bed. Just wait till she told Lavinia about it. Lavinia would simply not believe it. By the time she had run her bath she was in such a good mood she even allowed herself a couple of little extra drops of Floris essence in the water. A black and white floor! It was just too perfect even to think about. She lay in the bath and imagined Fulton on his hands and knees with his little cloth and his little bottle of Gumption, scrubbing away at all those tiles, while Elliott took all the telephone calls in his white cotton gloves holding the receiver three feet away from him while Fulton scrubbed away around his feet.

She met Lavinia Fellowes for lunch at The Ivy, wearing her new hat, a tiny affair with a small curling ostrich feather, a style which was currently very fashionable, but in fact was a copy of one she'd worn before the war. She was a little put out when Lavinia arrived also in a new hat, because really when ladies met for lunch there was only room for one new hat, and since the last time they'd lunched the Countess had allowed Lavinia to be the one, she considered Lavinia's action in also wearing a new hat most unfair. In fact she considered it really too bad. Still, at least they were not both wearing the same hat, for if they had been, that would have been the end of that.

But they made a pretty sight between them, the Countess realised, a couple of smart old ladies in hats and pearls, and they soon had all the waiters crowding round them, particularly since it was Lavinia's turn to pay, and Lavinia loved to show off. Sometimes she could be a little dreary as company, but today one of her best friends had been mugged in the Harrods car park, and this had cheered Lavinia up enormously, because Lavinia loved bad news, even more than she loved new hats.

Lavinia had no children, and the Countess envied her this. She'd often thought that her own children were a pretty mixed blessing when they were young, and now they were older she knew they were. If like Lavinia one had simply not had them, one remained in a state of delicious romance about the ones one might have had, and about how sweet and good they would have been. But if, as the Countess had done, one had gone through the whole dreary beastly business of child-bearing, and bringing them up, only to see them grow into quite the opposite of what their parents had hoped they would grow up into, then there was no way one could lie to oneself as Lavinia Fellowes could.

Of course Lavinia knew all about Mary and her dreadful little American, and couldn't wait to score over the Countess on that.

'Such a good-looking woman,' she said, with transparent insincerity. 'One would have thought she would have attracted *someone* by now.'

This always made the Countess feel sorry for herself, because of course Lavinia was quite right. A woman with her daughter Mary's looks and position in Society should have made the right match by now, and certainly should not be running around with queers and upsetting her mother by not going to funerals. At least her son Harry was married, even if he had chosen a frightfully plain girl whose idea of heaven was to roll around in hay barns and breed miniature Shetland ponies, which the Countess considered to be utterly useless things since they were only as big as dogs and yet you couldn't even have them on the bed. But Mary had neither children nor a husband, and seemed quite content to lead the kind of life that was really not one thing or the other.

'And how is Georgiana?'

The Countess replied that Georgiana her niece was very well, knowing that such little information would be insufficient.

'She's such a pretty girl,' Lavinia said carefully.

Which was invitation enough for the Countess.

Certainly Georgiana was pretty, she allowed, but what was the point of mere prettiness nowadays when the poor girl had no money? And as Lavinia should well know – which she did – there was not the slightest chance that Georgiana could get anywhere at all if she had no money. Apparently John Pemberton had been madly keen for a few weeks, and Mary had had high hopes for the liason, but he had soon cried off once he found just what little real substance there was behind Georgiana. Even a man as rich as Pemberton required that a girl should have a little *dot*, or even some jewellery, but of course the poor child didn't have a thing, and her father and mother of course couldn't care less. And if it hadn't been for Mary's kindness in taking Georgiana in, one just couldn't imagine what might have happened to her. As it was, there was little that Mary, or for that matter anyone else, could do to help her, except just hope and pray that the right man, older of course, would come along and Georgiana would find true wealth, not just some ghastly little jumped-up lawyer with a private income, which really would be both useless and quite unsatisfactory.

Now it was the Countess' turn to find out how things were going between Lavinia and her lover, for Lavinia was not only undisgraced by children, she was also graced by an elderly but active Polish lover who apparently made her feel eighteen again, which for the Countess was another source of irritation and envy. He was frightfully domineering like all Poles, and spent the whole time trying to get Lavinia to behave like a well-trained gun-dog, and throwing frightful rages if and when she didn't. Lavinia adored him, of course, and took great delight in telling the Countess how passionate he could be at the most surprising moments. The Countess was envious because she knew she should have a lover too, and if she had she wouldn't spend so much time being upset by facts such as her daughter not having married well, let alone at all. But the memory of Freddie, of her adored Freddie, quite prevented this, for she found she was not able to be unfaithful to his memory. She wanted to be able to look Freddie in the eye when they met again in the next life, and although she might fritter her time away quite happily till then, she did not wish to fritter it away with a lover, even though judging from how Lavinia looked, it obviously did wonders for one's complexion.

Lunch ended with a sorbet and on a sour note. Apparently Lavinia's house, which Mary had redecorated a few years ago, was going to be viewed by this film director. Lavinia told the whole restaurant how exciting it all was and the Countess tried to ignore this latest piece of information. She knew of the film director because Mary had told her on the telephone, but she wasn't going to let Lavinia know she knew, although Lavinia was insisting that *everyone* had heard of Kaminski. The Countess bet herself a private pony Lavinia never had until the moment Mary had asked her for her permission to view Charleston. Lavinia told the Countess her house was probably going to be used in a film, and that Kaminski was related very distantly to her present lover. The Countess made polite but obviously bored noises, while fitting a Sobranie into her cigarette holder, and thought to herself that nothing would ever surprise her as far as Poles were concerned. For even though, as Lavinia was always at great pains to point out, her lover was a Count, that fooled nobody, nobody with any sense that was, because everybody knew a Count. Besides, it irritated her, this insistence of Lavinia's to make her love affair so respectable.

The Countess also thought it was sheer cheek of Mary to take this wretched film director round people's houses, round everybody's houses but her own apparently. What on earth was wrong with Clayton Manor, the Countess asked herself irritably? And she made up her mind that from the moment she got home she wouldn't ring her daughter for a week. She was by now extremely cross, because it had become quite obvious that Lavinia was telling her all this in great detail because she knew that Clayton was not on the list. Her own daughter ignoring the house of her own birth was really too much.

Lavinia thought that this Kaminski, or whatever his name was, was going to be all the rage that summer, because he was purportedly extremely handsome, with a powerful presence. The Countess sniffed. Last year it had been an ageing pop singer who couldn't sing in tune who had been all the rage, and everyone had asked him everywhere. He too was said to be extremely handsome with a powerful presence, but personally the Countess had found him to be a boring little drunk. No doubt this famous film director would turn out to be exactly the same salad with a different dressing. Every year it was someone new and then, like last year's look, everyone forgot about them, and they disappeared into the blue beyond from whence they had come. That was Society.

And so to Fulton and Elliott's for tea, stopping first to purchase them some mille feuilles, which she knew would cause the most tremendous upheaval, particularly since the jam in the mille feuilles was red and not white. As she walked to their flat, she recalled how they had not wanted to ask her to tea until the curtains had been hung at the windows. And so of course she had insisted, saying that she simply had to come because she wanted to make sure they had got the 'drawing room warming gift' she had sent them, a large pot of lilies with bright yellow centres. It was important to do things in the afternoons because otherwise afternoons could be so terribly dull nowadays. She remembered how un-dull they had once been. Afternoons spent with Freddie had always been nothing but fun. Sometimes they would take a little picnic by boat across the lake to their private little island in the middle, which the Countess called Camelot, saying to Freddie that no man but him would ever be allowed on it, because it would invite bad luck. Sometimes she would read to him, because even though Freddie quite hated books, he loved to be read to, and luckily he was quite unaware that this was good for him. Other times they would sit with their coffee in the Orangery and talk over old times, and remember old friends, and the fun they had had. Fun had always been so important to their generation. It had not been a pastime, or a hobby, it had been an ideal. Fun meant you surprised your guests, or your guests surprised you. It meant you never said what you thought, or showed what you felt, because that might stop someone else having fun. And above all having fun made people try to look pretty for each other, and to try and make their houses look pretty, and life look pretty, and now that was all gone. She passed a new tower block and averted her eyes from it, for now it seemed all that was left was ugliness.

She walked on, looking instead for some of the old, but sadly few familiar landmarks that were still there, old and familiar, and threatened with extinction, like herself. If it had not been right in the middle of the Season, the news that her daughter was showing this wretched director round everyone's house but her own for a film would have sent her without delay down to Clayton, and she would have stayed there until someone had noticed. But she could not leave London at this moment, and besides, in reality she hated the country for any length of time. In the country one was always aware of people like the Weavers, whereas in town, although one was surrounded by thousands of Weavers, one was hardly ever made aware of them, unless one was related to them, but that couldn't be helped wherever one was.

When she reached Fulton and Elliott's block of flats she ignored the lift and walked up the stairs instead, carrying her box of pâtisserie in one gloved hand, and holding on to the polished brass hand-rail with the other. She thought to herself as she made the climb how fortunate it was that Fulton and Elliott were too old to 'come out', as she believed it was called, because the news would have been greeted by everyone in town with very loud yawns, and the idea of those little lavender and lace mothers of theirs living in their little cottages in Chipping Campden or wherever being solemnly informed that their elderly sons were not merry bachelors but gay bachelors was too funny for words.

Elliott opened the door. He was wearing a pair of grey

149

gloves, one of dozens of pairs he put on while his hands soaked in special handcream beneath them. It was a treatment he swore by, except that Elliott never swore because he was inexorably prim. Fulton on the other hand looked quite frightful as he stood awaiting her arrival in the middle of the drawing room. The strain of the past few weeks with the decorators was taking its toll, for he had dreadful bags under his eyes, which in themselves were bloodshot and showed up quite hideously against the glaringly white walls. Elliott of course looked wonderful, but then Elliott always looked wonderful when Fulton didn't. It seemed as if one drained the other.

'What do you think?' Elliott asked the Countess.

The Countess looked round and considered the room. It was all so white it was ghastly, and she was absolutely thrilled, because it was as horrific as she had warned them it would be. And with them all standing there on the black and white squared floor, well they just looked like rather odd pieces in a rather peculiar game of chess. One of the chess pieces was Lucius, Mary's queer friend. The Countess gave him her hand.

'Isn't it just too dramatic for words?' Lucius asked her.

The Countess was graciousness personified. At times like this she could afford to be.

'Wonderful,' she replied. 'Such fun.'

She always said that whenever she had to be charming, and didn't really know quite what to say.

'Aren't the flowers lovely?' she added.

She always said that when she was put out, and at this moment that was exactly how she felt. Put out. She had no idea Lucius was going to be there. It was bad enough finding out that her own daughter was snubbing her without going out to tea for a tiny relaxation and finding the same daughter's queer friend was there too. She gave Fulton the pâtisserie box and smiled at Lucius. There were only three mille feuilles, she explained, as she didn't realise there were going to be four for tea. Fulton said it was sweet of her and it didn't really matter because both he and Elliott were meant to be on a diet. The Countess looked at Fulton and knew this was a fib, because he was as fat as ever, and Elliott was already opening the cake box. There was something worrying Fulton however, and for a moment the Countess thought he might be worried lest the cakes showed up horribly against the all-white background, before she realised he was dithering about because he wasn't quite sure how to serve them. The Countess decided charitably to put him out of his misery.

'Do please let's be common and have them with cake forks, Fulton,' she announced, and sat herself down on the all-white sofa.

At once everyone was put out of their misery, and they all had Jackson's tea with lemon, cakes with forks, and discussed whether or not 'form' mattered, and what 'form' precisely was. Fulton thought the height of form was not knowing there was such a thing, but Elliott disagreed and said that was style, not form. The Countess reminded them that whether one ate one's cake with a fork or whether one didn't, or put frilly covers on one's lav seat, or served dinner with no side plates, et cetera, really did not mean a thing, any more than saying 'pardon', or lifting the little finger, or holding one's knife in the pen position, all these things were merely etiquette, and etiquette could always go by the board when it came to charm. She had known hundreds of people, she said, who had no idea of form, or etiquette, and yet who had been socially tremendously successful, because they had had the most important thing of all social graces, manners.

Being an American, Lucius was slightly excluded from this conversation, but he did not mind in the least, because he knew he would need all this later for his book. He did not mind, either, the slight distance he noticed the Countess put between herself and him as soon as she had arrived. It was not that she was just terribly charming to him, showing none of her usual hauteur, but she was more than terribly charming to him, she was alarmingly charming and this, he recognised uneasily, was certainly not normal. Normally she was dismissive with him, or merely ignored him, or sent him to fetch her coat like a servant, but today she was so sweet he realised suddenly just how much she thoroughly disliked him. He couldn't understand why, for he had always been so careful to be charming to her, so that she would not have to make any effort towards him. But this afternoon was very different. She kept telling him how funny he was, and the more she told him the drearier he became, which was obviously her intention. What a chilling and killing way the English had when they wanted to! Once or twice he saw Elliott looking at him sympathetically, and once when he took off one of his cotton gloves to show Lucius the effect of the special handcream, he touched Lucius on the arm by way of comfort. It was humiliating to be so well treated, and consequently to be powerless to say anything, for he was sure it had never been heard of socially for someone to beg someone else not to be so nice to them. He guessed that when Mary was a child, this is the way her mother would have treated her if she had been naughty. Far better, he thought, to be whipped and put to bed without supper, than to be humiliated with this chilling charm.

At last it was time for someone to go, and Lucius made sure that it was him. What a relief it would be to get home and soak in a tub of hot water and listen to Schubert, and restore himself socially in his own eyes once more, for if he stayed one minute longer he would be quite unable to live with himself ever again.

'A dear little person, I think,' said Fulton once he was gone, 'when he's on form.'

The Countess nodded and said nothing, then turned to look at Elliott. He was busy adjusting a small stick which propped up the white lilies with the bright yellow centres. He had now taken off both his gloves, and his hands very nearly matched the absolute white of the flowers. He said nothing as well, so the Countess was able to take her leave well satisfied.

chapter ten

Now that she was a widow, Mrs Parker-Jones found that the days went by very slowly, principally because there were no interruptions. Aidan had been a constant interruption in her life, and now without him there was nothing to grumble about, and also nothing to grumble at.

Mrs Parker-Jones felt like grumbling, for not only had she had to cancel Jennifer's dance because of Aidan dying like that, she had also had to forgo a major part of the latter end of the Season, and all she was left to enjoy was the miserable sight of Jennifer sitting around the place moping. The only good thing to come out of all this wretched business was that her late husband had very fortunately not had time to change his will, and consequently had left every single penny to her, to Clarissa, so from now on Jennifer had to do exactly as she was told or her mother would not be very forthcoming with her dress allowance, or with any other allowance as it happened. Her daughter however did not seem particularly aware of this as she sat around the flat getting under Mrs Parker-Jones' feet, wearing large woollen cardigans which she wrapped round her in such a way that she looked like an au pair, and not the daughter of Mrs Parker-Jones. Jennifer was taking her mourning far, far too seriously, her mother thought. It was of course typical of her generation, self-indulgent monsters that they were, forever saying 'right' to everything, and then forever doing everything wrong. And she had started to write poetry in lined books with 'Personal' written on them. Mrs Parker-Jones had disregarded this caveat and attempted to read some of them, but had not been able to make head or tail of them. Hardly a line rhymed, and Jennifer had used a lot of words Mrs Parker-Jones disliked intensely, such as 'despoil', and 'fructify'. Silly words that no one with any sense used any more.

But the worse thing of all to come out of her husband's untimely death was that Andrew Gillott no longer called because of the fact that she was such a recent widow. Before, practically every day, she had watched his large, impressive figure emerge from his motor car, and then she had almost run to the sofa to compose herself before the maid showed him in. But now she just stood looking out onto Sloane Street nursing only the vaguest hope that she would see him. Once she thought she had glimpsed his familiar figure emerging from the food shop opposite, where she knew he went sometimes to buy some game pâté. But she knew she was mistaken, for whoever it was did not even as much as glance up at her window, as Andrew most surely would have done, but simply climbed into a passing taxi and was gone.

Her daughter too, was no longer being visited by Nigel Bruce-Smith, and perhaps, Mrs Parker-Jones thought, perhaps this was the reason she was being really so depressing it just wasn't true. She wrote to him of course, almost daily, and he did at least write back. His letters were not very long, but they did now and then express his regret that he was not able to take her out during this period of family mourning. As for mourning, Mrs Parker-Jones thought it was old hat, but when she had once expressed this opinion to Andrew Gillott he was terribly shocked. He explained that proper people always observed mourning, and had more than hinted that not to do so might well prejudice her chances of 'getting on', as she liked to call it.

Mrs Parker-Jones did not wish to prejudice anything, least of all herself in Andrew Gillott's eyes. So she obediently sat about her flat with her daughter for the following six weeks, and although she thought a great deal about what extremely bad luck it had been for Aidan to go and die on her just when Jennifer was about to come out, she also realised that bad luck could often be good luck in disguise. Neither did she consider one penny of what she had given to Andrew as his fee to be wasted, even though she suspected it might be within her rights to ask for a small refund, since theoretically Andrew at this time should have been escorting them both through the rest of the Season's events, such as Henley, Wimbledon and Goodwood. However, she had not indeed asked for any money back, not only because she considered it would have been extremely bad form although, as she well knew, not everyone in her position would have been quite so generous, but also because Andrew might be upset, and that was the very last thing she wanted. In the back of her mind, she had also not been altogether certain as to how to broach such a delicate matter. She was not like Andrew's friend the Countess, whom she was quite sure would have no hesitation at all in simply demanding a substantial refund, just as she had had no compunction at all in asking Mrs Parker-Jones for her payment for the hire of her ballroom in cash all those weeks ago.

That was another thing about Aidan dying so suddenly that Mrs Parker-Jones resented, for it had meant that wretched Countess had been able to pocket Mrs Parker-Jones' cash and give her nothing in return. Here of course Mrs Parker-Jones had made no bones about asking for her money back, but the Countess had simply refused point blank, on a hastily scrawled postcard, giving as a reason the fact that her ballroom, if she had had enough notice, would naturally have been hired out to someone else, and that she was quite unable under the present economic circumstances to bear any more 'cash losses', just as if she was a branch of Woolworth's, and not a Countess. It really was extraordinary.

If she had had to admit it, Mrs Parker-Jones would have to say that on the whole the Season had not been what she had been led to expect it would be. She had been led to expect that it would be considerably more glamorous than it was, and that there would be far more people with titles going to each other's parties, instead of only the occasional title. And of course the clothes were not the clothes that they were in former times. She knew that, because she had suspected it and had her suspicions confirmed by Andrew. People simply did not have the money it seemed, nor did they have any style, which was far less excusable, for on more than one occasion she had mistaken her hostess for the staff, so poorly dressed had she been, with down-at-heel shoes and a dress that looked as if it came from some Charity shop. As Mrs Parker-Jones progressed through the Season it had seemed to her, although she would be loth to admit it to Andrew, that the more titled people were the less they appeared to bother about outward appearances. She considered that if you were a titled person, then you should dress so that you would be noticed as a titled person. People would know you were a Duchess just from looking at you. But in fact Mrs Parker-Jones had not so long ago been to an Art Gallery opening and seen a Duchess, and not a particularly old Duchess either, and she had looked just like Mrs Parker-Jones' cleaning lady. Mrs Parker-Jones had been dreadfully disappointed, and confessed this to Andrew later, but he had only sighed, which Mrs Parker-Jones took to mean that he also found people nowadays as disappointing as she did. Still, once August came, they were going down to their house in Surrey, and she had invited Andrew to come and stay because as even he had agreed, it would not be 'improper' by then, and she had told Jennifer to ask Nigel Bruce-Smith down also, so at least they both now had something to look forward to, besides endlessly dull days with endlessly silent meal times.

Andrew Gillott had been losing at the tables recently, and a great deal more than was his wont. This made him both cross and anxious. When he lost at backgammon it made him cross, because he was very good at backgammon and did not expect to lose, but when he lost at chemmy it made him anxious; since chemin de fer was a game of chance there was no way one could be good at it, and so for a skilled gambler to find himself both playing and losing at it naturally was a cause for anxiety.

He knew he was gambling because he was bored, and that when he was bored he played games of chance and always lost, and he knew that the reason why he was bored was because he was not escorting the frightful Parker-Jones woman and her dreadfully plain daughter around town at the moment, which somewhat surprised him at first, until he realised that the height of boredom was being bored stiff because you weren't being bored by someone boring. And this made him gamble even more (that and the fact that he had an overdraft even earlier in the Season than usual), and the more he gambled, the more bored he became, and the greater grew his losses. He had a theory that one could only pick winners in the paddock, or not lose at the table if one was gambling merely for the sheer enjoyment of doing so. If one did it for any other reason, namely to make money, or just because one was bored, one lost, and simply went on losing. He had formulated this theory from watching some of his excessively wealthy friends, who did not need to gamble for the sake of their bank balances, with the consequence that they always enjoyed their gambling and therefore nearly always won. Andrew was pleased with the sense of his theory, but naturally totally ignored it, because to observe it would have taken all the fun out of gambling.

Andrew had spent most of his small capital on his flat, which he considered to be an absolute essential if ever there was one. But the outgoings had soared so astronomically in the last year that he had been forced to realise that there could well come a time soon when if things continued to go as they were going, he would have to give up his flat and go and live on someone's estate in a tied cottage at a peppercorn rent. He faced this prospect with about as much relish as gentlefolk in the last century faced the idea of the poorhouse. For the idea of living in the country so far away from the vices he held so dear was an appalling idea. But he knew that it most certainly was very much on the cards for him, because he had seen it happen to so many of his chums of late. Practically every day at the club the news would filter through about how poor old so-and-so had had to fold up his tent and quietly leave town. It wasn't just that the quality of life in town had become so expensive, sitting about just living and breathing had become prohibitive. Gone were the days of a dozen oysters for starters at lunch, cocktails at the Ritz, and then on to dinner somewhere every night. Most of a chap's life nowadays seemed to be spent sitting on the edge of one's bed dreading the sound of the buff envelopes dropping onto the hair cord in the hall.

Nonetheless, August was still not a month to be seen around town, that at least was still very much a hard and fast rule. He knew some of his old cronies who no longer had anywhere or anybody to go to boarded themselves up in their flats for a month but Andrew, luckily, still had the odd bolt hole, and thus managed annually to escape town and subsequent social embarrassment. This year he didn't bother to tell anyone exactly what his plans were; instead he just said vaguely that he was going to cruise around a bit and play the field. People naturally did not question him too closely on the details lest he should do the same to them in return and thus blow all their cover – which was just as well, for had Andrew had to itemise his real plans for the month he could never have got out of bed in the morning let alone face himself in the shaving mirror. First, he was going to stay in Shropshire with his brother, who had gone mad and was trying to live off the land, which was impossible since his holding was practically non-existent. He kept his house shuttered up all year and served raw carrots and dog food for dinner every night. There were no bulbs in the electric lights and, although he still kept a butler, the butler always wore gumboots, due to the rising – and the constantly falling – damp.

After this brief but uncomfortable sojourn, Andrew would then go and stay with his sister, who would do nothing but talk about the dreadful conditions their brother lived in and this would irk Andrew so much he usually wished he was back staying with the brother again.

Not only that, but his sister, who had married a man with a very large fortune, was so irredeemably mean that by the time she had made one chicken last four days, and grudgingly poured one out the odd barley water, it made a person long for the generous helpings of dog food and flat pale ale which the brother served up.

So all in all, Andrew's proposed visit to the Parker-Jones' in the heart of Surrey, while about as stylish in Andrew's book as wearing a made-up bow tie, sounded positively hedonistic when compared with his other two engagements. He knew what the Parker-Jones establishment would be like from the address. The house would be an Edwardian copy of a country house, with an oak front door with a reproduction cast-iron medieval bell pull. Within there would be woodblock floors and low ceilings with dark stained beams, and there would be a large window with coloured glass in it halfway up the stairs. The stair carpet would be plum, of that particular shade one usually only sees in the dentist's. The guest room would be done up in glazed cotton copied from Colefax and Fowler, and there would be one room which was referred to as the 'rumpus' room. Outside there would be an unheated swimming pool round which they would have drinks and mosquitoes in the evening. The flower beds would be planted full of roses which didn't smell, and the edges of the flower beds would be cut out with a spade so sharply and tidily that one would quite expect to see nurses pushing patients in wheelchairs around the lawns. After the first drink Andrew would be longing once more for the ardours of Shropshire, or even the starvation rations served by his sister in Abingdon. He would be longing to see his brother's old horse ambling up the lawn for the fifteenth time that day, and his brother once more taking off his hat and flapping it at the old fool. He would long to hear his brother once again describing all the weeds, daisies, dandelions and ground cover, and would yearn to be sitting under the collection of family portraits (even though most of them no longer had any eyes, their grandfather once having shot them all out when drunk, mistaking them for his wife's relations). But all this longing was purely academic because Andrew knew he had both to go and stay there, and once staying there, he would have to stay there, because quite simply he had no real alternative. It was either that, or the flat with the blinds drawn.

Mrs Parker-Jones met him at the station wearing too much Chanel No. 5. She told him she had dispensed with the chauffeur, because she preferred to be informal in the country. Andrew immediately felt sick, and it wasn't just the horrible smell of the new simulated lambswool car seat covers, it was everything: her scent, the Surrey lanes with their depressingly neat houses, all with their individually hand-carved oak signs, and her way of driving in snatches, with her foot on the brake and her stupid head poked forward. His brother had an expression he always used for being sick. He called it 'throwing a map'. By the time they had arrived at the Parker-Jones' homestead, Andrew felt he could have thrown an entire atlas.

Since he had not uttered a word since she had collected him at the award-winning local station, he thought he now ought to say something, so he half-heartedly admired her flower arrangement in the hall. But by the time she finished telling him in detail how she managed to do it, and that the secret was in the special plastic carton, and that all the flowers in the house were from the estate – as she insisted on referring to the garden – he wished he'd kept to keeping his mouth shut. It completely baffled him how one simple remark could call forth such a torrent of incredibly boring explanation. All he had said was that he thought the flowers were quite pretty, and all she had to say by way of a reply was that they were from the garden, and then they could have been straight into the gin and tonics without any more ado. But no, not Mrs Parker-Jones. She had to go into all that about plastic cartons, and foam fillings, and banging the ends of roses with hammers and what-have-you. He breathed a small sigh of relief that he hadn't been fool enough to make a remark about her frock, or mention the news, or say what a charming house it was, which it wasn't.

Soon, as he had fatefully predicted, they were sitting beside the unheated swimming pool with Jennifer, an avocado dip and a positive army of mosquitoes. Andrew looked to the horizon, above the beds of standard roses and beyond the severely manicured lawns and borders. There was no reason to feel quite this miserable, he was sure, but he couldn't help it. He hadn't felt quite so much like having a damned good blub since his mother first waved him goodbye and left him standing all alone in the gym of his prep school. He didn't belong here, in this Surrey garden with this woman in her frock and her large plain daughter. He belonged in Jermyn Street, and St James's, and Knightsbridge, and Newbury, and the Yorkshire moors. He suddenly sighed rather loudly and obviously very audibly, because he found both his hostess and her daughter staring at him, but before they could enquire what the matter might be, Nigel Bruce-Smith arrived and saved Andrew from explanation.

Welcoming him, Mrs Parker-Jones announced that she had put him in the East Wing. Andrew looked at the house and could see no discernible sign of an East Wing, let alone a West Wing. He imagined therefore that the East Wing meant the bedroom on the right of Mrs Parker-Jones, and the West Wing meant the bedroom on the left. By now, furthermore, he was sure that 'the little boys' room', as she insisted on coyly calling the shared bathroom, would have a motor car on the door, that the towels would be monogrammed, the bed linen would be of a practical nylon mixture, and the bathroom suite would be avocado to go with the revolting dip they were eating.

Jennifer on the other hand was quite suffused with joy now that Nigel Bruce-Smith had arrived. She was quite overcome as she looked at him standing there so vulnerable in his dear sports jacket with the funny leather patches on the sleeves and holding a bunch of what looked like freshly cut flowers in the hand which wasn't holding his cigarette. Dear, sweet Nigel, who had written to her so often during those last few miserable weeks, and to whom she had sent all her best poems was here at last. He had come down all the way from London specially to see her. She just couldn't believe her luck. The only way she had been able to get over her father's death was by thinking of him, and although she had of course tried to support her grieving mother as best she could, there was no doubt about it, it was the thought that she might, one day soon see Dear Nigel again that had given her the strength to get through her ordeal.

It had been a difficult time for Jennifer in more ways than one, because try as she did, she could not help thinking that her mother had been the direct cause of her father's sudden death: had she not been so socially ambitious and anxious to climb the ladder from the middle of Society to its very top, Jennifer knew her father would still be alive to this day, ambling around the gardens and inspecting his standard roses with interest before taking himself off to the poolside where he would sit by himself quite happily until dinner with a whisky and soda and a good paperback. She knew her father had died as a direct result of her mother hurling the diamond bracelet at him, and she knew the reason she had done so was because she had pawned something which was not hers to pawn, and therefore, in the purest sense, that made her mother some sort of murderess. This was not a comfortable thought for Jennifer, and so she had made a mental compromise, something she had hoped she would not have to do until she was much older, and told herself that her father had slipped and fallen, hitting his head on the club fender, and she had quite put out of her mind the very horrid business of the bracelet and the subsequent funny mark on her father's cheek. She was not able to do this either easily, or quickly, but she was able to achieve it gradually, particularly when she learned that her father had left all his money to her mother, who thus controlled her daughter's destiny, and thereby indirectly Nigel

Bruce-Smith's as well. For Jennifer, although a plain girl, was not a stupid one. She was already aware from the little she knew of Nigel that he was not a young man with a great deal of money of his own; and, like a lot of young men who had not got a great deal of money of their own, he would not be exactly averse to the idea of marrying a girl who had, if not exactly a large fortune, a fortune large enough to enable him to buy several new sports jackets without patches. So, as she knew she was an irritant to her mother, she had been careful to keep from under her feet as much as possible during those difficult six weeks, because she was not going to encourage anything between herself and her mother except friendship, even though she was well aware her mother couldn't stand her. Because at this moment she knew it was quite possible, now she had got Nigel to come down and stay at 'Copyns', that seeing her advantages he would realise what a gain he could make by making her Mrs Bruce-Smith, and once Jennifer was Mrs Bruce-Smith she knew she could quite easily drop her mother without a second's thought since she knew perfectly well her mother couldn't wait to drop her the moment she was able to say 'I do' to Andrew Gillott. For Jennifer was familiar with her mother's amatory ambitions now that she was a widow, and particularly a widow out of mourning.

She quite approved of Andrew Gillott, for in a strange sort of way he and her mother were quite well suited, even though if one were to be critical it was perfectly obvious that Andrew both drank and smoked more than was good for him and that he was far too regular a habitué of the Claremont. However, leaving these somewhat minor minuses aside, there was no doubt at all that his presence turned her mother's moods from dark to light, and from storm into sunshine. Jennifer had written a poem about it, incorporating those very images. And now that he also was down at 'Copyns', her mother even smiled at Jennifer, or pretended to smile at her, just before she sent her to get some more ice, or to go and tell the weekend cook they were ready to dine, or to check the towels in the boys' bathroom, or take some fruit up to Andrew's room, or some biscuits to Nigel's. And the more she smiled at Jennifer, the more Jennifer smiled to herself, for she knew if everything went right for her mother then everything would go right for her.

Dinner was a great success and her mother laughed a lot throughout. Jennifer hadn't heard her laugh like that since the last time they had dined with Andrew Gillott, so she knew the portents were favourable. Her mother kept telling Andrew how funny he was, even when he made the most ordinary remarks, which appeared to please Andrew; and if Andrew was pleased, her mother was pleased. Jennifer watched her mother, smiling happily down the table at Andrew, as if she never wanted to take her eyes off him, which indeed she didn't whenever he was in the room.

After dinner, Nigel and Jennifer walked in the gardens together holding hands and smelling the roses – which didn't. Alone with Nigel, Jennifer suddenly knew that the time had come for her to give herself to him. She had always dreamed of giving herself to the right person, there in the garden at 'Copyns' with a new moon shining, and the sound of the bypass in the distance. But Nigel seemed strangely reluctant. First of all he said if they did it there they could be seen from the house, and then he said there were too many midges, and then finally to convince her said that making love out of doors was greatly overrated and so what was wrong with her bedroom?

Jennifer felt horribly let down. When she had imagined giving herself to someone in the garden at 'Copyns' it had not included dialogue about being seen from the house or being bitten by mosquitoes. But once she had recovered her happily not long lost sense of romance, common sense reasserted itself and she realised Nigel was quite probably right on all three counts, and he even grew a little more in her estimation. So they crept upstairs, with Jennifer's heart loudly beating, and having found her room without attracting any undue attention to their carnal ambitions, started to make love in the dark, while downstairs, Mrs Parker-Jones called vainly for them among the shrubbery and the scentless roses.

It never occurred to Mrs Parker-Jones, as it did at once to Andrew, that that pimp Nigel Bruce-Smith had fixed himself up with that plain daughter of hers and was probably screwing her right at that moment. It never occurred to her because like so many mothers of plain daughters she never thought for an instant that anyone of the opposite sex could possibly desire Jennifer, or that her daughter would ever do anything with a member of the opposite sex without first asking Mummy's permission.

Mrs Parker-Jones soon gave up searching for the lovers since she had more important things on her mind, and instead produced a bottle of very fine vintage cognac which apparently the late Mr Parker-Jones had been saving to drink himself some rainy day. Andrew at once got well and truly stuck in, for he had a weakness for vintage cognac, particularly when it belonged to another chap, and even more particularly when it belonged to some ex-chap who wasn't going to have a call on it any more. And the more he got stuck into it, the more he allowed Clarissa, as he now regularly called her, to tell him all about her loneliness; and as he only half listened he imagined that the roses outside the windows were really old-fashioned scented ones, and that the lawns were sprinkled with daisies, and that he could hear his mother's beloved voice calling up to his father, and that once more he was a small boy leaning secretly out of his nursery window to eavesdrop on the conversation which floated so sweetly up to him on the warm summer evening air.

Andrew had loved his mother so very much. She had been a beautiful creature full of the sort of natural English kindness that one just didn't seem to find now. She had a sweet voice, melodious and low, with not a sharp note in it, and she always seemed to wear frocks in soft materials, and carry a pair of secateurs in her garden-gloved hands. Hats with long ribbons, and the sound of little heels upon cobbled garden paths – these always reminded him of her. He drank again deeply from the hideous balloon brandy glass Clarissa had forced upon him, and thought that he would give anything to be a little boy once again in pyjamas.

Shortly after his third liberal glass of cognac, he had the vague sensation of being helped upstairs by a solicitous Clarissa. She led him up the stairs one by one, and as she did so he told her how much he had loved his mother, and how she had been the only person to be sweet and kind to him, and how much he missed her, particularly right at this moment. And Clarissa told him how she understood how much he had loved his mother, and how much she would like to be able to look after him just the way his mother had done, and Andrew found himself crying on her shoulder and telling Clarissa how much he loved her. And she helped him into his pyjamas and Andrew went to sleep holding what he imagined to be a rather large teddy bear, and which when he awoke a few hours later discovered to be a naked Clarissa.

chapter eleven

When Kaminski rang Mary to thank her for sending him the stills of the houses, he asked to see Stockton Hall and Westington Manor, but he did not ask to see Longborough, which greatly piqued Georgiana. For she realised then she must have put the photograph of Longborough in the wrong position, and that she should have placed her beloved family home on the top of the pile of photographs and not on the bottom. She couldn't say anything to Mary of course, because she was not meant to have placed the photograph of Longborough in the envelope at all. And although she knew that Mary would not really mind that she had, even Georgiana did not want to admit to herself how much she wanted Longborough to be part of Kaminski's film.

A few days later, when the owners had given their permission to Mary to show Kaminski round their houses, Mary had to ring him and tell him that she had fixed the appointments but would not be able to accompany him because she had to go to Scotland rather unexpectedly to see a client.

'Your cousin told me you only decorated for friends,' said Kaminski.

'My cousin was right,' replied Mary. 'But some of my friends are also clients.'

Kaminski thought that the situation was quite probably exactly the reverse and that Lady Mary was too English to admit it, but naturally didn't say so.

'This cousin of yours,' he asked her instead, 'would she come with me and my writer to see the locations? I mean she works for you, doesn't she?'

Mary said yes to both questions and called Georgiana on the house intercom to tell her she was to go with Kaminski to help him choose his locations.

Georgiana tried to sound as if she thought this was a very unexciting task, because she was afraid otherwise Mary might change her mind and go herself. But Mary had no intention of changing her mind, because her 'client' in Scotland was Lucius, and their trip was to be one of total pleasure. She couldn't wait to get out of London because her mother was getting on her nerves. She didn't know what she was meant to have done, but she had obviously done something, and the idea that her mother would no doubt very soon tell her what it was, was too tedious for words. Lucius had never been to Scotland. And September in the Highlands was quite sensationally autumnal.

If Mary was to be quite truthful, she had also got just a little tired of having Georgiana round the house the whole time. It wasn't that she wasn't sweet and willing, which she was, but she was always there. And there really couldn't be any real privacy between her and Lucius while she was. Lucius knew it, and Mary knew it, and she only hoped it wouldn't be too long before Georgiana knew it and got herself fixed up with a nice affair or something. Helping people was only so much fun, but after a while they really had to help themselves. Both she and Mamma had been frightfully disappointed when Georgiana had lost Pemberton – and to Poppy of all people – but now it really was up to Georgiana, and Mary hoped and prayed that Georgiana would realise this and move out.

Georgiana was very well aware of her obligations, and also of the need to find somebody. But unfortunately, just at this moment, no one seemed to be materialising who was remotely suitable. It still slightly annoyed her that Poppy had taken Pemberton, because he would have been the perfect answer to her problems, even though physically she would have had to make the most enormous concessions. It wasn't that she had no friends: she had made dozens of new friends. She had an abundance of new acquaintances and admirers. Her address book was crammed with names – far, far more than she would ever have dreamed possible when only a few months ago she had first arrived to stay with Mary. But the trouble was none of them was rich enough to be able to afford Longborough, and even if they had been rich enough, they would not be interested in a girl who – as her aunt constantly reminded her – had hardly any even moderately good jewellery.

She had spent August with the Countess at Clayton, and the Countess had been in extremely bad form the whole time she was there, her main cause of complaint being that Mary did not come down often enough to see her, although whenever she did come down she then complained that Mary was coming down too often. She disliked all of her country neighbours, and yet she constantly asked them in to have drinks with her in order, it seemed to Georgiana, to complain about them as soon as they'd gone. She asked Georgiana to garden every morning, and when Georgiana complied, the Countess complained that all she ever did was garden, and wondered aloud why it was that a girl of her age should only be interested in gardening, when she herself when she'd been that age had only been interested in men. She hinted that this was probably the real reason why Georgiana had not yet enjoyed a great success with anybody of consequence. The Countess constantly warned Georgiana of the danger of leaving things for too long, and held up her daughter Mary as a good example of what could happen to a girl who let things go on too long at an early age. By the end of August Georgiana found herself, quite respectfully, disliking her aunt.

Georgiana knew her aunt was right, of course, which is what irritated her. (The Countess had a way of outlining other people's problems so succinctly that it left very little room for further discussion.) She also knew that Mary's fate, because she had money, was considerably more enviable than someone like hers, for Georgiana's only visible means of support was herself. She had learnt a great deal from the Poppy-Pemberton incident, most particularly that a girl should never ignore the sound of bare feet on a wooden floor in the corridor outside her bedroom. But certain things still surprised her about Poppy and Pemberton, mostly the fact that she knew Poppy did not have to sleep with Pemberton, but in spite of that she had, and apparently was still doing so, and this being so it meant she must be doing it for pleasure, which Georgiana from her point of view, saw as being totally immoral.

She thought of all this as she waited for Kaminski to arrive in his drawing room. There was a round marble table in front of her, supported by a carved dolphin. Georgiana thought it was probably reproduction, but it contained some books, so Georgiana picked one up to pass away the time and it fell open easily at a page. While she was reading the page where it fell open, the maid showed in E. F., Kaminski's writer. He was slightly out of breath and so was the man Georgiana was reading about. She closed the book and put it down. E. F. picked it up and glanced at the spine.

'You into soft porn?' he asked her.

'I'm sorry?' queried Georgiana.

'You don't have to be,' said E. F. 'I just wondered whether you were into this stuff. This sort of soft porn.'

'Is Mr Kaminski making a film out of this book then?' Georgiana asked, picking the book up once more.

E. F. found it inwardly hysterical to hear Kaminski referred to in such perfect tones as 'Mr Kaminski'.

'No, no. No, "Mr" Kaminski doesn't make motion pictures of airport books,' E. F. replied. "'Mr" Kaminski is an "auteur".'

'Oh,' said Georgiana. 'He writes as well, does he?'

E. F. thought this was too good to be true. Kaminski should really be here to hear this for himself, but he was taking a person to person from the Coast. He thought maybe he should try and explain to her little ladyship that an *auteur* was a film maker who not only directed but wrote, and in some cases even appeared in his own films. And then he thought he wouldn't bother, because it occurred to him it would be much more fun to watch Kaminski go through the day with this chick who had not a clue who he was, and that if he tried to explain exactly who Kaminski was and what he was at, it would spoil the fun of watching Kaminski having to explain himself to her or rather, as would be the case with Kaminski, trying not to explain who he was to her, for when you were Kaminski you didn't have to explain who you were to anybody. Kaminski's name was sufficient introduction for hostesses all over the world to find room for him at their tables. No one had to add the fact that he directed films when they introduced him. Not like when they introduced E. F. Tyrell, his name was always accompanied by the information that he was a writer and that the host was sure the guests had all seen some of his films, and forever met with the standard retort that the person E. F. was talking to was not even aware that people actually *wrote* films. No no, Kaminski was simply introduced as Kaminski, because simply everyone had heard of Kaminski. Everyone except this amazing broad here with her amazing English accent. Up till recently, she'd probably thought

Kaminski was the name of a cheap automobile made in Poland.

At which point the great man himself entered. He stood for a moment in the doorway, and Georgiana looked up at him and smiled. E. F. watched from his sideline, fascinated.

'Good morning,' Georgiana said.

For Chrissake, you'd think this girl had just quoted something out of Keats or somebody the way Kaminski was looking at her. If he didn't know the man better, he'd have sworn Kaminski's heart was beating faster, although it was quite plain from the way the chick was handling him that hers most certainly wasn't, or if it was, she was too goddammed ladylike to show it. She'd just looked up at him once, then returned to idling through her book.

Georgiana sat between them in the back of Kaminski's chauffeur-driven Rolls. E. F. got the feeling that the young lady didn't think this was quite proper, for it meant that the sleeves of both his and Kaminski's jackets kept touching her bare arms, and once or twice when the car cornered slightly too fast she was thrown up against one of them, in the best Hollywood Romantic tradition. And every time she was forced to lean against one or other of them, she would apologise. Even so, E. F. had to admit she kept them well entertained by describing the house they were about to visit, its present occupants, its former occupants, its origins and its past history so deftly, that if E. F. was not mistaken, reading between the lines, she was relating to them about as much hard and soft porn as any successful author could ever hope to cram between one of his hard or soft covers. If E. F. was reading it right, the house originally had been a gift from a grateful nation to a very successful general. The successful general had a son who was a lousy soldier but great at pulling women. He'd pulled them so successfully that he'd contracted the clap and subsequently died from it, as a result of which the house passed to a cousin, who had married a girl who was really in love with someone else, and for a long time they had happily practised troilism until they had all dropped dead. The house had then passed to a gentleman who had been in love with one of his half-sisters, as a result of which he had gone mad, but not before he had been married off to a girl with an enormous fortune who had brought with her to the house all the fantastic gold plate on display in the State Dining Room. And so on until the present day, when it transpired the wife of the past incumbent had been able to reroof the entire house by courtesy, Georgiana hinted delicately, of her skills in the boudoir.

As the car drew up in front of the house, E. F. looked out at its magnificent façade. It was fantastic, he thought – the history of the place from the time the first brick was laid was purely pornographic. He was, however, greatly relieved to find the present incumbent of this famous house absent, for had she shown them round and not the estate manager, E. F. reckoned he would have found it difficult to be properly reverential about all her late husband's distinguished ancestors, knowing what he did about them. As it was he kept stopping and staring at every portrait, and looking at the subjects depicted on the canvases with new eyes, for beneath those robes and uniforms he now knew once beat the hearts of gangsters, murderers, homosexuals and troilists, and this was a great big eye-opener for a simple Boston Irish boy.

Kaminski looked at Georgiana as she walked beside him round the house, because being small she kept having to run to catch up with him, and this rather gave him the impression he was being escorted by a child. Occasionally, as she was telling him some new detail, she would look up at him anxiously, as if to reassure herself he was still there, or that he was listening. He grew more and more silent as she talked, because he wanted to remember every detail, not just of the house – he could return to the house any time he wished – but of her, for he now knew that running beside him was the very experience which he had not yet had, the unknown adventure he had suspected he had needed when he began his planning of the remake of the Bolst silent with E. F., namely that of having an affair

172

with someone who not only didn't want him yet, but quite possibly might not ever want him.

She walked round the grounds with them, and Kaminski took pictures while E. F. smoked and chewed gum. Kaminski took pictures of the house but not of the girl, E. F. noticed, rather as if he was afraid to try and capture her essence in a still, lest the very quality he was so arrested by might become frozen into an incongruous expression and distress him. E. F. found himself watching the girl more and more, because she did things that not even Bolst's totally unselfconscious heroine did, things born out of sheer pleasure, or childhood habit, or maybe because at that moment she imagined she was on her own and the two men were too busy to notice. She jumped in puddles. In all his long and weary life E. F. thought he never could have imagined the day when Kaminski would become fascinated by a girl who jumped in puddles when she thought nobody was looking. And Kaminski, whose past mistresses had been drawn from the constellation of stars, and who liked his women to be intelligent, and sophisticated, and erudite, and able to speak at least three languages, *and* mix a perfect martini, spent half an hour with this little girl rushing from one side of a bridge in the gardens of this great house playing some childish game with sticks.

There he was, the great international film director, seriously playing at whose stick would arrive on the water first the other side of the bridge. E. F. wished he could show all the serious cineastes this scene, instead of having to sit and watch it on his butt. He wondered what Kaminski was at? Maybe it was all for the film; but more certainly, knowing Kaminski, he was doing it because he wanted to lay her; but most, perhaps, because he couldn't help himself. As far as she was concerned, he who prided himself in such adventures on always being the Black Knight had in a matter of a few hours become the Black King to her White Queen. If E. F. had produced this as a storyline for Kaminski a couple of months ago he'd have had it chucked back at his head. But now here he was, playing childhood games and oblivious to anything and everything else around him. The simple hook in the story for the audience of one was now of course would she, or wouldn't she? All right, so nowadays everyone did it, with the possible exception of his Aunt Alice in Palm Springs, but this funny little girl could prove another exception to the rule. And if so, what would the great man do? And, what was much more imprtant to E. F., how could they continue to work on the picture if she didn't? He hated having to use his imagination; he far preferred to work from life and just lift it a little. But it could well be if she didn't want Kaminski, or if Kaminski couldn't break through the puddle-jumping, stick-racing barrier soon they would not get to first day of shooting, which meant no real money for E. F., which in turn meant hell from his wife Gloria, and when Gloria gave a man hell, boy, it was purgatory.

They had lunch in a local restaurant. She chose trout with almonds, and put a piece of lettuce over the fish's eyes, because she thought they were staring at her. E. F. had news for her; the fish wasn't the only one. Kaminski didn't take his eyes off her, but she didn't seem to notice. Kaminski took in every detail of that meal, and when she blew bubbles into her lemonade through her straw, E. F. wished Bolst could have been there to see it. Bolst's girl had danced, and made love, she had teased, and mocked, and loved, passing from one man to the next until her final experience which combined her greatest physical moment with her death, in what *Les Cahiers* had described as the final amoral statement in a life which had only one solution. She had not jumped in puddles, or blown bubbles with her straw, or asked a possible candidate for her bed if he didn't find his beard a little prickly in summer.

E. F. almost felt sorry for Kaminski, which was a far from normal feeling for him. He felt Kaminski was being mauled quite badly by his White Queen. For a Black Knight to find himself recast as the Black King, vulnerable to every move and helpless under constant attack must be terrifying. And yet he could see Kaminski was loving it, relishing every masochistic moment, and because he was, he was suddenly so apparently vulnerable.

Then they moved on to the second house, to Westington Manor, where the two men were once more treated to more ancestral details, although they were somewhat less sensational than the last set of details, as was the house itself. In the Long Gallery, Georgiana told them that old houses were lovely for children on rainy days because the wooden floors were good for racing across on tin trays, and that old rooms were better for hide and seek, as was old furniture. E. F., who had been brought up in a tenement block, believed her. He could easily have hated her for telling him about a childhood he had not experienced, but he did not; for although there was such a patrician air to everything she said, on the other hand the way she said it was almost melancholic, as if such childhoods were not the answer to everything.

E. F. did not have to ask Kaminski which house he favoured for they both knew the first one was the one they had been looking for. It had everything. It had the Palladian Style, it had the pictures, it had the furniture, and finally, darting in and out of the Romanesque pillars, sliding past the solemnity of it all on a metaphysical tin tray was their heroine, the sprite from the Bolst silent, with the same innocent force of destruction about her. And each time she slid past Kaminski it seemed to E. F. that she put out a hand, and that he put out a hand, but that she still always managed to stay just out of his reach.

Back in London, when they pulled up outside her cousin's house, Kaminski got out of the car and followed her to the door. E. F. watched as he spoke to her without hearing what they said, and he saw her smile at Kaminski, and he knew Kaminski wanted to be asked in but she was not going to allow it, and so Kaminski got back into the car and they returned to his apartment in silence.

'You dining with anyone in particular tonight?' he asked Kaminski when they arrived.

E. F. knew with whom he would like to have been

dining, and Kaminski knew that E. F. knew. Kaminski shook his head.

'Me neither,' said E. F. 'How about a session?'

A session was E. F.'s way of describing work. He saw Kaminski looking almost grateful for the suggestion. E. F. knew that with that Russian temperament of his, if he was left alone Kaminski would plunge into a black despair, so he suggested work because he knew at times like this it was the perfect antidote. Some men went to brothels, Kaminski cut open a new ream of cream paper.

Besides, if they worked, E. F. knew Kaminski could talk about the girl. They would call her Louise in the script, as they would call Kaminski Philippe, and this way Kaminski could tell E. F. exactly what he was feeling without embarrassment, and for once E. F. would listen without any of his customary derision.

Kaminski asked how Philippe would approach Louise. E. F. said because he had become obsessed with her so quickly, a man like Philippe, who was so used to having what he wanted when he wanted it, would approach her very directly. But how? Kaminski enquired thoughtfully. This was a very different kind of creature. E. F. told him a totally fictitious story of how a man he had once known had become similarly obsessed with a girl, so much so he'd started watching her house night and day, driving himself crazy with desire and frustration when he saw her returning home with other men, but unable to leave, until in the end she had had to let him in. Women were like that, E. F. told him. They always gave in. Louise was not a woman, Kaminski reminded him. She was a girl. E. F. shrugged and said girls were just women in the wings.

'Tell me why Philippe wants Louise that much,' Kaminski asked.

'That's easy,' said E. F. 'Because he hasn't had her. Or rather he thinks he can't have her. This guy's laid everything, so of course he wants this ridiculous creature who's coming on as if he doesn't even exist. It's classic.'

'Classic,' Kaminski repeated, nodding. 'Classic or classic cliché?'

'Oh come on, Kaminski! Classic classic! Like that goddammed house we saw today! That could have easily been just another grand house, but it wasn't. And why wasn't it? Because it's classic. And that's Louise's thing. She's so goddammed original she's no cliché.'

They worked on, E. F. watching Kaminski walk up and down, and up and down as he convinced himself of his own story, at the same time trying to subdue himself into a state of patience. He could not risk losing this girl, not just because he desired her but because she was their film. But the shape of the story, and its denouement – E. F. knew full well that all depended on how Philippe got to lay Louise. So sensing the great man's impatience, and knowing what depended on the outcome, E. F. suggested dinner. Kaminski declined the invitation, saying he wanted to work a little longer. E. F. left, knowing that Kaminski would not stay in the apartment. He knew him too well.

He knew Kaminski would let himself out of the apartment and would walk to her house, where he would stand in the shadows watching, hoping to get a glance of his Louise. And if by chance she returned home with another man, he would watch in an agony of desire, just as E. F. had described. If she asked the man escorting her in, Kaminski would stand in the shadows working himself into the required state of jealousy and passion. And then he would walk back to his apartment again, let himself in, and sit all night drinking on his own and wondering how patient he was going to have to be. The idea that the girl might be with another man would gnaw away at him, because once Kaminski set his needle to self-destruct, he was always pretty thorough. Then by morning again he would have worked himself into a sufficiently patient state to recommence working. That was Kaminski's way. It was not, however, E. F.'s way. E. F. was going off to dinner, and afterwards he was going to call that large woman who'd given him the come on at dinner last week.

chapter twelve

Georgiana had accepted an invitation to go to a Charity
Auction with Pemberton and Poppy, and since they were
now an established couple, she was able to do this without
any embarrassment. Besides, she was curious. She was
curious to see how Poppy looked, because even though
Pemberton was by no means her first lover, she knew that
to date he was her most regular. She didn't really think
about Pemberton himself or how she would feel when she
saw him because, since he had represented the first real
failure, he had completely ceased to interest her.

When Pemberton's butler showed her into the drawing
room, Georgiana discovered Poppy in her jeans and
Pemberton in evening dress. It was fairly obvious they
were having a quarrel.

'Just get away from me,' Poppy was saying to him as
Georgiana came in. 'Please just get away.'

'You cannot go in your jeans, Poppy!' Pemberton had
replied rather slowly. 'Look. Georgiana's wearing a
frock.'

He said it in just the same tone that Nanny Sydmouth
used to use when cajoling Poppy out of one of her 'turns'.
Neither of them paid any further attention to Georgiana,
so she sat on the sofa and daydreamed until one or the
other of the lovers decided to give in. She was well used
to Poppy's tantrums. When she was small she used to
throw plates and glasses if she didn't get her own way.
Georgiana rather hoped she wouldn't throw any of
Pemberton's stuff because it all looked rather good.

'You make me want to scream,' Poppy said to
Pemberton, who looked suitably affronted in a fairly
controlled sort of way.

Poppy then turned to address Georgiana for the first time.

'He makes me want to scream.'

Georgiana thought this was fair enough comment because Pemberton had had exactly the same effect on her. To allow Poppy to do so out of earshot she retired to the temporary peace of the cloakroom.

Pemberton sighed when she returned.

'Poppy is not coming,' he told her. 'We'll have to go on our own. Hope you don't mind.'

Georgiana did mind, she minded quite dreadfully, but of course she was far too polite to say so. She minded because standing there all alone with Pemberton in his drawing room she had suddenly realised how crushingly boring he was, and that the reason why Poppy was refusing to change out of her jeans, and had taken to painting nude murals in the loo was because she had come to exactly the same conclusion. Georgiana suddenly felt quite sorry for Poppy, being stuck with Pemberton but being quite unable to rid herself of him, because of course form required her first to find herself another lover before chucking Pemberton or it would look as if she had been chucked by him, and Poppy could never stand that.

On their way to the Auction, Pemberton moaned on and on about Poppy, complaining about how completely impossible she was, and Georgiana shut off, and thought instead about the day she had just spent with Kaminski. She realised he had been very taken with Stockton, the first house they had gone to, and that in all probability he would choose it, because it was everything he had described to Mary that he wanted. But she wasn't interested in what he wanted. Georgiana was only interested in what she wanted, and she wanted Longborough to be chosen for his film, so that Longborough would be done up and restored, and Georgiana would be able to stand in the house of her ancestors knowing that it lived again.

Had Kaminski been like Pemberton she would have known how to approach him, but he wasn't like

179

Pemberton, in fact he wasn't remotely like any man she'd ever met, because he was so serious. She felt daunted by the idea that if she wanted him to look at Longborough she would have to come right out and ask him directly, and she was afraid of asking anybody with such fierce eyes anything, let alone anything direct. She also baulked when she considered the reality of the situation, because taking him to Longborough would mean he would see the crumbling façade, and the broken glass in the Orangery, and she would have to take him to meet Nanny in the West Wing. It took all of her courage just to think about it.

The Charity Auction was immensely dull, and would have proved so even if one had never been to one before. Georgiana was bored and also a little embarrassed now to be seen with Pemberton but without Poppy, so it was a great relief when the ordeal was over and Pemberton dropped her back outside Mary's house. She knew Mary was out so she was planning to sneak down to the kitchen, steal a bowl of cereal and sit and finish the Barbara Cartland she was reading. Pemberton drove off in his Ferrari, and for a moment she stood to look up at the evening sky. On such nights she always used to stand out on the lawns at Longborough and stare into the universe, wondering what was to become of her, and whether she would ever be free of the smell of damp, and mice droppings, and the cobwebs and the holes in the roof; but tonight the few stars she could glimpse in the sky over London only reminded her of the diamonds she did not possess and made her suddenly melancholy.

A voice from behind her, from across the road suddenly interrupted her reverie. She turned and saw Kaminski standing below the street lamp opposite. She stared at him for a moment and then smiled, because she couldn't quite think of what else to do.

'How extraordinary,' she found herself saying, 'I've been thinking of you all evening.'

She immediately wondered what on earth had prompted her to say such a thing, because it sounded so forward.

Kaminski on the other hand made no reply, and just continued staring at her.

'It was such a nice day,' Georgiana added, by way of hopeless explanation.

'Who was that?' Kaminski suddenly asked, pointing in the direction of the now-departed Ferrari.

'Nobody,' said Georgiana, shrugging. 'Just my cousin's lover.'

Kaminski continued to stare at her, fascinated. He crossed the street and came and stood beside her.

'Have you got a lover?' he asked.

Georgiana couldn't understand for a moment why he should want to know and, because he looked so serious and intense, suddenly started to laugh.

'I want to know,' he persisted, putting a hand on her arm which stopped her from laughing.

'Have you got a lover?'

'No,' she replied, 'but I wish I did.'

Then suddenly for no reason known to herself, she put her hand up to his face and touched his beard. She had never before admitted to anyone that she needed a lover, and now that she had, she felt that they had already made love, such was the sudden intimacy of his question and her subsequent answer. She had not, however, been brought up to consider men such as Kaminski suitable as lovers, and now that she was standing there, touching his bearded face, she realised she had already gone too far, and she was frightened.

'Do you want to come to my apartment?' he asked her.

This was so direct that it made Georgiana momentarily quite breathless, as if he had just punched her, not opportuned her. She stared up at him, and felt an unfamiliar helplessness creep over her as if she was now out of control of her destiny, her life no longer a motor car with just herself at the wheel.

'I said do you want to come to my apartment?' he asked her once more.

Somewhere in the near distance, Georgiana could hear

the sound of Mary's Porsche arriving back from the dinner party she'd been to with Lucius. In a minute she would be drawing up at the kerb, Lucius beside her, and they would be patronising her as usual, and no doubt they would ask Mr Kaminski in for a drink, and send Georgiana down for the ice. She had no choice.

'Quickly,' she said. 'Now.'

She said it so softly for a moment Kaminski wondered whether he had heard her right. But there was no doubting the fact that she was running away from the house ahead of him in her pink dress, and as he ran after her he thought that if he were shooting this scene he would do it with an aerial shot, so that the camera could just follow the pink of her dress in the darkness, weaving in and out of the cars and the people.

Eventually, when she considered herself out of reach of the house, she stopped, and Kaminski hailed a taxi. In the cab she sat at the far corner of the seat away from him, staring out into the dark streets, and when they arrived at his apartment waited obediently while he paid it off and then followed him inside, into the lift, and up to his apartment where she stood waiting for him as if she knew exactly what was going to happen and was no longer in a position to do anything about it.

Georgiana was determined that this time she would not be as silly and as naive as she had been with Pemberton, and that she would try to be as sophisticated as possible. But perhaps because she was only nineteen she couldn't help feeling that she would really rather prefer to be sitting in a dressing gown in a nursery somewhere eating a bowl of Rice Crispies. She wondered what she should do next. She remembered a film she had seen once where the girl went into a next door room and changed into the man's dressing gown, and she thought that being a film director perhaps this would be what Mr Kaminski would expect her to do. So she looked surreptitiously out of the corner of her eye to try and spot where the bedroom and bathroom might be.

Kaminski sensed she was feeling lost, and so he went and poured himself a drink and let her find the scene.

'Would you like anything?' he asked her.

'As a matter of fact I would,' she replied, looking at him.

'Your customary lemonade with a straw perhaps?' he said.

'No,' she replied. 'As a matter of fact I would rather like a bowl of cereal. If you wouldn't mind.'

Kaminski went and fetched a bowl of cereal and reckoned that not even E. F. would have thought of that one. Philippe, on the point of seducing Louise, has to fetch her a bowl of cereal with the top of the milk. And most certainly neither of them would have thought that on Philippe's return Louise would be discovered standing, looking completely lost in his bath robe.

Kaminski sat and drank his scotch and watched her eat her cereal, as the owner of a new puppy might watch it having its first meal. E. F., he decided, was wrong. This was no sexual butterfly, at least not yet it wasn't. For a brief moment he almost felt guilty for desiring her, although she herself seemed fearless. And then she smiled and he really couldn't wait any longer, and only when he stood naked before her did her eyes seem to grow too large for her tiny face, and he just had time to admire the dark skin of his own body against the white of hers before they started to make love.

chapter thirteen

When Andrew Gillott awoke in the same bed as Mrs Parker-Jones, for a moment he could not quite believe that what had happened had indeed happened. He tried going back to sleep in the faint hope that it was all a terrible dream, but reawoke to find Clarissa standing beside the bed smiling at him, and dressed from head to toe in a purple mu-mu with matching towelling slippers. She gave him the *Sunday Telegraph*, then went and drew the curtains.

He looked at her back view as she tied the curtains neatly back and wanted desperately to cry. He wanted to cry and he wanted to run away, for the weekend was becoming even more like his first week at prep school, only he had the feeling that this time pinching himself hard and saying 'perspicacious' as Nanny had taught him to do would be of very little help. And it was pointless asking himself how it happened, he knew that full well, any more than asking oneself why one had fallen off one's horse. The answer was always the same. You or your horse had put a foot in a rabbit hole, except in this case Gillott got the uneasy feeling he had stuck both legs in the warren. It was perfectly horrendous. It wasn't that he was averse to being fixed up at weekends, or on house parties, because he quite welcomed such accommodation. What he resented was the feeling that on the previous evening he had not so much been fixed up as nailed, and completely against his will.

He looked at his bedmate. Clarissa smiled back at him brightly. Andrew shut his eyes. It was worse than looking at her mu-mu. She put a breakfast tray down on the bed and he looked blearily at the food. It was disgusting, the sort of breakfast he called boarding-house grub: cornflakes with white sugar, an overcooked fried egg, thin curling toast and the kind of tea which always has little clots of milk floating in it which one can never remove even with the edge of one's teaspoon. He hoped he had not foolishly promised to stay longer than the weekend, and then remembered doubtfuly there had been talk of a week. Next weekend now seemed about as far away as the last day of term always did on the first, when it seemed as if a life sentence stretched ahead, full of hideous certaines, like being shoe-blacked, or beaten up in the bogs. He would have to have lunch and tea and dinner with her every day, and because she didn't even keep horses, he'd never be able to escape her prattle for one minute. He would be forced to listen to her views on everything from socialism to herbaceous borders, until the urge to cut his throat would overcome him and he would be found dead one morning slumped over the vanity unit in the boys' bathroom. He knew this would inevitably be his fate, for she had from this morning on taken to calling him Andy, an appellation which he loathed even more than he could possibly say. He asked her not to, but she just smiled whimsically at him and stuffed some cornflakes in his mouth, an act which she obviously considered both naughty and sexy. Then she went and ran a bath for him and Andrew slid down between the Peter Jones matching bedsheets in deep despair.

As soon as she came back and took the tray off his bed and disappeared to give it to the kitchen, Andrew defied the pain in his head and leaping out of bed, made for the avocado-suited bathroom and locked himself in. It was the only place he was totally safe from the wretched woman, and Andrew determined upon taking more baths in the next few days than he had ever taken in six months. He stared at the towel she had carefully laid out for him, with the frightful double lettered monogram, and decided he would have to send himself an urgent message. It was the only answer. A long weekend would be bad enough, but the best part of a week would be inconceivable. He lowered his vast frame into the bath. The water was warm, and smelt of pine. They used to collect pine cones when they were children at Christmas, and paint them gold and silver and hang them on the tree. He ran the hot tap onto his foot by mistake and swore, which brought him some relief. He picked up the Sunday paper. At least she took the *Telegraph*.

When Mrs Parker-Jones returned and found the bed deserted, she remade it lovingly, with hospital corners as she had always been taught to do. She was getting the cover from the chair by the window when she saw Nigel

185

and Jennifer in the garden, walking towards the shrubbery. Jennifer was wearing a mini dress which personally Mrs Parker-Jones deplored, because it did nothing for her legs at all. But this morning the sight of it only helped to make her mood better than ever. It was nice to know that it wasn't only the mini-dressed brigades who could find love. She saw Jennifer put an arm round Nigel and pull him into the shrubbery. She hoped her daughter was not being too forward with this young man. It really didn't do to be too forward with young men, and most certainly her late father would never have approved of such behaviour. She knew it could only be for the best when her late husband's place was taken by another man, hopefully a suitably authoritative one, because young girls needed guidance since sadly they did not have the same respect for their mothers as they apparently did for their fathers. Only this morning for instance, she had detected a distinctly impertinent look on Jennifer's face when she had enquired as to whether she had had a good night, and she had giggled, which really was rather immature, and asked her the same question back in a way which was more than a little suggestive. It had not been at all nice.

Of course it was comforting that Jennifer did not have any private means, for no doubt judging from her present behaviour, her rank impertinence would have been even more in evidence. With Aidan's estate in her sole control, Clarissa could sell or pawn at her will. But unless her daughter took that impertinent look off her face she most certainly would not be passing any of the proceeds her way, of that she was quite certain.

They had just started Saturday lunch when the telephone rang for Andrew from Lord Pemberton. Andrew must return to London at once, although Lord Pemberton gave no clue as to the reason for the urgent summons.

Mrs Parker-Jones was devastated. What on earth could Lord Pemberton want at such short notice? And on a Saturday in London, in August? But she did not dare question Andrew because he had a closed look on his face, such as she had read about in books. She wondered perhaps if there was anything more to this wonderful man that she did not already know about. Perhaps he was employed on secret government work? Or perhaps he was as indispensable to Lord Pemberton as he had become to her? And although she was bitterly disappointed that he had to leave so soon, she quite understood that he must answer the summons, because Lord Pemberton lived in Chester Square, and had three estates, two of them in Yorkshire.

The worst aspect of his departure was not only the fact that he was leaving just as their relationship was beginning to flower along the lines Mrs Parker-Jones had so devoutly hoped that it would, but it meant she was going to have to spend the rest of the week watching her daughter throwing herself at Nigel Bruce-Smith in the faintly unattractive way she had recently developed. She wished Andrew could take Nigel back to town with him, but it was not something she found herself able to suggest, for so closed was the look on his face when she waved him goodbye that for a moment she thought he must be ill. However, he did solemnly promise to ring her that same evening, which was some consolation.

When Andrew reached London, the first thing he did was telephone Pemberton and thank him for his help. He really didn't know what had inspired him to ring Pemberton from the village Post Office and ask him to send the message, but he thought it must have been divine inspiration, because normally Pemberton would never have been anywhere near London at the weekend. In return for the favour he invited Pemberton to dine at his club that evening.

'Can't tell you what it meant, your man ringing,' Andrew explained to him as they sat perusing the menu. 'Must have been just like those poor sods felt when Mafeking was relieved.'

Pemberton nodded and continued to try and find something faintly attractive amongst the dishes advertised on the menu. He had a very strong desire for something tasty, for the months spent living with Poppy had been gastronomically disastrous. Poppy seemed to think that dinner either had to be taken out at some infernally noisy place where a chap couldn't hear himself order let alone think, or else had to be taken at home from a random mixture of sunflower seeds and half-cooked rice. It had taken him quite a while finally to shift her, but now she was gone at last. It hadn't been an easy matter, because Poppy came from the sort of family which would cut a chap stone dead for booting out the only daughter, and although Pemberton himself was not exactly inconsiderable, he did have a nervous disposition *au fond*, and the idea of having to spend one's time avoiding Sydmouths of varying kinds was enough to bring on his allergy.

As a matter of fact, in the end he thought he'd handled it really rather well, because he'd managed it without anyone, least of all Poppy, detecting him at it. It had come about through Pemberton selling off one of his fleet of motor cars, for the chap who was buying (a real goer with an enormous gold ring and a rather vicious Alsatian which sat chained up in the back of his Aston) had called at the house. Poppy had been in one of her very worst moods, insulting Pemberton's mother on the telephone, while pretending that she thought it perfectly acceptable to entertain lunch guests in her dressing gown.

From the look on her face when the chap arrived in his frightful light suit, Pemberton knew at once he was exactly what Poppy would want next, and so he'd play right into her hands. Pemberton asked the man to return the following evening with the money in cash, and then he'd left the car keys with Poppy and gone out, making sure that he did not arrive back until the small hours of the morning, and making sure that Poppy knew of it. This of course would be more than the bored Poppy could stand, and if she was going to sit around in her dressing gown all evening drinking, he knew she would ask the car dealer to join her, which of course is precisely what Poppy did, and things had developed quite nicely from there until the great day had dawned when Pemberton came home and found a note from the stupid bitch on the hall table.

Happy though he was at that moment, he was too much a man of the world not to have heeded the lesson it had taught him, and he vowed he would never again start an affair with someone so casually. In fact he confided to Andrew over dinner that he thought he most probably would never ever again start an affair.

'You'll feel different soon, old boy,' said Andrew, chucking a cutlet bone back into its dish. 'You're only feeling like this now because the silly bitch has just nipped you on the ankles. Always the way with women. You vow you'll have nothing more to do with them, and then damn me if you don't wake up the very next week in bed with one of 'em.'

He gave Pemberton a melancholy look, and Pemberton nodded. He felt sorry for Gillott. It wasn't his fault he was the younger son and had no money. In fact he knew he was even shorter of dibs than usual, because someone had told him Gillott had been gambling more than ever and with even less luck than was customary.

'Know what you should do,' he said to Andrew. 'You want to find yourself a rich widow. Only way out for you, you got to face it.'

Gillott was faintly appalled, but he knew Pemberton was right. The irony was that he couldn't explain to Pemberton that the vital message had helped him to flee from the very salvation Pemberton was recommending for him. The idea of having to settle for Clarissa Parker-Jones was too terrible to contemplate. and yet judging from the mountain of buff envelopes which greeted him on his return from Surrey, the uncontemplatable might yet indeed have to be contemplated.

'What about yourself?' he asked Pemberton, thinking that he might embarrass him slightly on the question of his not having yet produced an heir, and thus take the heat off himself for a while. 'Isn't it about time you got hitched and thought about producing the odd heir?'

Pemberton nodded.

'*Touché*,' he replied.

He then explained to Gillott why it was he was so

luckily in town when Gillott had chosen to telephone him for help. The decorators hadn't finished getting rid of the last traces of Poppy. He had them paint out all the erotica in the downstairs cloakroom straight away, because he could swear they'd been a major contributory factor in bringing on his mother's sudden stroke the month before. But they'd got a bit delayed redoing the kitchens, which Poppy had left in the most devilish mess, due to her habit of constantly sacking the staff and bringing in all these odd bods from agencies and so on, who'd pretended to clean, but in fact had spent all day smoking and drinking and reading his magazines, with the consequence that when she left his kitchens looked more like those of a large London hotel at the height of the season. Then he'd had to send for one of those frightful people who come and buy the contents of wardrobes when someone dies because Poppy had left all her stuff behind when she fled with her car dealer, after which he'd sent down for one of the finest clarets and drunk the whole bottle by himself in celebration.

'I tell you,' he said to Gillott in conclusion, 'by the time that car dealer chap's had her on the premises for a few weeks he's going to find one Alsatian's not enough. He's going to need a whole pack of the beasts.'

But Gillott was not one to be easily sidetracked, and deftly steered Pemberton back to the subject of his marriage lines.

'Yes, but what now, old boy?' he asked him.

'What now?' mused Pemberton. 'Marriage, I suppose. I'm not as young as I was, though I'm not as old as you, of course. But there's the name, do you see? Got to think of the name, so I suppose I've just got to get on with it.'

'My mother,' Pemberton said returning to the subject as they drank their port, 'thinks we need to add bone. Says as a family we've become too interbred. Says we need to add a bit of common.'

'Plenty of that about,' said Andrew, unstopping the decanter.

'You must know someone with a sister with a bit of

190

bone,' said Pemberton. 'I need someone nice and quiet with good wide hips, a nice smile, not much upstairs, and able to play the joanna to me in the evening. And keep a kneeler for gardening by the back door. You know the sort of thing.'

Andrew thought the sound of a woman with nice wide hips who kept a kneeler by the back door sounded perfectly frightful, but it really was not for him to say, because one man's meat was another man's whatever.

'Tell you what,' Pemberton said suddenly after his third glass, 'we could come to an agreement.'

'Don't be such an oaf, my dear chap,' Andrew replied. 'Wouldn't hear of it.'

'Be doing me quite a favour, you know,' said Pemberton. 'This business with Sydmouth's daughter's quite knocked the stuffing out of me, so far's the opposite sex are concerned. Couldn't you cast round a bit? You know – spy out the land? Be frightfully grateful.'

'Look,' said Andrew. 'I don't mind fleecing foreigners and the stupid bourgeoisie. But chums, no. Certainly I'll look around for you. But forget the fee. Wouldn't dream of it.'

'Silly bugger, Gillott,' said Pemberton. 'You know you're skint.'

'Skint I may be,' Andrew replied with as much massive dignity as he could muster. 'But broke I ain't.'

They then moved to more comfortable chairs in order to drink their brandy, and settled in to discuss the most recent equine news, since this was of consuming interest to them both, particularly since at Goodwood the form had been turned completely upside down, what with the horse that ran twenty-ninth in the Derby beating an odds-on Irish certainty, and a certain five-year-old handicapper trotting up in a canter after being unplaced in his last four outings and thus landing an enormous coup for one of Lambourn's best known betting stables. So thus the evening ended on a convivial note and both of them returned to their respective residences convinced that the world was a far better place than it had been four hours previously. Andrew felt that the task of finding a suitable bride could indeed be quite an interesting one, and Pemberton felt that now he had confided his problem to Gillott he could quite safely shelve it, so that whenever his mother brought up the business of his producing an heir, bringing out her beastly little 'begat' book, he would be able to tell her that everything was well and truly in hand, while he took himself around town enjoying himself more than he had been able to do so in the previous few months.

He knew now that Poppy had forced him into becoming the most dreadful bore, and when he thought about Georgiana he felt quite sorry for her, but he still could not consider her as a possible candidate for bridal honours, however impeccable her lineage, since he had never quite got over the way she ran away from him that famous night. And indeed had she not deserted him in such a thoroughly peremptory manner he would probably not have got himself embroiled with Poppy Sydmouth, so really if it came down to it, it was actually all Georgiana's fault in the first place, and if anyone should be paying to have his downstairs cloakroom redecorated it should be her and not him. He then took himself to bed feeling agreeably aggrieved, and with his conscience in quite satisfactory shape.

At the same time as Pemberton was brushing his teeth and slipping off his monogrammed slippers, Andrew Gillott was sorting through another pile of bills which had been placed on his desk by his cleaning lady during his absence and which he had therefore not noticed. Even without the benefit of one of those ghastly little pocket calculators which accountants and salesmen flourish eternally under one's nose the whole time now, Andrew was able to ready-reckon that things had got a little out of hand, even for him. It wasn't just his bookmakers, his wine merchants or even the car hire people. This time they all seemed to have it in for him, the butcher, the baker, the candlestick maker, the ruddy lot. And as for his telephone bill – it looked more like Pemberton's monthly income than the telephone bill for one rather weary old bachelor. Any minute now, he gathered, they were coming to cut the wretched thing off. But before they could it rang.

When Andrew heard who it was, he wished it had already been cut off. It was Clarissa Parker-Jones, his 'teddy-bear' from the night before. She wanted to know what Pemberton's problem had been and how he had been able to cope with it. She sounded anxious as if she thought he might be in deep trouble. Andrew kicked a pile of buff envelopes under a chair and thought he had news for her. He was in deep trouble. She wondered whether there was anything she could do for him. Andrew, staring at the dirty haircord on the floor, thought there was plenty she could do, judging from what he could remember of the previous night's events, but he wasn't sure that was quite what he wanted.

He dropped his voice to a confidential level and merely told her Pemberton needed him to talk over highly confidential matters. Clarissa was suitably impressed. She also hoped that the confidences might soon be shared. But Andrew, knowing his women, would never dream of telling her exactly what he and Pemberton had discussed, because knowing Clarissa Parker-Jones' conceit, she would doubtless push herself forward as the most likely candidate for bridal honours, and he'd be stuck with the embarrassing business of telling her she was far too long in the tooth.

Next she wished to know exactly how long it was going to take to solve Lord Pemberton's personal problems. Andrew's reply was deliberately evasive, because he wanted to keep the beastly woman down in Surrey as long as was possible, and if he told her he wasn't coming back down there to stay with her for the rest of the week, she'd be up to London like a flash tearing the clothes off him before he could say Tote Investors.

'Jennifer's behaving dreadfully,' she then informed him.

Andrew couldn't find it in his heart to blame the stupid girl. Surrey seemed to have that effect on everyone. It was worse than that it emerged. She was 'throwing herself' at Nigel Bruce-Smith.

'And now,' Clarissa added, 'now she's informed me she's hoping he's going to propose to her.'

At that moment, Andrew realised that things had gone too far. Nigel Bruce-Smith was a pimp, a gigolo. Not even Jennifer Parker-Jones deserved to get hitched to such a cad.

'Can't have that, I'm afraid,' he told Mrs Parker-Jones quite brusquely. 'Can't have that at all. Found out a great deal about that young man, and if I was you, I wouldn't have him in the house a minute longer. And I'd check the silver before he leaves, too.'

Clarissa Parker-Jones wanted to know at once exactly what he had found out, which Andrew knew of course she would. So he told her that a friend of Pemberton's had told him the creep took money to lay people's daughters. Clarissa Parker-Jones gasped. She was deeply bourgeois about such matters, and the very idea of it to her was so shocking it rendered her speechless, which was Andrew Gillott's most favourite state for her. He put down the telephone and knew that not only she but also Nigel Bruce-Smith would have a sleepless night, because there was no doubt about it, Clarissa would turn him out of her house as soon as she could find him. It was really quite cheering to think about, and so Andrew went to bed satisfied, having kicked yet another mound of freshly discovered buff envelopes under yet another chair.

chapter fourteen

Georgiana placed her hands over her eyes as she awoke, and stared through the shreds of pink light which filtered dimly through her fingers. She was wide awake, but she didn't want to open her eyes quite fully yet. She could feel the softness of the fur rug over her, and the cool of the black leather sofa against her bare skin, and distantly she could hear the sounds of early morning London as they drifted up to her, the clank of the milk cart and the soft cooing of the pigeons. And she could feel somebody watching her. And last night was not so far away that she didn't know that the somebody must be Kaminski.

She thought as she lay there that in a way it was actually quite surprising that it was Kaminski, for it had never occurred to her that he might desire her, but now that it was clear that he not only had desired her all last night, but might indeed desire her again quite soon, she thought it best to remove her hands from in front of her eyes and look at him. So she slid on to her tummy, and smiled at him. He stroked the top of her head, and then putting a hand to his beard, continued to watch her, and Georgiana gave a contented little sigh, and went back to thinking about the fact that she had now, officially as it were, run away from Mary's house, and that in a few hours time Mary would discover this, and would not know where to find her. This excited Georgiana, because she realised she might have done what she had always rather wanted to do, which was to cause a scandal. A small scandal admittedly, but enough of one to make it impossible for her to go back and live with Mary, and Mary would in turn realise just how ungrateful she was, and Lucius would have to find someone else to go and make his coffee whenever he wanted some.

It had been perfectly all right for Poppy to go off with Pemberton, but it would be very different when they found out about Georgiana and Kaminski, for Kaminski was a gypsy compared with Pemberton, and he had literally stood at her gate the night before, and she had run off with him. She yawned. Goodness, she felt hungry. Her night with Pemberton had not left her at all hungry, but Kaminski's lovemaking had left her famished. She looked at him and when she saw he was still watching her, moved nearer him under the rug. It was strange to have made love in someone's drawing room. She had not given much thought to which room people normally made love in, but she idly supposed it usually to be the bedroom, because she doubted that many people had very large and comfortable black leather sofa beds such as the one she was now lying on with Kaminski. In a way, he was her first real lover, for one couldn't count Pemberton and his paunch. She wondered what would happen to her next, and whether Kaminski would want her to stay. She knew that a lot of men apparently disliked having their women as permanent fixtures, and that they really only liked their women to stay when they wanted to make love, because Poppy had told her so. But while she would of course quite understand if he asked her to leave, she devoutly hoped it would not be until after they had had breakfast.

Watching Georgiana awaken, Kaminski was fascinated by her lack of any self-consciousness. He knew now that most of the women who had occupied his bed and his time up until now had just been ordinary women, for their first thoughts on wakening always concerned their hair, or their make-up, and they would confuse the issues of the night by telling him they loved him, and they would then insist on making and bringing him a breakfast which they liked but he didn't. This girl was different, for she had done none of these things, neither had she told him she loved him, nor demanded to know whether or not he loved her. She was it seemed devoid of sentiment, and knowing as he did now just how new love was to her, it made it even more surprising that she made no attempt to wrap it all up in the pink and white tulle of romance.

She now lay across him, suppressing the odd and occasional yawn, happy to wait for him to tell her what to do. And so he lifted her up gently onto the cushions, placing her carefully so that she looked decorative and so that her face caught the early light. Then putting on his bath robe, he went and made them both breakfast, the way he liked it, fresh orange juice, coffee and eggs, but for her he put a bowl of cereal on the tray. A few minutes later, watching her earnestly eating it up without looking at anything except the cereal in the bowl, he quite suddenly desired her again, so she carefully put down her unfinished cereal, and he put down his undrunk coffee.

That particular morning, E. F. was early for work. E. F. was never ever early, and Kaminski, who was feeling just a little tired, thought it was typical that E. F. who was usually late should be early, early enough to see Georgiana now fast asleep under the fur rug on the sofa, and early enough for Kaminski to have only just finished showering and dressing, and before he had either the time or the heart to wake her. She lay there with her cheek upon her hand in a sleep that was at once artful and artless. Kaminski put his finger to his lips as E. F. shouldered his way past Juanita in her surgical sandals, and then looked back down at the sleeping figure.

E. F. stopped in his tracks and stared at the scene before him. For him to say he was surprised he would have to accuse himself of underwriting the emotion of the moment, which was something for which E. F. was certainly not well known. Philippe had laid Louise already? He just couldn't believe it. He looked at the way Kaminski was looking at Georgiana and he saw that he was going to have a very good chance indeed this time of reaching the first day of shooting, for the great director was looking at the girl with the kind of tenderness he usually only reserved for his own inventions.

'So what is this?' E. F. hissed.

But Kaminski said nothing, and looked so impassive that E. F. realised he had to be in the middle of a close up on a long take.

'Come on, Kaminski,' he tried again. 'What is this?'

Kaminski did not bother with a reply, allowing a glance to suffice. He knew E. F. knew he would, so there was nothing more to say.

'Go on,' said E. F., because he wanted to hear every last moment of it. One minute the great man was following her round like a puppy, and the next minute he'd had her. That was quick, even for Kaminski.

Kaminski paused. It would have been easier for him to describe the past twelve hours to E. F. in cinematic terms, beginning with a close up of himself waiting in the shadows, then a long shot of the Ferrari arriving outside the house, another close up of himself watching the girl get out, then a cut to the other side of the car and a medium shot of the girl as she shut the door, then pushing in till he got close to her face, very close when she saw him waiting there, and then that sequence from above of her running down the street in her pink dress, and him just walking after her, and the taxi ride, and the arrival at the apartment. But he couldn't, because just reviewing it like that in his mind transported him back to the essence of the events themselves. So he told it directly and simply, like a story outline, although as detail he included the moment she had first touched his beard and said that she wanted a lover.

'Right,' said E. F., as always eager to categorise. 'She's a nympho.'

Kaminski sighed. E. F.'s view of women was that they all had to be either nuns or nymphomaniacs.

'No,' said Kaminski. 'No, she's not a nympho.'

'Okay, so she's a butterfly,' E. F. retorted. 'She's a sexual butterfly, just like Louise. And just like Louise she's searching for fulfilment through sex.'

'No, she's not,' said Kaminski. 'And she's not a sexual butterfly.'

He suddenly remembered her physical innocence, and if he had not always as a matter of course considered remorse a wasted emotion, he might have experienced a little of it.

Kaminski merely shrugged.

'Louise,' he said.

'Sure,' said E. F. 'I know this is Louise. But – I mean – for Chrissake.'

He looked down at the sofa bed. The girl looked at once virginal and abandoned. She suggested romance and promised fulfilment. She was the perfect study for a painter, or a director. And she was lying so still and motionless that for a moment E. F. thought perhaps her heart might have stopped and that she might already have met the same end as Louise, for he knew very well it was not just an idle rumour that Kaminski was a lover whom women found it hard to rival. He'd had to deal with far too many weeping damsels in distress not to know that. Kaminski might have problems in other areas, but not in the bedroom. His mistresses never forgot him, and because they were not able to forget him they never forgave him. E. F. had been able to acquire some very nice pickings from Kaminski's left overs because of this, for E. F. knew quite well that a handy shoulder to cry on was worth a good head start in the race to the bedroom.

But this one was different. He had never before walked in to start work – and early for once – to find Kaminski delaying their start because he didn't want to wake some girl he'd laid the night before. Even when on the previous evening they'd been kicking round the idea, he never imagined the scene would be quite so quickly realised. Kaminski beckoned him into the kitchen, and E. F. followed him in on tiptoes, which was not something E. F. was used to doing, just as he was quite unused to the sight of Kaminski making coffee for them both, and making sure the kitchen door was tight shut so that their voices did not waken the girl.

'Okay,' E. F. said after some small talk. 'So how did you manage it?'

He thought for a moment that Kaminski was going to clam up on him, because he had that funny look on his face which he normally reserved for the times he was just about to tell E. F. he needed a rewrite. Kaminski watched the coffee dripping through the filter before he answered. But E. F. was not impressed with the loaded silence, because he knew Kaminski had to tell him or they both had no picture.

'Come on,' E. F. urged. 'How did you do it?'

'I went to her house,' Kaminski replied. 'After you left me last night, I simply went to her house. I told you.'

'You mean you went and waited outside her house?' said E. F.

If E. F. had been sentimental he might have thought he detected a slight shift in Kaminski's attitude towards Louise that morning as they started their discussions. As it was, he simply thought Kaminski was holding out on him in order to make him work harder for his money, something he often did when things weren't going quite as smoothly as either of them wished.

'Girls like Louise, they're pretty stupid, right?' E. F. enquired.

Kaminski thought for a long moment before replying.

'Remember the girl in that Anouilh play?' he said. 'I forget her name, but at one point she tells how the old man who lives opposite watches her bathing every morning. And describes how they both take so much pleasure in it.'

'I remember,' said E. F. a little too quickly, which showed that he didn't.

'That girl's no more "stupid" than Louise is stupid. She's sensual, pagan, maybe even just generous.'

E. F. shrugged. This was all the rage, 'generosity'. Every Hollywood tart you read about had recently been described as being generous with her body. It was a fashionable euphemism, and it faintly depressed E. F. to hear Kaminski using it where normally he would be so much more direct. E. F. decided on another angle.

'I'm still not altogether sure why Philippe's so knocked out by this girl, besides the fact that she appears to elude him.'

Kaminski thought about this while he drank his third cup of black coffee.

'I told you yesterday,' he eventually replied. 'She's not like anyone else he's ever met.'

'Come on,' E. F. protested. 'What's she got – stripes or something?'

Kaminski returned to brooding. How could he possibly explain to E. F. something he knew E. F. could never understand, and wouldn't even want to understand? To E. F., love equalled sex, and sex you could buy, you could hire, or you could be given for free. To E. F. it meant something which released him from his wife, from his work, and it made him forget for a moment what a disappointment he was to the person who mattered to him most – himself. What it didn't do was ever involve his mind, except to work out the logistics of where, when and how. The difficulty for Kaminski was that to him sex was also sex, and the fact that he showed more discretion than E. F. as to how he went about getting it did not, he realised, make him really that much different from E. F., and therefore it would have been difficult at this moment to tell E. F. that he did not understand because that would be patronising, even though it was the truth. Besides, it was professionally necessary for E. F. at least to feel he understood why Philippe felt like this about Louise even though Kaminski knew he never really could, because E. F. had the kind of mentality which would dismiss Dante's Inferno as the fantasy of a pyromaniac.

It was difficult ground anyway, attempting to analyse the nature of love. Kaminski had always accepted that love could not really be properly evoked. Moments prior to love, and moments after it, maybe. But not the actual moment, that had to remain a mystery, because if one could retain it as a specific memory then it would no longer be necessary to rediscover the mystery. There was no point in discussing this aspect of love with E. F., for his understanding of love was purely physical, with the one single exception of a girl called Mary O'Brien, who had worked in his mother's café when E. F. was, as they say in Ireland, but a gossoon, back in Boston. Occasionally, with the help of his favourite scotch, E. F. would still bawl his eyes out for Mary O'Brien, for his father had got her pregnant, and she had died in childbirth. But besides her, there had been nobody else, and E. F. could only understand discussions about women in magazine terms. And so Kaminski saw that it would be better to leave aside any analysis of the metaphysical aspect of Philippe's affair with Louise, and change the subject to a discussion about locations.

He asked E. F. which of the two houses they had seen he considered best suited for their purposes.

'I told you,' E. F. replied. 'There's no contest. Number one has it. Christ, it's magnificent. It's got everything. Style, Classicism, class. I mean, Jesus, what a location for a love story.'

'Are we working in here this morning?' E. F. continued, looking round the kitchen and realising that a change of subject was indicated.

'You stay here for a moment, while I go and wake her,' Kaminski replied.

Then he pushed the kitchen door open quietly and went out, leaving E. F. whose curiosity needed no arousal, with an excellent vantage point from which he watched the fully dressed and dark bearded Kaminski lift a naked girl with pale skin from under a dark fur rug and carry her through to the bedroom.

A very good scene. E. F. thought to himself, and perfectly executed. Normally whenever he saw scenes like that shot, the girl being lifted was about fifty pounds overweight, or the actor doing the lifting was a faggot with no muscles and the whole thing had to be cheated. But this little girl was just a slip of a thing. And Kaminski had no trouble in lifting her. Kaminski would have had no trouble lifting up most women, for he was still in first-class shape, a condition he'd kept himself in since he was a young man working down the mines. There was nothing like a spell as a miner, thought E. F., for building up a guy's physique.

For the second time that day Georgiana awoke in strange surroundings, and as Kaminski pulled the sheets over her, she saw he was almost smiling at her. She went back to sleep, to a sleep made even sweeter by the knowledge that where she was was very naughty. She had run off with a gypsy and was all bare in his bed to prove it.

Kaminski returned to the drawing room, leaving the

202

bedroom door slightly ajar as you would for a child who had not yet quite fallen asleep. He glanced at E. F. who was settling his overweight frame on to the sofa, and hoped he would not have to endure the usual diatribe about E. F.'s sexual adventures of the previous night before starting work proper, for his own nocturnal adventure had only served to heighten his natural fastidiousness, and the thought of having to hear about E. F.'s fat woman was not something he looked forward to with any great pleasure. But he need not have worried, because the sight of Kaminski carrying the girl had driven all memories of the fat woman out of E. F.'s head, and he was only anxious to sit down and start straight in because that way E. F. knew he would find out all about it.

Kaminski went to the table and picked up the photographs Georgiana had brought him round to inspect when first he met her. He picked them up, then glanced through the half-open bedroom door at the figure now well asleep in the bed. He wished he could get rid of E. F..Not so as he could make love to her again, but just so that he could sit and watch her, as he had done earlier. It was not surprising that he found it impossible to describe to E. F. what Philippe felt for Louise, because what he himself felt at that moment for the girl in the bed was quite impossible to describe, and he suspected that the moment he could convey to E. F. exactly what these emotions were would be the moment they would be gone, and the girl in the bed would mean as much to him as his maid.

'I suppose she does belong somewhere,' E. F. remarked, seeing Kaminski staring through the door.

Kaminski did not reply, but just continued to stare. E. F. now felt vaguely irritated by her presence, and wished that Kaminski would tell her to get dressed and go home, or that he would ring her cousin or her aunt and tell them she was with him and that they would demand her instant return. No such luck. Kaminski had absolutely no intention of sending her home, neither had he of telephoning any of her relations to inform them of her whereabouts, and that she had run off with him the previous night.

'You know you can't run off with something like a Lady Georgiana Longborough, Kaminski,' he said half-heartedly, 'and not expect anyone not to notice.'

Kaminski did not understand what E. F. meant. Kaminski had not run off with her, she had run off with him. It was up to her to make her own arrangements, and if she didn't want to make any, that too was up to her. He said nothing of this to E. F. He simply ignored the interruption and continued the discussion about locations. E. F., however, refused to give up.

'You'll have Interpol here, Kaminski,' he persisted. 'It could prove embarrassing.'

But Kaminski now had that closed look on his face again, except this time it was his number five closed look, the one he always assumed whenever E. F.'s agent was trying to up his fee, and when Kaminski was determined to let E. F. know there were plenty of other writers around, and if his agent kept pestering him about money, one of those other writers would be sitting in E. F.'s chair the following day. E. F. knew this look of old, and he knew there was no point whatsoever in continuing to do battle with Kaminski when he was wearing this look. Kaminski was not just half Russian, he was half Tartar, and that, E. F. reckoned, was what produced the number five closed look. Anyway, why should he care if the stupid bastard got pilloried by the whole of British Society just because he was knocking off one of their élite offspring? Who cared? E. F. was there to do his job and write a story. He sat back on the sofa exhausted, and wished it was martini time already. So much headwork so early in the day was bad for the brain. And he roundly wished the sleeping beauty to hell, for now her presence was quite obviously a distraction, and not an inspiration.

The telephone rang and Kaminski answered it. E. F. for a moment thought the Cavalry had arrived, because apparently it was her ladyship's cousin making discreet enquiries as to whether Mr Kaminski had liked either of the houses he had just viewed. Kaminski kept his cool quite admirably, and if there was one thing E. F. admired about Kaminski, it was his cool. For having politely informed Lady Mary which of the houses interested him most, in the very same tone he told her that if she was worried about her cousin Georgiana she wasn't to be, because Georgiana was with him. At which point the great man replaced the receiver, and left E. F.'s imagination to run riot as he imagined the repercussions this piece of news would have on Lady Mary and her intimate circle.

Maybe she wouldn't mind, maybe she'd even be relieved. But one thing was quite certain, whatever she felt, she'd be letting an awful lot of people know that she didn't mind, or that she was relieved, or that she was neither. E. F. knew she'd be dialling all those telephones of hers at once if possible, and sending out messages like she was Western Union, and the whole of London would be hearing about her young cousin and this screwball film director before he and Kaminski were into their second martini.

Kaminski walked to the window and looked out of it.

'I think we won't work today after all,' he announced.

E. F. shrugged and put down his pencil. That was fine by him, enough had already happened to flesh out a bit more of the story line. So he welcomed the stoppage. He could ring his fat lady, and they could lunch in that noisy Italian café in Beauchamp Place, and after lunch he'd allow her to charm the pants off him.

As for Mary, she realised after she replaced the telephone that the sudden discovery one has been harbouring a serpent in one's bosom is a really quite agreeable sensation. She had begun to suspect that this might be the case, that Georgiana was but a viper in deb's clothing, but even so the final realisation still came as a bit of a shock. Naturally she rang her mother immediately, and although they had not been cordial to each other for some time now, as soon as the Countess heard how Georgiana had simply run off to this man's house, with not a word to Mary, and that Mary had not even had the courtesy of a call from her the next morning to tell her where she was, she agreed

205

that Mary had been most disgracefully and cruelly treated, and immediately rang off so that she could ring her friend Lavinia. Before she hung up, she told Mary that really she was not in the least surprised, because when Georgiana had stayed with her down at Clayton, she thought Georgiana was developing a rather sly manner, and had suspected that she had been planning something, because she spent all her time gardening.

Meanwhile, Georgiana slept quite dreamlessly, and Kaminski waited for her to wake. While he did, he listened to Rachmaninov's Piano Sonata No. 2 in B flat minor, because of course it fitted his mood quite perfectly. He suspected from her cousin's tone when she had learnt the whereabouts of Georgiana that Georgiana might, on waking, find herself forced to yield to her family's pressure, but in his heart he hoped she would stay. And yet he would not influence her, indeed he must not influence her decision, for to do so would be to destroy her purpose in his life.

As he listened to Horowitz, he wondered what her reaction would indeed be, whether she would yield to the family, or whether she would simply climb back into her pink dress, call a taxi, and disappear out of his life as abruptly as she had entered it. He watched her, and he listened to his music, and finally, since she showed no sign of waking and by now it was early afternoon, he wandered out to the shops and, defying the gods, he bought her clothes. He bought them in her tiny size, wondering what he could do with them if she didn't like them, because he knew no other girls as little as her. He bought her silk, and cashmere, and a great deal of underwear he judged she would not have worn before, for it was slightly out of her age bracket, and then he returned to his apartment and found the maid sitting on the bed.

He frowned at Juanita and indicated that he wished her to leave. Juanita smiled back at him. She approved of men as authoritative as Kaminski, and she also understood that such men should have young mistresses.

'What were you talking to the maid about?' Kaminski asked Georgiana after Juanita had gone.

'I wasn't talking to her about anything,' Georgiana replied quite truthfully. 'She was talking to me.'

Nonetheless, she understood at once that he did not like her talking to anybody else.

'Your cousin telephoned,' he told her.

Georgiana stared at the gift-wrapped boxes.

'I told her you were with me.'

She looked up at him and gave him her mischievous smile.

'Good,' she replied.

Kaminski pushed the boxes nearer her.

'These are for you,' he said.

Then he went to run her bath.

chapter fifteen

The news that Georgiana Longborough had run off with a film director was not long in reaching Mrs Parker-Jones, and it came as some comfort to her, for at least it meant she was not alone in her maternal cares. Her heart went out to poor Lady Mary and even to her mother the Countess, for although it was bad enough to have one's daughter leaving home the way Jennifer had, for someone to run off the way Georgiana had, just like that – and in the middle of the night with a man from show business – must come as a shock, even to the very best and bravest.

It was only to be expected of course that Jennifer's best friend Georgiana should behave like this towards her quite obviously caring relations, for Jennifer herself had behaved quite shockingly to her poor grieving mother, and no doubt the girls had encouraged each other in their wildness. Girls of that age were really quite insane and likely to do anything on the spur of the moment.

Everyone knew that, and what everyone also knew was that they always lived to regret it. Jennifer would live to regret leaving her mother like that, just as Georgiana Longborough would live to regret treating her poor cousin and aunt as she had. Time would tell, it always did, and Mrs Parker-Jones for one was quite happy to sit back and wait to see what a mess they were about to make of their lives.

Jennifer had left home for no better reason, if you please, than the information Mrs Parker-Jones had passed on to her about that gigolo Nigel Bruce-Smith's intentions towards her. No sooner had Mrs Parker-Jones informed her of the sort of creature he was, and that he took money for immoral purposes, than she had packed her bags and left 'Copyns', telling her mother that she never wanted to see her again just as if it was her fault and not that dreadful young man's. And later, when she had persuaded Andrew Gillott to write to her daughter and tell her directly himself what he knew, and that he had positive and written proof that this was how the young pimp made a living out of the Season, Jennifer had written back saying – and Mrs Parker-Jones felt really quite faint at the memory – saying that it only meant he was the same as Andrew. Mrs Parker-Jones shuddered to think what would have happened to her relationship with dear Andrew if the sweet man had not had such a wonderful sense of humour, for on receipt of Jennifer's most insulting letter, he merely threw back his head, laughed, and said '*touché*'. Which Mrs Parker-Jones considered to be so Christian and so broad-minded that it had served to increase her affection for him from three-fold to four-fold.

There were, however, worse things in store. For, following Jennifer's sudden and dramatic departure, came the news that she had not only taken to sharing a flat but she was also working somewhere in order to support herself, something which she had quite definitely not been brought up to do. Not even Mrs Parker-Jones had had a job, and her whole attitude to Jennifer's life had been

208

completely governed by the fact that she wanted her to have a better life than she had, and not end up slumming it, which she was undoubtedly doing. So all in all, when Mrs Parker-Jones learnt of Georgiana Longborough's misdemeanour, it gave her no little comfort.

John Pemberton also gained some comfort from the scandal, for it confirmed his fast-growing belief that Poppy and her cousin were both mad, which hardly surprised him since he had been told by someone at his club that both the Longboroughs and the Sydmouths were descended from the notorious heiress Meg Minchampton, who had brought insanity into both families – something which personally, after his experiences with the two girls, Pemberton had absolutely no trouble believing. Pemberton discussed this blot on their family escutcheons with Andrew Gillott over a game of backgammon, and Gillott agreed that there'd always been something a little touched about the Sydmouths. He also told Pemberton that apparently the Countess was being sent round by one and all in an attempt to get Georgiana to come to her senses, (that is if the girl had any, which personally Gillott doubted, and Pemberton without any trouble agreed).

'Just hope the poor bugger's got his armour on when she comes to call,' Andrew said, as he lost yet another fifty pounds to Pemberton.

Kaminski had put off working with E. F. for more than a few days by the time the Countess telephoned him and asked if she might call. He was not in the least surprised by the request, only curious as to what she might have to say. However, he decided to send Georgiana out for the morning, and keep E. F. with him, for he had not worked all these years in the film business without knowing the value of a witness.

He did not have to tell E. F. the reason for all the cancellations over the past few days, nor did he have to fill him in on the chain of events, because the cancelled working days were testimony to that. He also knew that E. F. would not remonstrate with him, because when they resumed working, the experiences Kaminski had just experienced would be more than ample recompense for the lost days. Of course he would not share everything with E. F., at least not verbally. He would not for instance dwell on her elusiveness, and the feeling he had that whatever he did to her or that they did together, she still managed to keep out of his arm's length. He had thought, at the beginning, that making love to her might mean he could solve his obsession with her, and that discovery might lead to *ennui*. But it hadn't. At least not yet.

That very first evening, when he had bathed her and dressed her in her new clothes, that would make a good sequence, he realised, shot in total silence, just as it had been in the original. Bolst had shot that sequence from outside, through the window glass, staying only on Louise's 'innocent' expression. But Kaminski thought that when the time came he too would shoot through the window glass but also from inside the room, so that you could see both of them and both of their expressions. Another scene E. F. would really enjoy, the scene where the girl makes the man up, putting him in one of her earrings and blackening his eyebrows. That was a scene E. F. would appreciate writing, and all the more for knowing that it had happened. Kaminski knew he would also enjoy it for another reason, because when he learnt of it E. F. would know that he wasn't the only man who became ludicrous in the hands of women. E. F. would particularly enjoy the moment when Louise laughs at Philippe. The script would record with undisguised glee the man just sitting there in his make-up being laughed at. But to earn his enjoyment, first E. F. had to bear witness to Kaminski's meeting with the Countess.

The Countess made her entrance suitably dressed in mauve, and E. F. had to admire her style, for she wore a small hat with a veil which covered the quite startling cool of her eyes. Kaminski extended his hand which she touched only briefly, and then they all sat down. E. F. merely received a brief nod. The Countess understood that Mr Kaminski had her niece staying with him?

Kaminski acknowledged that she was correct. The Countess understood that her niece had arrived at Mr Kaminski's a few days ago, apparently rather suddenly. Mr Kaminski agreed that this was exactly so. The Countess wondered if Mr Kaminski understood just how hot-headed her niece was and just what a mistake she was making, and whether Mr Kaminski realised she was only nineteen. Mr Kaminski replied that he well understood she was nineteen years old. The Countess then sighed and Kaminski nodded. The Countess said that she was herself no longer young, and was quite used to scandal, but that nonetheless her niece must be returned at once.

E. F. was enjoying this, and found this last part very funny, for it made the girl sound as if she were a parcel, or a borrowed article of clothing. But if Kaminski found it amusing, he certainly wasn't showing it.

'Mr Kaminski,' said the Countess, laying her gloves carefully on her lap. 'Gone are the days when a girl has any great need of a reputation, except in the case perhaps of Royalty, and even then not always. We both know that. But the fact is that my niece and you – it is just not suitable. And if the Press get hold of it, that would be boring. Very boring. Her mother certainly wouldn't like it.'

This was the first time Kaminski had heard Georgiana's parents mentioned, for he had not considered her to have any up until that moment. He felt disappointed, because the existence of parents posed a threat. Parents could take Georgiana away from him, and before he and E. F. had finished their first draft. Parents could point out far more effectively the unsuitability of such a relationship. Parents could prise her away from him.

The Countess continued. She did not, she said, have to tell Mr Kaminski that her niece was very strictly brought up, nor did she have to tell him that she was used, like all girls in her position, to obeying a certain set of rules. Kaminski knew this, he had known this from the start. But for the first time since the beginning of their relationship, for the very first time since he walked behind that running pink cloud, it was coming home to him that the end could well come long before he wished it.

E. F. was unaware of anything like this, and was merely enjoying witnessing a scene which he knew he would also later enjoy writing. It was gold, pure gold, with the Countess calmly bringing to bear hundreds of years of natural authority, against Kaminski who himself was no mean authoritarian. The Countess might be a Countess, but Kaminski was an Emperor. If a hack had been writing this scene, E. F. knew this was the moment when the bedroom door would have opened, and the girl would have appeared, half-naked and tousled, probably with a sheet wrapped round her, and the audience would then be invited to watch a tug of love. But not in this scenario, for as E. F. had been informed, the cause of this semi-royal confrontation was out shopping somewhere, wearing the elegant new clothes her lover had bought her, and choosing food for what she announced was to be a *fête champêtre*. E. F. also had some news for the Countess. He wanted to say to her if she thought she was used to having her own way, and watching people junp when she said jump, wait till she saw Kaminski. Kaminski could command silence out of mayhem, and mayhem out of silence. He could call up armies when he wanted them, and revolutions when he needed them. If he so desired he could make the Red Sea close back over the fugitives, and send Moses back up the mountain for a rewrite. The Countess was small beer. She might come from a background which had lasted for a thousand years, but Kaminski had lasted in films for over thirty, and in Hollywood terms, that was also a thousand.

'Mr Kaminski,' said the Countess with some finality, 'I do not think you understand me.'

E. F. noticed that people always said this when they meant the exact opposite. Kaminski had obviously also noted this, judging from his reply.

'On the contrary,' he said, 'I think I understand you very well.'

'In that case,' countered the Countess, 'I want you

to know that in my opinion you are acting with great irresponsibility.'

'Countess,' said Kaminski, 'you must appreciate your niece has not been abducted. My front door is open. Earlier this morning Georgiana walked out of here. It could be that she will not return.'

Clever, thought E. F. Very neat.

The Countess rose and walked to the door.

'I hope for my niece's sake, Mr Kaminski,' said the Countess, 'that she does not. But in the meantime, I have to tell you that I find your attitude most uncooperative.'

That came as no surprise to either of the men. The Countess was only echoing the complaints of producers down the years. Lack of cooperation was Kaminski's trade mark. It was like accusing a lion of having a roar.

The Countess, however, was not quite finished. Like all experienced directors, she saved her best shot until last.

'I believe you are hoping to film at either Stockton or Westington, Mr Kaminski,' she stated, deliberately not asking it as a question.

Kaminski assured her that this was indeed the case, and most probably Stockton.

The Countess put a hand on the door.

'Then perhaps it would be best if you understood that the owners of both of those houses are great personal friends of mine, and of course under the circumstances it would be quite impossible for them to even consider hiring their houses out to you for your film. And I'm afraid to say that would go for most of the other houses owned by friends of mine.'

She didn't even bother giving Kaminski one last look, E. F. noted with glee, but just turned, exited and was gone.

E. F. looked at Kaminski who was looking at the door.

'I get the feeling,' he said, 'we've just heard the sound of doors closing to us all over England.'

Kaminski said nothing but crossed to the double doors which opened out on to the small verandah which overlooked the street below. He was back in waiting, and if it had not been raining, E. F. knew he would have been out there on the balcony, watching for Georgiana's return. Instead, he just opened the French doors and watched the Countess' large car departing, and while he did so, E. F. made some important notes on the scene he had just witnessed.

Kaminski in his turn knew the chances were that Georgiana would not return. It was the first time she'd been out of his apartment since the evening she had arrived, and he imagined that once out there again in the streets she knew so well, and fully clothed for the first time in so many days, she might simply disappear on the same mad impulse which first brought her to him. He found himself wondering whether she was not after all just a sequence which he and E. F. had been working upon, and if that were so by now they should be having their customary martinis, so he returned inside and went and made the drinks.

Then they heard her voice in the hall thanking Juanita for helping her in with her things, and for Kaminski suddenly it was Christmas, and he had a kaleidoscope and he was looking at all the pretty little bits of coloured glass, and he could hear his father and his friends throwing their glasses into the fireplace, as he now was throwing his.

E. F. was throwing his when Georgiana came in.

'It's for luck,' E. F. explained to her.

From the look on Kaminski's face E. F. thought for a moment he was going to break every glass in the place, which he hoped he wouldn't because he was looking forward to at least one more martini.

The girl was changed. She had lost her uncertainty with Kaminski, but not her mischief. That was still there, and E. F. saw it was the mischief that had the great man so enthralled. But she'd changed all right. Kaminski cleverly hadn't kept her in the clothes that she'd first worn, that very English style. That had gone with the uncertainty, and E. F. saw, marvelling at Kaminski's taste, that he had recostumed her in clothes which were definitely a little too sophisticated, which made her look even more young and fragile, and which coupled with her insouciance, gave her the look of someone who had just escaped from school wearing her mother's clothes.

That took taste, E. F. thought, a great director's taste, and suddenly his mood turned from admiration to uncertainty as he realised, judging both from her return and the look on Kaminski's face, that they were going to be hard pressed to finish this script. For here she was, laying out a picnic on the carpet, as if they were out in a field somewhere, and pointing out to them that it was raining, and that they would have to put macintoshes on if they didn't want to get wet. E. F. saw any hopes of getting to first day's shooting, let alone first day of typing, fading very rapidly.

'Your aunt was here,' Kaminski said quite casually as they sat down to picnic.

E. F. watched for her reaction, which was interesting because she didn't have one. She carried on just as if nothing had been said, laying out the food, and unstopping the white wine.

'She wants you to go home,' continued Kaminski, obviously now used to her ways. 'She doesn't want you to stay here.'

Georgiana looked up from the picnic.

'What do you want me to do?' she asked Kaminski.

'For the moment,' he answered carefully, 'I want you to stay here.'

E. F. thought as propositions went that was the plainest he'd heard. But what a risk! He wasn't asking her to stay for as long as she wanted. He was asking her to stay for as long as he wanted, and no longer. After that, that was it, out. The impudence was amazing. So what was her answer? Nothing. She just put up a hand and gave Kaminski's beard a little tug, and then went on eating. Kaminski put his hands together in their praying position and sat back in his macintosh and stared at her. And E. F., in his macintosh, imagined that the rain seemed louder than ever, and he hadn't worked with Kaminski for all this time without knowing that he always used rain for his love scenes, and in that case it was obviously imperative for E. F. to finish up his picnic lunch and go.

chapter sixteen

Since Poppy Sydmouth had left Pemberton he had been in a state of mind comparable to a person who has recently contracted and recovered from a bad dose of 'flu, namely he was left in a mood which hovered between relief that the attack had passed and exhaustion due to the state the attack had left him in. To take his mind off how he felt, he cleared out several of his houses. He also made lists of things to do which he knew he did not want to do, and making the lists helped to confirm that he would never do them. His mother was getting on his nerves on top of everything, fraying any nerves that were left to be frayed after Poppy had finished with them. She told him he should take more time digesting his food, which depressed him inordinately, and she told him that he needed some new suits and was going thin on top.

She also told him she didn't think that his butler was up to much except things he shouldn't be up to, that the silver looked poor, and that it would be better not to have electricity to cook on. She informed him that in her opinion the valet service was overcharging him, that the fruit did not taste, that she couldn't understand a word the Portuguese cook said and that furthermore her bedroom was a silly shape. As a result Pemberton found himself spending more time outside his house than he had even when Poppy had moved into her mad phase and was wandering about the place in nothing but a body stocking and a pair of ballet shoes.

His appetite was also starting to fail him. He kept getting the sensation that he was eating cotton wool, which his mother blamed on the fact that the cook spoke no English, but which Pemberton took as yet another symptom of his fading appetite for life in general. Even his friends at the club seemed to have lost their zest, and looked more and more to him as if they also knew that they had, which they undoubtedly had. Few of them nowadays said anything remotely witty to him, and even fewer anything original, and he not only felt that he had heard all their stories before but, from the way they told them, that they had too.

He thought of becoming a great collector, except that he had no idea of what he wanted to collect, and so each week he found himself leafing through *Country Life* in the vain hope of finding something rare and beautiful which needed collecting and which would fill him with the desire indeed to do so; but perhaps because he already owned so much he found it difficult to differentiate between what was rare and what was ordinary. He had houses, he had horses, he had furniture, he had paintings, one of which was on permanent loan to a museum so he knew it must be pretty good; but what he did not have was any idea how to appreciate what he had got because it had all been inherited. He had simply gone into his father's business, and as an occupation that had about as much kick in it as the dinners the Portuguese cook prepared for him every evening.

And so he found himself all too frequently wandering the streets of London in the afternoons, resisting the impulse to fall asleep in a chair in his club, and quite able to resist any desire to return home. Sometimes he wandered into Harrods on the pretence that he needed some collar stiffeners, and sometimes he wandered into a cinema and pretended to watch a film, but they were far too often American, and he could never understand what the characters said to one another in American films. Once or twice he even found himself walking in the Park just near the Daisy Walk where his nanny had let him sit on a bench and talk to the other children provided he kept his socks clean. It was as if, now that he was older, he was reverting to his childhood ways, because he had grown tired of all his others. He would go to Harrods and travel up and down the 'moving stairs', as Nanny and he used to call them, or visit the toy shop where he had been allowed to buy balloons, and once he went to stare in Jackson's window in Piccadilly as he had when a child, only to find to his great consternation that Jacksons was no longer there. And he noticed that his choice in socks was getting paler and paler until very soon he would be wearing white again. He felt he was no longer in control of what he did. Rainy days meant museums and art galleries, and sunny days meant walks in the park. Since he was still nursing the idea of being a great collector, he often visited art galleries, and although most of the works he saw were modern, and although rather like American films he found them hard to understand, he continued to visit the galleries in the vague hope that a miracle might happen and he might one day see something he liked and wanted to buy.

One day he wandered into a small gallery which he had never visited before. The girl behind the desk stared at him as he came in and then, since he obviously looked quite lost, asked if she could help him. He looked at her and saw that she was a nice comfortable-looking girl with a round face, and that she wore a sensible suit and sensible shoes, the sort of outfit that a chap could see she'd have no difficulty in going for a good walk in.

'As a matter of fact there is something,' Pemberton had replied. 'I'd like to know if anybody ever buys this sort of stuff.'

He turned and pointed his umbrella round the gallery.

'I always maintain,' he continued, 'that I know everything about Art, but I don't know what I like. Which is what led me to wonder if anybody ever bought any of this stuff?'

The girl studied him quite seriously.

'That's very naughty of you,' she said.

Pemberton was quite surprised. It was a good few years since anyone had told him that he was naughty.

'Why? What's so naughty about that?' he asked.

'To point your umbrella round like that,' she said, 'and talk about people's paintings as "stuff".'

'Sorry,' said Pemberton. 'But I've seen rather a lot of this stuff lately, and I can't say I understand it.'

'That's quite probably because you haven't tried,' the girl said rather crossly, making the appreciation of art sound like a form of potty training.

'I have,' Pemberton replied. 'I've tried damn hard, I'll have you know. If you're meant to be selling it, perhaps you can make some sense of it for me.'

The girl sighed and looked at Pemberton as if he was an errant schoolboy.

'If you look at a sky at sunset,' she asked, 'do you "make sense of it"? If you look at fresh green grass, do you "make sense of it"?'

Pemberton was stumped. He'd never actually looked at a sunset for any length of time, or for any other purpose than to see if it augured well for the weather, and the same could be said for grass. He only looked at the grass to see if there was any goodness left in it for his horses.

'Don't get you, I'm afraid,' he replied. 'Don't get you at all.'

'Colour,' she patiently explained, 'can just be colour. It doesn't have to "make sense". It would be silly to expect it to.'

Pemberton wasn't really listening to her, but instead was looking at her. She had rather nice blue eyes which went with the colour of her blouse. Pemberton would have liked to have told her so, but ever since Poppy his social confidence had gone, and because he feared a rebuff, he put the subject of the colour of her eyes to one side and instead went for the blouse.

'I like the colour of your blouse,' he said suddenly. 'It's jolly nice.'

The girl blushed, and Pemberton liked that as well. He found it charming. Poppy never blushed. And Pemberton really rather liked a girl who could blush nicely. When he was a boy they had had a nursemaid called Marjorie, and she used to blush. He used to love to make her blush, particularly when there was a thunderstorm and she used to take him into her bed. He could never smell coal tar soap even now without thinking of Marjorie.

'I wasn't really talking about blouses,' said the girl slightly reprovingly.

'I know you weren't,' said Pemberton. 'But I was. How about coming out to dinner with me this evening?'

Jennifer blushed an even deeper shade of red and looked at the floor.

Of course this wasn't the first time she'd been asked out to dinner since she'd started working in the gallery, and she knew that one of the hazards of doing such a job was that men were inclined to treat you like the hat-check girl. But the idea of having dinner with someone who looked as if he could afford not just the hors d'oeuvre but the entrée and sweet as well was just mouthwatering. For the past few months since she had left home, she had lived on hardly anything more than thin white bread Marmite sandwiches, hot chocolate and tinned tomato soup. The diet had been rather enlarging, but life in a large draughty flat, with three other starving girls was no appetite suppressant, and lately mirages of what Jennifer called 'decent food' kept appearing in her imagination at not infrequent intervals.

'I'm sorry,' Jennifer said, her cheeks now ablaze with embarrassment, 'but I'm afraid I don't know your name.'

'I don't know yours,' said Pemberton, his social confidence returning. 'But that doesn't stop me from asking you out to dinner.'

'Jennifer Parker-Jones,' said Jennifer.

'Really?' said Pemberton, looking at her quite kindly. 'Well, we can always do something about that. Mine's John Pemberton.'

Jennifer now went an even deeper red, for she knew at once this was Georgiana's friend who had run off with her cousin Poppy. In fact she had met him all too briefly at Georgiana's cocktail party, but she could see he didn't remember her, which was not surprising because when they were introduced he was busy staring over her shoulder at Georgiana, and she most certainly wasn't going to remind him that she had been the rather fat girl in a rather nasty dress with a large bow on it. Nor was she going to be fool enough to tell him that she knew exactly who he was, for lately she had grown really rather tough, and she knew now that there were a great many things that were far better kept under your belt, and that other people kept a great many more things from you, and that money bought everything, including love. Besides, she rather liked John Pemberton. He wore nice clothes which didn't make you feel inferior or old fashioned, good sensible suits and shirts which were obviously hand-made, just like her father's had been.

'Where would you like to go for dinner?' he asked her when they got outside.

He hoped she wouldn't suggest one of those frightful Italian trattorias with rotten food and rude waiters, where even the napkins seemed to be made of pasta.

'I'd like to go to the Connaught,' she replied.

Pemberton could have proposed to her there and then. At last he had met a girl who wanted to eat somewhere decent.

'Good,' he said. 'I'll send my car for you. Where do you live?'

When she told him, and after he had written it down in a small pocketbook, he stared blankly at what he had written.

'Never heard of it,' he said.

'That's very rude,' said Jennifer.

'Sorry,' said Pemberton. 'Didn't mean it to be.'

Then he wished her goodbye for the moment, and walked back to his house in a state of great excitement. For the first time for a very long time he felt as if something nice was going to happen to him, and he thought it had everything to do with meeting a girl who wished to dine at the Connaught and who didn't mind confessing that she was hungry. That in itself was a rare and wonderful thing. Girls like Poppy never felt hungry. They went to gymnasiums and every now and then ate a handful of raisins. When he got home he went straight up to his room and locked his door, so that his mother could not disturb him. He thought he would lie down on his bed, have a good sleep and wake up with a good appetite for the evening ahead. But first of all he rang his chauffeur on the intercom and instructed him to pick up Miss Parker-Jones at her rather odd-sounding address at seven o'clock on the dot.

At three minutes past seven o'clock, Jennifer climbed into the back of Pemberton's Rolls and settled back contentedly. She had always liked the way motor cars such as Pemberton's smelt of leather and expensive cigars and now, finding herself back in the atmosphere which had been so familiar to her as a child, she realised she did not ever want to leave it again. Living as a single girl in London without any private income was an unattractive, toughening way of life, and having let it toughen her into adulthood she thought now might be the time to give it up. Not that she intended ever speaking to her mother again, or to people such as Nigel Bruce-Smith whom she now knew did not like her for herself, but she could see that Pemberton had not the vaguest idea who she was when he had asked her out, and that was reassuring. Also, because he was very rich she need have no fear that he was being paid to do so.

Sitting across the table from him later at the Connaught, she realised that although he was middle-aged he was handsome, and he had such an easy way with everyone it was obvious everyone liked him, even Georgiana's rather crusty old aunt, who was dining with friends at the next-door table.

'Heard about Georgiana Longborough, have you?' Pemberton asked Jennifer half-way through the meal. 'Run off with some film bod. No one's speaking to her, you know.'

Jennifer had not heard it from Georgiana, but she had

heard about her. Eveyone had, because it had been in the *Daily Mail* only a few days before.

'Course they're all as mad as March hares, that lot,' Pemberton confided in her. 'The Longboroughs, the Sydmouths. All as mad as March hares. Got this bad cross, don't you know. Mad Meg. Expect you've heard of her?'

'No,' said Jennifer, and ordered some pudding.

Pemberton told her the story while Jennifer ate her way through a good sensible-sized helping of pudding, and as he talked to her, the memory of his recent conversation came back to him, for he found himself talking to a girl who not only was not even distantly related to Mad Meg, but who from looking at her undoubtedly had bone. If she'd been a horse, he would have described her as classic hunter-type, go all day in the field, jump anything, then come home and mop up all her grub, as she was doing now, and no more would be heard of her till morning. A damn good doer all round. Pemberton had great affection for the classic hunter-type. You knew where you were with them. Not like those nonsensical arab-types, with their dashing from one water hole to the next as if their lives depended on it. Poppy had been one of those, and one was quite enough for any man, thank you.

After dinner they had coffee, Jennifer had a Cointreau, and Pemberton had a pale fine champagne cognac. He was not a snob, because he had no need to be, but even so he had been comforted to see that Jennifer had appreciated the wine over dinner and not gulped it down as if it was spa water, like some of the girls he'd taken out just recently had. And now, as they sat talking comfortably to each other, from the way they were getting on together Pemberton thought they could have known each other for ages.

Of course his mother would not approve of her. She'd get out her wretched little 'begat' book, and look her up and find her nowhere. He'd have a hard time there, of that there was no doubt. But he knew a great deal more about breeding than his mother did, and he knew if he'd made the mistake when he was younger, as a lot of his friends had, of marrying some thoroughbred filly, the chances were that with his blood lines they'd have produced a squib. He didn't have an overdeveloped sense of duty, but he had enough to know that that would have been a pity; after all the hundreds of years of careful breeding that had gone into producing him, and from careful study of his family tree, he felt sure that it was due to the judicious adding of a bit of common every now and then that he was as sane as he was today. Not that he relished the idea of a loveless marriage such as his parents had enjoyed, but he did like the idea of combining his own predilection with a sense of family duty, and looking at the size of Jennifer's wrists, he felt that with her this was eminently possible. He certainly had no intention of forming a marriage alliance with families such as the Sydmouths or the Longboroughs. That would be something his bookmaker would give him a thousand to one against, and even then the odds would be cramped.

Pemberton's mother was still awake when he returned, as he knew she would be. He tried to creep past her door, but she heard him and called him in. He went into her bedroom and found her sitting, as usual, propped up in bed with the latest *roman à clef* in hands whitened against the lace sheet protector, and head whitened against the cream lace sham, the whole effect being ruined as always by the lipstick-smeared cigarette smouldering in the ash tray.

She was not in a good mood. But then, as Pemberton reminded himself, lowering himself onto her bed, nowadays she never was in a good mood.

'You realise what time it is?' she asked him, as if he was still fifteen.

Pemberton knew well what time it was. It was one of his stronger points, for he had a collection of very expensive watches to help him keep an eye on time's winged chariots. He also knew how late it was, and just hoped

224

to himself that it was not already too late for him or for his heirs, because he knew he must rid himself somehow of this positively Volumnian figure before it got to the point where he himself would meet some unheroic end brought about by sheer despondency. In his mother's presence he had no stature. He had no age, he had no position. And as long as she was still alive, in any of his many houses, he would have no peace, and for him she would be a far more intimidating figure than any old man with a long white beard and a sickle.

Being near her chilled him, and he longed to see her once more as he had used to see her as a boy, a figure distant down the railway platform as the school train left for St Timothy's. And now tonight the chance to escape had arrived, because he had found someone who once again gave him undemanding warmth like a nursery fire, and who he was sure would let him sit in old slippers and toast metaphorical muffins, only this time no one would be taking him from her as they had taken him from Marjorie. This time there would be no school train, no tear-soaked pillows, but just endless bundling, as Marjorie used to call it.

He nonetheless kissed his mother dutifully on the cheek. She in turn did not move her face at all, but simply embraced the air beside his ear with her brilliant lips.

'Goodnight,' she said.

Having dutifully visited her to wish goodnight, and having dutifully kissed her, Pemberton now dutifully left her bedroom, hating her all the while. She had almost spoiled his day, as she almost always managed to spoil everything. He remembered how when he once won a cup on Sports Day she had told him she was not surprised, for as she was always telling him, he could do anything if he tried. No wonder he had put off getting married for so long. This loveless woman who was his mother had been a stern warning against that most unholy state. She considered life to be intolerable, and was determined to make everyone else's life as intolerable as her own. But this time Pemberton was determined that she should not succeed, his classic hunter-type would see to that. Already even her name 'Jennifer' seemed to have a special ring to it. He whispered it to himself as he walked away from his mother's bedroom, and the repetition of the name seemed to negate the malevolence within the room he had just left.

Jennifer lay in her bed thinking over her evening with Pemberton. It had been a great success from all points of view. She had eaten well for the first time in many months, and she had felt happy and relaxed at the same time. The torments and tensions which had been brought about by her love for Nigel had finally receded, and the dismay she had felt on making the discovery that all the time he was being paid to take her out had vanished. Sitting opposite Pemberton as they ate their way quietly through dinner, she knew that he was thinking of her in a more permanent light, for they had established an immediate cosiness between them which for her part Jennifer had not felt since she had sat upon her father's knee and slid marmalade fingers down his trouser legs. No doubt they would get to know each other better, but she very much hoped they would be able to maintain this state of cosy warmth between them, despite the minor inconveniences of running five houses and three estates.

She knew Pemberton could give her the security she so badly needed now that her father was gone, and she could produce the children he needed, but not before she had obliged him to send round his Rolls or drive himself round in his Ferrari to her flat many times, for the lesson she had learnt both at her mother's and at Nigel's hands had made her realise that nothing that was not hard won was treasured. She would not do anything so foolish as to make Pemberton frantically jealous, for he was too middle-aged for that to be good for him, but she would make him pant a little as he climbed the mountain towards marriage, so that he would not be deceived into thinking that he was a bargain, just because he was rich.

At the same time Pemberton was lying in his bed and

wondering what he could do to rid himself of his mother. Her immediate exodus from his life was no longer just rather necessary, it was utterly imperative. He wondered whether the sudden discovery of death watch beetle in the house might not drive her away, for she hated the presence of workmen, but then he realised she would simply take refuge in another of his houses. Then he thought he might pretend he had to go away. Once he was out of the house, he would merely move into his club; since his mother rarely went out nowadays it would be perfectly possible for him to live at his club undetected by her. Then he remembered how boring he had been finding all his fellow club members of late, so he rejected that plan as well. Perhaps he might contract something highly infectious, which it would not be a good idea for her to nurse? But then he remembered that as far as he knew he'd had all those sort of things as a boy, and he couldn't imagine what this mythical disease could possibly be, and in desperation he finally fell asleep pushing her off a first floor balcony which, while highly improbable, at least enabled him to fall into happy repose.

As it was of course, the next day his mother was still very much in evidence, so instead of inviting Jennifer round for a drink, Pemberton telephoned her and arranged to meet her at her flat, a suggestion with which Jennifer was only too delighted to concur, for she was already planning exactly the same sort of move. She had already determined that Pemberton should have no illusions about the exact state of her circumstances.

And that evening, when Pemberton arrived finally at her flat, having lost himself at least half a dozen times while trying to find it, he was determined not be shocked. When younger he himself had lived for a while in a flat, during what he liked to refer to as his 'bumming around period', although it wasn't quite the sort of flat in which he found himself now, nor indeed had his flat been located anywhere near the area of London which he had had to search out so thoroughly in his A-Z. It was an amazingly uncomfortable and cheerless apartment, full of large and uncomfortable pieces of furniture. Even the table where his drink now stood wobbled desperately every time one picked up or put down one's glass, and under Jennifer's strict eye Pemberton was having a lot of trouble not spilling the quite frightful beverage which Jennifer had just poured him. But he wasn't fool enough not to know that he was on trial, that she was challenging him to complain, or to be so appalled he would drop her, or not see her again after a few dates, and rather than this deterring him, he found himself admiring her guts. He was being asked to jump through a set of hoops. For once in his life it was he who was undergoing examination to see if he was up to the mark – rather like a three-day eventer before the final phase – and not, as usually was the case, vice versa. Naturally this enamoured him even more with the girl.

Since his mother no longer ventured out in London except for the odd chauffeur-driven visit to Harrods and the haberdashery counter, it was perfectly possible for Pemberton to undergo his trials in secrecy, for he had become determined that nothing should interfere with his wooing of Jennifer. He knew Society too well, and while he had been perfectly prepared to be the gay dog for as long as it suited him, now that he had decided on making a late marriage for the sake of his descendants, he was determined to do it in privacy. Besides, all too often he had seen chums of his at the club out of their minds over some woman or other but minding their own business and going along their own way, having their future happiness wrecked as soon as their friends found out about their love-sick state. They would all seek out the poor unfortunate woman, and then report back in chorus that they considered her too thin or too fat, badly bred or badly overbred, frigid or loose, too tall or too short, and before the poor chaps knew what was happening, they found themselves calling the whole business off. It just wouldn't do, and Pemberton felt far too deeply for Jennifer to allow that to happen. She was just what he had been looking for, and he wasn't going to let any friend of his go and stick his nose into his affair and ruin it, not even poor old Gillott, fond as he was of the silly bugger.

It was for this very reason that Pemberton let Andrew keep popping round with suggestions of possible future Lady Pembertons. Over a large tumbler of Pemberton's best malt, he'd shove old copies of the *Tatler* under his host's nose with red rings round various photographs, and list the women's assets, physical and financial, often in front of Pemberton's mother who took a great interest. It all added spice to Pemberton's secret affair, which was already going wonderfully, since Jennifer was by now giving him quite a stiff time. Plenty of kissing and cuddling, but strictly nothing more. Normally of course, this sort of thing would brown Pemberton off, and whenever girls had tried this on him before, they'd got pretty short shrift. But Jennifer was different, because he wanted to marry Jennifer. And since it was pretty obvious from the strict way she dealt with him that she was keen on him too, it wouldn't be long before he summoned up his courage and popped the question.

Once or twice at the club, after the port, he'd felt tempted to tell old Gillott about his feelings for Jennifer, but happily thought twice about it and never did, mainly because one of Jennifer's greatest concerns was for privacy, which amused him no end. She seemed almost embarrassed by the fact that the seventh Marquis of Pemberton was wooing her so ardently and persistently. She would ask him to park his Ferrari round the corner from her flat so that her flat-mates would not see it. She would make sure he called only when the other girls were out, and she would only go and see him in the country if she was allowed to travel down on the train by herself, and return to London the same day. Pemberton found this most refreshing after years spent being pursued by girls whose eyes literally lit up when they learnt the size of his estates, and who only wanted to leave their various houses or flats when everyone else could see who was picking them up. Sometimes when they were alone, which they nearly always were when they were not dining, Jennifer would call him John, or sometimes 'Naughty Pember' which he both loved and preferred, and sometimes she would call him 'Duke', apparently after John Wayne, because she said he reminded her of him. This simple intimacy greatly improved Pemberton's state of mind, which satisfied Jennifer, as she had told him she considered that he needed 'elevating'.

So finally when he did propose and she accepted him, sitting by the wishing well in the garden of his favourite house, Pemberton thought he had never known such happiness. He was also greatly relieved, for much as he had tried to pretend that a refusal to his proposal was impossible, deep down he knew from the dance she had led him that it was in fact very much on, and the chances were fairly even that he might lose his new found Marjorie. The notion was quite appalling to him, for he knew now that a return to his old life would be out of the question. The days of Poppy Sydmouth were a nightmare when compared to the time he had spent with this warm and gentle person.

'Since you're sitting by a wishing well,' he said, shortly after she had accepted him, 'I suppose you really ought to make a wish.'

Jennifer looked at him thoughtfully. She knew he wasn't going to be everything she had always wished for, but he had quite enough of what she wanted to make them both happy, and because of this she thought she could manage him quite successfully. So she shut her eyes and wished.

'I wish, I wish, I wish,' she wished, 'I wish that we could get married quietly, and live here without seeing anyone for as long as we both wanted.'

Pemberton sighed, more deeply than he had ever sighed before. She was magnificent, quite magnificent. Not only a girl in a million, but a girl in fifty million. Imagine – she would rather no Guards Chapel and white tulle, no wrangling mothers, no beastly cake that no one can ever get their teeth into (or sometimes out of) and no confetti

230

in the boot of the Rolls which even the best of chauffeurs took months to remove. Just himself, and herself. Pemberton felt a lump rising to his throat, and his eyes began to tingle.

'From now on,' he said huskily, 'what is mine is yours.'

'Naughty Pember,' said Jennifer, pinching his cheeks, 'you know you'd have to ask your trustees.'

'Not to get married I don't,' he replied.

Jennifer slipped her arm through his as they walked back up to the house. Things were going to be even easier than she had dared hope, she thought, because if he had said no to her idea of a quiet wedding and insisted on the full and proper business, it would have meant that she would never really be able to get Pemberton out of the clutches of that frightful old mother of his. But as it happened, she'd been able to get him to agree without a struggle, and so from now on she was quite certain that it would be plain sailing with any other decisions she might wish to make.

For instance, she didn't really like the informality of the gardens through which they were presently strolling. She knew they had been planned by somebody famous to look like a landscape, but they weren't really the sort of gardens she enjoyed. She didn't like just rolling lawns and large trees, she would far prefer to see lots of neat round rose beds such as her father always favoured. And she would like to have a nice rockery somewhere, and a wooden summerhouse where she and Pember could enjoy tea together. And that was only the tip of the iceberg, because the house itself needed a great deal of work done inside. The hall seemed dreadfully cold and uninviting with its plain walls and flagstoned floor. It would be greatly cheered, she thought, by a red flocked wallpaper, or perhaps even a nice floral patterned one, with large roses on it. And she had already planned what would be his suite and her suite to be done in a nice mix'n'match fabric and paper, and their two bathrooms would have corner baths with gold dolphin-shaped fittings. She looked at her future husband and squeezed his arm. She was going to make him so happy. Then she noticed his feet as they reached the steps of the house.

'Oh naughty Pember,' she said reproachfully. 'Wearing our best shoes in the garden.'

Pemberton sighed happily. She was quite, quite irresistible, and she was all his. For the first time since he was a boy, he was a happy man.

chapter seventeen

The Countess looked at her accounts, which she kept in code at the back of a small leather diary, which in turn she kept locked up in her wall safe, for she never trusted staff not to read what they could when they could. According to the figures the Season had been a moderate financial success as far as the hire of her ballroom had gone, and as far as the distribution had also gone of her privately printed book containing all the essential information aspiring mothers-in-law to the nobility need to know. But of course it had been a dismal failure as far as her family was concerned, and this she felt deeply.

Georgiana had made an ass of herself, and what was worse she had done it in public, and now there was no course open to her but to do whatever she had to do in the full view of the entire world, which was horrid. The Countess hated publicity, except of the very discreet kind which simply stated one had been to a wedding or a private view. Not the kind that allowed every Tom, Dick and Harry to know what one was doing and who one was doing it with. That was not at all the thing. Then there was this business of Mary going to live abroad, just because that dreadful little American she had hanging on her coat tails wanted to write his book, so nothing would do except for her to go and live on Capri with him, and look after him while he typed out his beastly little memoirs of a London Season, which would undoubtedly be full of thinly disguised people purporting not to be the people they actually were, which really was of very little interest because she was quite sure nobody would buy the wretched thing anyway.

And then there was this irritating business of Andrew Gillott owing her money, and that *was* irritating because he had owed it to her for so long. It wasn't that the Countess was mean, she just liked to keep things square, which was not one of Andrew's particular predilections as she knew very well, for he appeared to spend the whole time robbing Peter to pay Paul, or more precisely the banker to pay the bookmaker. She knew the only course open to him now was to marry, because if he did not marry he would very soon end up exiled on some remote Greek island, waiting once a week for the delivery of back numbers of the *Telegraph* which she knew would not suit him at all, for she certainly couldn't imagine how Andrew could possibly manage from day to day knowing that the rest of the world knew the results from Epsom, Newbury and Sandown and that he didn't.

The Countess realised there would be little point in dropping a delicate hint to Andrew for he simply wouldn't notice, any more than he would notice a change in the weather unless it was bad enough to cause a radical change in the going. She therefore decided to summon him round, give him a very large drink and tell him in the only terms he would understand – namely, those an officer would use to men about to go over the top:

'You're going to have to get married, old boy,' she said.

Andrew looked at the Countess, and then drank quite a lot of his drink. Unfortunately, he knew she was right, for only that morning yet another batch of buff envelopes had arrived threatening all sorts of procedures and penalties if he continued to refuse to pay. In reality he had known it for quite a long time, which was probably why he'd been going to so much trouble to find a suitable bride for his friend Pemberton, because truth to tell he'd really been sizing up the field for himself. The only difference was that in his case he knew that half the fillies he'd recommended to Pemberton wouldn't look twice at him, even if he'd sprung from Nearco himself. Pemberton was all right. He was so well-heeled he only had to glance in their direction and they'd rush at him. Andrew Gillott was not in the same league, and he knew it.

'I'm not exactly what you'd call a bargain, you know,' he replied to the Countess. 'I haven't a bean, and I don't like women.'

'Don't be so silly,' the Countess said. 'No men like women. Men only like each other, while women hate each other and only like men. Which is why there's such a necessity for Society.'

'Nevertheless,' Andrew said, 'you know what I mean.'

'And you know what I mean,' said the Countess. 'What about that beastly little woman?'

'Which beastly little woman?' faltered Andrew, suspecting he knew her identity.

'That beastly common little woman,' replied the Countess.

Andrew groaned.

'I couldn't,' he protested.

'You're going to have to, old boy,' the Countess persisted. 'It's either her or the workhouse.'

'You have no idea what she's like,' said Andrew miserably.

'There's a lot to be said for marriage,' the Countess continued, ignoring his protest. 'Just because it makes people miserable doesn't mean it isn't good for them, you know. She'll drive you mad, but she'll put up with you, and that's exactly what you need. Someone who'll put up with you. Got a lot to recommend it.'

'She's got a house in Surrey called something frightful,' Andrew moaned. 'And she wears purple gowns when she brings you breakfast. You don't know what you're asking of me.'

'She's got money, hasn't she?' the Countess said. 'Not a lot, I'm sure. But a damn sight more than you have. She's the sort of woman who'll do what you want and when you want it. And when she doesn't, you can always go to your club. And they tell me when her husband died he left her the lot, so there's no fear of her dropping dead on you and leaving you penniless because it's all gone to the heir.'

Andrew sat in his chair and contemplated his own vast frame. He knew the Countess was putting the screws on him, and he knew that such was the size of his outstanding debt to her that she was perfectly able to call the shots. So if she wanted him to marry the beastly little woman, marry her he would have to. And if it meant that he could pay the Countess off and also settle that pile of buff-enveloped accounts, then it might not be such a frightfully bad thing in the long run. He'd got himself into this corner of course, but even so he still couldn't help feeling sorry for himself, and quite frankly at that moment he could have done with a quiet blub. He drank his second stiff drink and considered the advantages and disadvantages. Clarissa worshipped him, so maybe he would be able to continue doing just what he wanted to do and when he wanted to do it. She had a flat in London which was only a short walk – or a taxi ride if she was paying – from his club. This meant he would be able to off-load his own rather miserable flat and pocket the proceeds. Clarissa would pay all his bills without question, and best of all would settle with his bookmaker before he got warned off. That was the credit. The debit was Clarissa herself, and the thought that he would have to spend a largish portion of the rest of his life in her appalling company. And then worst of all, there was Surrey.

'What shall I do about Surrey?' he asked the Countess as they sat finishing their lunch.

'You can't do anything about Surrey,' replied the Countess. 'No one has ever been able to do anything about Surrey. It's got far too much gorse. We can, however, do something about the beastly woman's house. We'll get Mary or one of her friends to do it up.'

'I wouldn't be too sure,' said Andrew gloomily. 'You ain't seen it.'

The Countess bit delicately into her Bath Oliver and ignored any further protests. Her mind was quite made up on the matter of Andrew availing himself of this moderately wealthy widow. Such an opportunity would not come someone like Andrew Gillott's way very often. Besides, by the time Mary or her friends had got hold of the house and rag-rolled the walls, and stripped back the doors, and removed the excess ironwork, and the strictly shaped flower beds and the nasty gold dolphin-shaped bathroom fittings there would be no recognising the place. Andrew might even be able to ask friends down without having to go and hide in the carefully manicured shrubbery. The Countess would most certainly visit him, once he repaid his little debt of course.

She smiled down the table at him. She knew from his woebegone expression that she had carried the day, and if she could have found it in her heart to feel sorry for him she would have done. But as it was she couldn't, for she knew he had brought the whole thing on himself, and the price he had to pay for it was marrying the beastly little woman. Naturally, in due course the Countess would let the woman know exactly how much she was in the Countess' debt, and eventually she would even allow her to ask her to Surrey. But until then Andrew was going to have to be a good boy and swallow the dose of medicine.

After lunch he departed with an expression more befitting someone in deep mourning, and the loan of a few hundred pounds to buy a ring for his proposal bid. Shortly afterwards Fulton and Elliott called, to collect a parcel the Countess had had made up for Mary on Capri. They were intensely interested in the Countess' affairs at the moment, as the Countess knew, so she drew out their visit by feeding them little bits of information about Andrew Gillott and Mrs Parker-Jones and other odd bits of gossip and scandal, so that they broke their rule and stayed not only for tea but dinner as well, even though it was their sauna night.

She was sending out a parcel with Fulton and Elliott to Mary full of an assortment of little things she knew her daughter would miss, such as Jackson's tea, Fortnum and Mason's Christmas pudding and lavender sachets for her underwear drawer. Little things she knew would make her turn away from the azure Italian vistas and long once again for English lawns and Minton china. She hoped that by sending her a constant bombardment of such parcels homesickness would overcome Mary, and she would return to England and give up her silly little American queer, who seemed to spend more time choosing Piazza clothes than writing, at least according to Fulton. The Countess missed her daugher. She missed her telephone calls. She missed grumbling about her and she missed grumbling to her. Since she had gone to Capri she had felt older, and more bored, and worst of all more boring. Queers were all very well for short periods of fun if one was an old lady, but finally their company was tiresome, mainly because they disliked women so. And although the Countess felt no particular loyalty to her sex, nevertheless she had once been a fairly active member of it, and she felt a certain affection for the woman she had once been, which was not something one could share with queers and popinjays. Besides, when Mary was around she could enjoy herself again, because without her all her rooms seemed darker, and she laughed a lot less.

Fulton and Elliott it emerged had not just stayed to hear her news. They stayed to tell her some. Georgiana, it appeared, had lent Longborough to her film man for his film and in return, so they had heard, he was going to restore the house for her. There was even some talk of getting a man down from Christie's to restore the house exactly to its former state.

'That,' said the Countess, 'is always a mistake. Some of those original colours are so violent. It's like dressing a woman up in eighteenth-century costume nowadays and expecting her to wear a wig full of fleas.'

Fulton and Elliott laughed and clapped their hands in delight. 'Even so,' added the Countess, 'how extraordinary.'

This of course, would also put Georgiana in her debt,

237

she thought to herself. Because if she had not induced all her friends to refuse the loan of their houses for this man's film, he would never in a million years have chosen Longborough, and Georgiana would never have got her house restored. Georgiana owed her aunt a great debt therefore, and later she would not hesitate to remind her niece of the fact.

'Aren't film people extraordinary?' she said to no one in particular.

And because she said it to no one in particular, nobody bothered to reply.

chapter eighteen

Georgiana had not told Kaminski anything of the state of Longborough before she took him down there. She told him only that it needed some repairs, and left him to see the exact state of the house for himself. Since she had last been down, it had certainly not improved, although happily her parents were away so they were able to wander quite freely within, and peer through cobwebbed doorways and stare out of dirty windows without interruption.

As for E.F., he had never seen anything like it. The dust was so thick on the furniture it had practically gone solid, and as for the guana on the window sills (as his Aunt Alice would call it), it had become so complicated it was almost decorative. The bedroom carpets were as thin as cobwebs, and there were already more than enough real ones hanging round the place to keep a pack of tarantulas housed for life.

'For Chrissake,' he muttered to Kaminski, 'I keep expecting Miss Havisham to appear.'

In the event a type of Miss Havisham did appear, in the shape of old Nanny Longborough, who served them all tea out of faded china, and called Georgiana 'Lady Georgie'. E.F. held on to his cup as if it was a Mae West in a boiling sea, for it was the only clean thing he had touched since he had entered the place. Fortunately the tea was warm, which was just as well because the house was so damp. It was also very cold, far colder than the mild day outside. In fact it was so cold they had all kept their coats on.

The two men left Georgiana talking to her nanny while they walked out through the grounds. From a distance, viewed from the edge of the ha-ha, the house was impressive. And if E.F.'s bones had not been aching from the cold of the interior, he might have been warmed by the mellowness of the stone. He might have also been pleased by the serenity of the elevations, had he not witnessed the squalor inside. At this moment, all he wanted to do was get back in Kaminski's car and drive back hotfoot to London.

They didn't need this place. For even though the Countess had been able to shut an awful lot of doors in their faces, happily there were still others, others which were just as suitable to their purposes as Stockton had been. Much as E.F. had grown to appreciate Louise, he certainly did not appreciate the house of her ancestors.

'What a location,' he said to Kaminski. 'I mean, can you imagine? The camera'd go straight through those rotten floorboards. And you'd have to light night for day it's so gloomy inside.'

Kaminski ignored him and put a hand to the side of his face. He looked at the house, and then he looked at the small figure emerging from it and making its way towards them.

'It's perfect,' he said.

Now E.F. knew he'd gone crazy. His mouth opened so wide that if he hadn't just chucked away his cigar it would have fallen out. Being a writer who prided himself on not writing lines like 'what do you mean?' and 'what on earth are you talking about?' naturally he shrank from using such expressions himself. So he just stared speechlessly

239

at Kaminski instead. The screenplay they had been working on, albeit slowly, was set against a background of extreme luxury. When Philippe made love to Louise, silk curtains blew in the wind, and they never drank out of anything but the finest cut glass. Even yesterday when he had managed to collar Kaminski for a few working hours, they had decided to set the murder scene where Phillippe finally murders Louise against the background of an orchestra which has been hired to play for them in a next door room. If they used this house, the only person Philippe would be able to hire would be a blind fiddler in a fur coat.

'Please,' he finally said to Kaminski, 'tell me you don't mean it.'

But the stupid bastard seemed to be deaf nowadays. And yet he couldn't tell Kaminski to knock it off, because he knew Kaminski was feeding on the situation, and if they wanted to better the Bolst, which E.F. thought to be highly unlikely, he had to let Kaminski go as deep in as he wanted with the girl. What they hadn't reckoned on was the girl herself, and more precisely her house. For obviously she would not have bothered to bring them down here if she did not want them to use it. And they couldn't possibly use it as it was. To restore it would cost a great deal of money. And at the moment money was scarce, even to Kaminski. Personally, E.F. felt like chucking the whole thing in, but what he felt like and what was possible were two different things entirely, like sex and marriage.

'I don't think it's quite right for you,' said Georgiana when she arrived where they were standing.

She looked back at the house wistfully. It had taken all her courage to bring Kaminski down here, and now it was over and she had showed him round she just wished they could go back to town and she could forget that she had brought him to Longborough. She felt just as she used to feel as a child, when she had brought girls back from boarding school to tea and had immediately regretted it and wished that she was back at school.

When she had first entered Kaminski's life she had been obsessed with the idea of getting him to use Longborough for his film. But now they were there at the house, she wanted to forget that this was the reason why she had become involved with him in the first place. One day she would bring the house back to life again, but not because of Kaminski. Because now she didn't wish him to see the depth of her ambition. And just as she had put aside all other considerations from the moment he had told her he wanted her to stay with him, now she even put aside Longborough.

She knew that none of her friends or family could understand why she had done what she had done, and she shared this inability to understand herself. Kaminski was not the realisation of any of the ideals she had nursed and, although she thought he liked her, he never spoke of love and neither did she. And yet, when they made love she knew she experienced something that was definitely not ordinary. When she was alone, she saw how unsuited they were for each other, but when he was there it was impossible to keep the absurdity of their relationship in the forefront of her mind; for when they were together something in her was satisfied, as if in the presence of his enormous energy she could set aside her own personality, and rest peacefully in the shadow of his.

Had he not known Kaminski so well, E.F. could have kissed Georgiana for telling them that the house was not suitable. Knowing Kaminski, the idea that she thought the house was wrong would make him all the more determined to use it.

'You're wrong,' Kaminski told her. 'The house is perfect.'

E. F. groaned all the way back to London, and not because he was hungry. He didn't care if it meant a rewrite, and he didn't care if it meant he had to stay in England longer. What he cared about was that Kaminski, who up till now had been exemplary about women, was now discovered to be as weak as E. F. himself, and that was not good. He was doing exactly what the girl wanted

241

and when she wanted it, and the fact that Kaminski had made such a good attempt at disguising this did not prevent E. F. from feeling sadly that yet another illusion had been shattered.

Georgiana looked out of the car window at the passing countryside and could not believe that Kaminski had meant what he had said about the house. But then she did not understand the nature of the business Kaminski worked in. She began to a few days later when he started working on Longborough with his set designer. This rather shocked Georgiana for she had never before considered Longborough to be anything else but a house. Now apparently it was a 'set', and her parents were 'props' who had to be moved out of harm's way to the estate manager's house, while the furnishings and paintings were restored and revarnished to suit the whim of the designer, who apparently was even unhappy about some of the exterior aspects of the house, to the extent that he added a couple of false windows and bolstered up the real ivy with plastic stuff.

That they worked fast there was no doubt, and for the next few weeks Longborough was a hive of activity, with painters and plasterers and carpenters running round all over the place. Kaminski took her to see what he'd had done to the once derelict stables, and Georgiana was amazed at how quickly they had worked. She stared at the newly painted walls, rehung iron mangers and replastered ceilings. Even the name plates of horses long departed had been restored and repainted, with all their names carefully picked out in gold lettering, including that of Bantry Bay. Nothing was missed anywhere in the house or grounds. Cornices had all their broken and frayed edges renewed, and gold leaf was painted on gold leaf, until Georgiana had the feeling that if she didn't keep an eye on things they would remove Nanny and give her a complete face lift as well.

Naturally Nanny did not approve. The 'men' got under her feet, and she did not like them parking their vans in the front, which most certainly would have not been

allowed in the old days. And when Nanny and Georgiana's parents walked through the main rooms after they
were finished, they all agreed that the pictures had been
over-varnished and over-cleaned, and that as far as the
decorations went, although quite obviously the designer
had been careful to keep to the original colours, they did
not have the necessary 'faded' look which was so essential
if a house was to keep its period feel. There was no
arguing that the structural repairs were simply first class,
but Georgiana's mother was not at all happy with the
colour they had chosen for her bedroom, and they all
thought it would have been far better had they not done
up the nursery in pink but stuck to yellow which of course
was the correct colour for an Upper Class nursery. Georgiana's mother was also surprised at the kitchen, for she
thought so much use of brass made it look rather like a
pub. Still, they would all get used to it in time she
supposed, but really it wasn't like home any more, was
it?

Georgiana agreed completely that it was not like her
home any more and was deeply thankful. In fact it was
so unlike the Longborough she had known that she found
it quite difficult to prise herself away and return to
London with Kaminski. But he insisted, saying that once
shooting started soon she would be able to stay at Longborough all she wanted.

So she returned with him to what she mischievously
called her 'prison'. And while he worked on the script
with E. F. he set her to plan a ball for the film. She might,
he said, ask some 'real' people along to mingle with the
extras.

This idea greatly appealed to Georgiana who realised
that here was an opportunity to snub all the family and
friends who had dropped her. So she snubbed them in
the best possible way which was to invite them all to the
ball and watch them accept with alacrity, for they could
not bear to refuse. She knew they would all have to
come to Longborough, and although most of them would
undoubtedly find, as her parents had done, that the

pictures were over-varnished and that the period feel was too new, nevertheless her good fortune would make them all so cross that every time she thought about it she knew she would do anything for Kaminski, because he had made it all possible.

The Countess was among the last to accept, and when she did she accompanied her acceptance with a short note to the effect that she could not understand why Georgiana should require the presence of an old lady such as herself at the ball, and please to tell the 'director person' that the insurance company would not allow her to wear her real diamonds so she would only be wearing the replicas, which of course most people did nowadays, and anyway waltzing with a Securicor man was not her idea of how to spend an evening.

Georgiana herself was not to be filmed dancing at the ball. She did not understand why, but she accepted that Kaminski did not want her to be, even though he insisted on choosing a dress for her. It was scarlet, and would be worn by the girl chosen to play Louise when they returned to Hollywood, so she must be very careful not to damage it.

'This is new,' E. F. had groaned in reaction to this piece of information. 'We don't cast for talent or beauty any more. Now we're casting for size. "No actress with big feet need apply." '

But Kaminski's obsession with Georgiana had overtaken him, to the point where he thought he could even abandon his work for her. It was not just that he could not bear her to talk to the maid, he could not bear her to talk to anyone, and just as he had envied the taxi driver who had carried her home that very first evening, now he envied one with whom she exchanged even a few words, the assistant who brought her coffee on the set, or a prop man who wished her good morning – anyone and everyone to whom she spoke and who spoke to her – until it seemed he would not be happy unlesss he could be her clothes and she could wear him. And although they were making good headway with the script, and very soon they would wrap up the filming in England and return to America, he found he could no longer look that far ahead, even though it was all too soon. He had wanted Georgiana to become an obsession, instead she had become a compulsion.

Meanwhile there was the ball, and to it came all Georgiana's friends and relations, with the notable exception of Mary, who wrote to Georgiana from Italy saying unfortunately she could not make the journey because she was busy typing out Lucius' oeuvre, entitled *The Bay Tree*, a *roman à clef* which was due to be published in America the following year. That was not precisely the only reason, she added in a postscript. It was also because England had become strictly out of bounds since Fulton and Elliott had stayed with them a few weeks before, and Elliott, by dint of making a pass at Lucius, had discovered that in fact Lucius was not gay, with the consequence that he had run back to tell the Countess, who had immediately ceased all further communication with her, besides an initial dozen air mail letters crammed to bursting with phrases such as 'the disgusting nature of your association'. The P.S. ended at that point in a flurry of exclamation marks, and Georgiana thought how much it was in Mary's style to write her a communication where the P.S. was longer than the letter. Personally, feeling as she did about Lucius, Georgiana thought the Countess was right, but her vigorous objections to her daughter living with someone who in fact was now not a homosexual were nowhere near as riveting as Jennifer Parker-Jones' reasons for not attending the ball. Her letter arrived shortly after Mary's and was stamped and crested so elegantly that Georgiana had to look at the signature twice to appreciate that it was indeed from her rather plain friend.

Since Georgiana did not take *The Times*, she did not know that a formal announcement had appeared in the columns to the effect that the Marquis of Pemberton had married Miss Jennifer Parker-Jones quietly, and that they would be having a private party for friends later in the year. Georgiana thought it would be very good for Jennifer to be a Marchioness, for she was the sort of girl who could only improve with precedence. And besides, it would be such a source of gratification to her frightful mother, not to mention Andrew Gillott who had had the unenviable job of steering her through the Season.

In this respect, Georgiana could not possibly have known Mrs Parker-Jones at all well, for on being told the news of Jennifer's marriage to his old friend Pemberton by a still amazed Andrew Gillott who had known nothing of the romance at all, Mrs Parker-Jones had screamed. There was no other word for it, Andrew had later told a group of friends at the club, the woman had screamed, and if that wasn't cast iron proof that all women were mad he didn't know what was. A man from no background on being told that his unmarriageable daughter had become a Marchioness would have got out a bottle of pop and celebrated.

Seeing Clarissa behave in such a manner should have been enough to make Gillott call off his own wedding, if he hadn't already paid for most of the arrangements. After she had screamed, she had torn off to her bedroom, babbled for most of the night about life being unbearably unfair, and then had turned on Andrew and told him that it was all his fault, as if he had been scheming it all the time, which he most certainly had not been doing. Of course he'd tried to reason with her when he had managed to calm her down, but it had been to no avail, and her temper had been nothing short of abysmal ever since, so much so that he had seriously considered booking single rooms for their proposed honeymoon in Kenya, for he thought they might at least start as he intended they should go on. When he was well in his cups he had to admit to himself that, were his fear of the Countess not greater than his fear of Clarissa, he would call the whole thing off and blow the expense. But when he was sober he knew that he could not possibly contemplate it, for to jilt Clarissa meant he would have to exile himself on account of his debts, and the idea of abroad gave him an even worse attack of the shivers than the sight of Clarissa in her heated rollers.

Georgiana's invitation to the ball did at least go a little way to restoring Mrs Parker-Jones' good spirits, and for that Andrew was most thankful. It gave Clarissa some comfort to know that Georgiana had not made a good match, just a temporary misalliance, which her aunt and the rest of her relatives all trusted would soon be over because to have the name Vladimir Kaminski appearing on the Longborough family tree was simply not on. And since Georgiana now at least had somewhere respectable to entertain, a good and suitable match must surely follow, if not sooner then later. For, as the Countess had often observed, girls who made later marriages often made better ones, since their silly notions of love and romance had been replaced by then by sensible ideas of self-advancement, which really was much more the thing.

Lately the Countess had been experiencing an almost pleasurable sense of déjà vu, as if she had been to earth before and lived another life. It could well be something to do with her advancing years, she thought, but whatever it was, as she surveyed the lists of the names in Society nowadays it seemed to her that so many were the same names as could have been found on the lists of long ago. It made one feel as if one must be part of a predestined *placement* arranged by an Almighty Host. New money had come in, of course. There was no doubt about that at all. But like new blood it was quickly absorbed into the system and the mixture remained much as it was before, with Society's clock standing still with both hands pointing, as on Georgiana's engraved invitation, to the words 'Supper and Dancing'.

chapter nineteen

Of course E. F. thought the idea of asking a whole lot of Georgiana's society friends down to the wrap party was crazy. They wouldn't mix in, they'd get in the way, and they'd make the kind of stupid remarks that put hard-working backs up. And if Kaminski thought extras stole from the set, wait till he saw these people. These people were like locusts. E. F. had heard it on good authority that if you asked any of them to dinner you had to chain the knives and forks to the table. And if you gave a party nowadays, first you cleared your house. But Kaminski was not in the mood to listen to E. F. When was he ever? No, he just went around wearing his number six closed expression, which personally E. F. felt was *not* flattering.

And he had shaved off his beard. It made him look younger, which made E. F. extremely nervous, for if Kaminski had seized on the idea that it was necessary for him to look younger, then he knew that Kaminski was in far deeper with that girl than even E. F. had thought. He did not like that idea, not one bit, in fact he positively disliked it. When a man becomes really involved with a girl, especially a girl who is that much younger, it is not good for that man, for given time he inevitably becomes parted from his friends and his work, and in the end he ceases to be altogether. He had seen it happen too many times before to want to see it happen to Kaminski. But for the moment Kaminski was not listening. He had to have her by his side the whole time, and if she moved away from him he would want to know where, and where had better not be too far. E. F. had had far too many affairs to think that it was necessary to go as far as Kaminski was going, such as keeping on the orchestra which had been hired for the film to play at the party, and even keeping behind some of the prettiest extras just because Georgiana thought they might look decorative. This was lunacy, and E. F. grieved to see the great man entranced by such frippery. Okay, so the script was turning out fine, with Kaminski adding details which were so authentic they could only be autobiographical. So E. F. couldn't condemn the affair as much as he would have liked, because it had saved him a great deal of headwork, and at his age that was something to be grateful for. It had also meant that he was able to see a lot of the fat woman, even though she insisted on dining practically daily in Beauchamp Place, so that E. F. thought if he ever saw another *truite en papillote* he would have to be carried out screaming.

The wrap party was a success from the opening. It had to be, contrary to E. F.'s gloomy prognostications. It had all the right ingredients to make it successful: stars, but not too many of them, Society, but only a sprinkling, people who liked to talk and people who liked to listen, and most of all that special end-of-term feeling that a 'wrap' party always had, the work celebrated because it was over, and mourned over for the same reason. The sprite looked a picture in her scarlet gown, chosen quite purposefully by Kaminski to make her look that little bit too sophisticated of course, but nonetheless beautiful. This was all good, except what was happening to Kaminski. He was enjoying himself, and that was something Kaminski never did, or at least was never seen to do. He was dancing every dance, and he was seen on two or three occasions to be smiling. He and E. F. had always privately agreed that only fools smiled, so E. F. was appalled. Kaminski was behaving out of character, and E. F. felt as every writer feels when they see someone behaving out of character. He wanted to put a stop to it.

'Come and have a quiet drink in the library,' he said to Kaminski when he got a chance late on in the party.

It would not be long before breakfast was served, and Kaminski was watching Georgiana dance for the second time with someone much younger than himself, which was perhaps why he followed E. F. quite obediently into the library, and closed the now impeccably stripped and polished double doors.

'You know,' E. F. said, 'this place is so immaculate now I still can't believe it isn't actually a set. I keep thinking if I go up behind one of these walls I'll see stage weights and braces.'

Kaminski smiled again, and E. F. shook his head and poured them some brandy. Perhaps it was because Kaminski had shaved his beard off that he seemed to be smiling more. E. F. hoped this was the explanation.

For a moment they both nursed their brandies in silence, listening to the hired orchestra playing the last waltz. The music crept under the library doors and mingled with their cigar smoke, which in turn curled and filtered out of the open windows towards the large oaks in the grounds.

'Some party,' said E. F. finally.

'Yes,' said Kaminski.

'Still, it's not over yet,' said E. F. 'Got a helluva lot to do when we get into the studios.'

'We have,' said Kaminski.

They fell into more silence, and E. F. saw that Kaminski was only passing the time with him out of politeness, because his mind was still quite obviously where Georgiana was. This was something E. F. had never seen before. Girls never came between Kaminski and his work.

'When it's finished,' Kaminski said slowly, 'I'm coming back, E. F.'

'You'll probably have to, once you see the rough cut,' joked E. F., who knew what he really meant.

'I'm coming back anyway,' Kaminski said.

E. F. thought what a lousy line that was. If he submitted a line like that, Kaminski would send him away with a flea in his ear. He leant forward to attract Kaminski's attention.

'You can't live in England, Kaminski,' he said. 'It's too damn cold. You need warming up. Live in England and you might as well go back to Siberia, with your temperament.'

Kaminski ignored him, so E. F. realised that he would have to try again. Kaminski had got it bad, there was no doubt about it. And even though as a writer E. F. wished everything upon Kaminiski that a writer wishes on his director, as a human being he had no wish to see Kaminski go to the wall without some attempt at mediation.

'I suppose you've got to say she's beautiful,' he said.

'She's more than that,' Kaminski replied. 'She's unattainable.'

And his hand went up automatically to his now hairless cheek.

Exactly how attainable did a girl have to be to be attainable, E. F. wondered to himself? But publicly he just nodded in agreement, and continued to pursue his aims with a well-practised eloquence. For if there's one good thing about being a scriptwriter, he thought, it's that words in the form of dialogue come easily to you. They may not come good, but they certainly come easy. And so he praised Georgiana to Kaminski at length and with the skill that comes of spending six hours every day practising with words. He praised her youth, and then he just touched upon the fact that it was a pity that girls never stayed girls. Sometime, maybe tomorrow, maybe next year – sometime they all finally became women, and when you came home at night, there they were checking their shares in the share index, and telling you about what they heard in the hairdresser's, which was not what you wanted to be told when you came home at night. Girls, when you thought about it, said E. F., went from butterfly to chrysalis, which was not the right way round.

Kaminski poured himself another brandy. E. F. was fat, moderately talented, and right. Georgiana would change, and it would not be for the better. How could it be? She was perfect as she was, she wasn't going to become any more perfect. He could not bear the idea that the object of his brief obsession would change into something different, and yet he knew he had to face it head on, for to imagine that she would stay as she was was ridiculous, and yet he did not think that he would like the woman that she would, perhaps inevitably, grow into. Perhaps a little socially aware, a little shrill sometimes, complaining about the maid, or bored, growing from a youthful phenomenon to a certain type.

'These people,' E. F. was saying, gesturing to the doors, 'the people out there. They're charming, and fickle, and stylish, and they want you at their tables. And yet as you sit down, they can't help pulling the chairs from under you.'

Kaminski drank his brandy and then threw the glass into the fireplace. E. F. watched, satisfied. He could retire quite happily from the scene now, knowing that Philippe was about – metaphorically – to destroy Louise.

But even E. F. had realised that Kaminski had to make love to her once more before he killed her off. He waited until they were back in London and back in his apartment, where he had first made love to her. She was so exquisite that afternoon, as she lay there in his arms, that even Kaminski doubted if he would be able to recapture that changing light, and the way her body moved, and how willing and innocent she was in the way she pleased him. And he realised with something approaching guilt, that she had never asked anything of him. Just like a good child she had never bothered him, or annoyed him, or once been jealous. It made it practically impossible for him to end it, but even that she helped him with, because for the very first time she asked to know the story of the film he was making. And this was also typical of Georgiana – that she could have been so uncurious about his film until he was just about to leave her.

She was not so lacking in intellect that she could not see that Louise was her and Philippe was meant to be him. Because not only did he make no attempt to conceal it from her, describing in cinematic terms their own meeting, but he was most careful to show her where his film story had changed from the Bolst silent, until he got to the very end where he told her he had chosen to revert to Bolst's ending, with Louise lying dead in Philippe's arms.

'But I don't want her to die,' she cried. 'Please change the end.'

'All love affairs must end,' he told her. 'And they end either in death or in parting. That way they always end beautifully. Any other ending would be wrong. Any other ending would be "common".'

This appealed to Georgiana as Kaminski knew perfectly well it would, and although she wanted to tell Kaminski that she loved him, she knew it would only make her cry more, and she could see he wouldn't like that. She really didn't understand why their love affair had to end, only that Kaminski had said she must do something beautifully and not be common. She tried to think of Longborough, now looking as she had always wanted it to look, but it seemed to her all she could see was an old house with new furnishings, now that Kaminski was going.

'If you must go,' she told him, 'then I must die. Like Louise. That would be beautiful.'

'Death is only beautiful on film,' he replied. 'In real life it is invariably fatal.'

'I know what you're doing,' said Georgiana. 'You're leaving me so that I have to grow up. But I don't want to grow up. I want to be with you, like this always. Like we are now.'

Kaminski tried to tell her that she would never grow up, that she would always be young, and beautiful, lying on her rug, or jumping in puddles, or blowing bubbles in her lemonade. That she'd always be walking beside him, half-running, half-skipping, her mischievous face lighting up into a smile as soon as she saw him. She was going to be preserved on celluloid. But he knew she would not understand the word 'celluloid,' so he said film instead.

Georgiana thought about this for a moment.

'You mean like being in a book?' she asked him.

'Yes,' said Kaminski. 'Exactly like being in a book.'

And so a few days later, Georgiana bought an evening paper and turning to the Diary page, saw a picture of Kaminski and E. F. leaving for Los Angeles.

The item was headed:

'FAMOUS DIRECTOR FLIES OUT'

She then read the item in the Diary.

'Kaminski and *moi* have greatly enjoyed our stay in England,' joked screenwriter E. F. Tyrell. 'It has been most enjoyable, and most appropriately,' he added, pointing up to the sky, 'we're flying off into the sunset.'

Georgiana looked at the picture again. Kaminski had started to regrow his beard, and he was wearing a jacket she did not remember him in. He held an airport bag in his arms such as people are always pictured arriving and departing with. Perhaps they would meet again. Or maybe in a few years they would pass each other in the street, and as in the photograph, he would be wearing clothes she did not recognise, and she would no longer be wearing the clothes he had chosen for her. Those would be hanging in the back of her wardrobe in plastic bags with zips on them, and she would not have worn them for a long, long time, for they would now be far too young for her. Perhaps for a moment they would think they recognised each other, and then perhaps they would walk on pretending they hadn't. Kaminski the famous director passing a lady in a suit.

She picked up a pair of scissors, and slowly cut Kaminski's picture from the newspaper. Then she took it and pasted it into her favourite book, just beside the words that said

'The End'.

Bette Pesetsky
Author From a Savage People

'May Alto supports three children, and one ex-husband, by ghost-writing. One day, she learns that a client called Quayle has been given the Nobel Prize – for a book called *Eine Leerstelle* which, of course, she wrote.

May has written her whole life – her mad, revolutionary mother, her aunt Giselle, her uncle Trasker – into every work she has ever touched. Quayle has done nothing more than sign his name to the product. What can May do to claim her deserts but attempt a spot of blackmail?

A fine and funny novel, as passionate as it is clever'
NEW STATESMAN

'An inventive, provocative tour-de-force' PUBLISHERS WEEKLY

'Briskly clever . . . funny and fast-paced and absorbing' WASHINGTON POST

Elaine Dundy
The Dud Avocado

'American girls are just like avocados . . . a hard centre with the tender meat all wrapped up in a shiny casing . . . so green, so eternally green'
   Paris in the Fifties is the setting for the story of a girl called Sally Jay Gorce. . .

'Scandalous and entertaining . . . both funny and true' EVENING STANDARD

'A champagne cocktail . . . just such a draught has been prepared by Elaine Dundy' THE OBSERVER

'The writing, like Sally Jay herself, has high spirits and is laced with astringencies a class and a half above the wisecrack' THE TIMES

'As delightful an examination of how it is to be twenty and in love and in Paris as I've read' SUNDAY TIMES